Valentine wound down his window and nodded to the uniform at the roadside. The Police Constable seemed to do a double take when he caught sight of the DI. "Sir." He gulped the word, then steadied himself. "I wasn't expecting ... "

Valentine held up a hand. "Just lift the tape, son." He had no time for reunions.

As he drove towards the dump entrance, he spotted the "Scene of Crime Officers" white tent, the officers in their spacesuit livery, and the usual hubbub of hangers-on and dicks-in-the-wind.

The first to approach the officer in charge was DS McAlister. He slitted his eyes, then took two firm steps in the direction of DI Valentine.

"I heard you were joining us, but I didn't want to believe it."

"Look, spare me the welcome party. What have we got?"

DS Rossi dismissed the white-suited crime scene officer and made for the newly formed enclave of officers gathering around Valentine.

McAlister spoke. "White male, late fifties and dead as dead gets."

"Is that a medical opinion, Ally?" said Valentine.

Other Bold Venture Press
mystery titles you will enjoy

PRIMAL SPILLANE by Mickey Spillane
THE LAST REDHEAD by John L. French
CANCELLED IN RED by Hugh Pentecost
THE 24TH HORSE by Hugh Pentecost
I'LL SING AT YOUR FUNERAL by Hugh Pentecost
THE BRASS CHILLS by Hugh Pentecost
STRICTLY POISON by Charles Boeckman
A DATE WITH THE EXECUTIONER by Patti Smith
FLYING BLIND by Howard Hammerman
NO FREE LUNCH by C.J. Henderson
SOMETHING FOR NOTHING by C.J. Henderson
NOTHING LASTS FOREVER by C.J. Henderson
NO TORRENT LIKE GREED by C.J. Henderson
BET YOUR OWN MAN by C.J. Henderson
THE KILLERS ARE COMING by Jack Bludis
NAME OF THE STRANGER by Johnny Strike
HELLBENT ON HOMICIDE by Gary Lovisi
HARVEST OF HOMICIDE by Gary Lovisi
THE LAST GOODBYE by Gary Lovisi
THE END GAME by Gerrie Ferris Finger
WOLF'S CLOTHING by Gerrie Ferris Finger
GANGSTERS OF THE RAILS by E.S. Dellinger

ARTIFACTS of the DEAD

A DI Bob Valentine case

TONY BLACK

DI Bob Valentine mysteries
by Tony Black

Artifacts of the Dead

A Taste of Ashes

Summoning the Dead

Her Cold Eyes

ARTIFACTS OF THE DEAD

Tony Black

First published 2014 by Black & White Publishing Ltd

Bold Venture Press edition September 2019

Copyright © Tony Black 2014

ISBN-13: 9781070676272
Retail cover price $12.95

The right of Tony Black to be identified as the author of this work has been asserted by him in accordance with the Copyright, Designs and Patents Act 1988.

A CIP catalogue record for this book is available from the British Library.

For Cheryl
and Conner

Prologue

The bulldozer emitted a chugging noise as its caterpillar tracks pushed through the refuse. White parcels of cardboard and plastic carriers toppled into the broad, fresh footprint of the earth mover. A grey-to-black cloud of smoke hung in the wide trail, fresh bursts from the vertical exhaust pipe adding a slug-line smear to the blue skyline. The jagged sawtooth of the Isle of Arran **off the coast of Scotland** looked a long way out at sea as the driver crunched the gears a final time and brought the vehicle to a halt.

In the cab, a shabby portable radio — it looked like dump-find — sat on the dash, blaring a West FM jingle, as Davie ferreted for a pack of cigarettes. He whistled something from the terraces, a line about "honest men" that had been stuck in his mind since Saturday.

"What's this, now?" Davie clamped the filter tip in his mouth and lit up. As he did so, he eyed the fast-approaching quad bike, the orange light flashing above on its pole.

"Bastard, won't give me a moment's peace." He turned the key in the ignition and felt a shudder as the bulldozer came to life again. As Davie tucked his cigarette packet into the top pocket of his shirt, he smashed a fist into the grubby dash. "Five minutes, for a smoke. I was only after a bloody smoke!"

Davie kept his eyes to the front and tried to ignore his supervisor on the fast-moving quad bike. He bit the cigarette between his teeth and tucked his head further towards the filthy windscreen.

As the supervisor edged closer his driving became more erratic, aggressive, almost. He clearly wanted to say something to the man at the earth mover's controls; he waged an arm to attract his attention.

"Davie." The supervisor's roars were closer now.

The driver pretended to be oblivious to the commotion that was rapidly drawing near his open side-window. It was one small victory he was allowed: to be able to play dumb and irritate the boss.

"What's that? Slow down, is it?" Davie felt a glow in his cheeks as he slammed the gears again and forced the dozer blade deeper into the rubbish pile. What would he want, anyway? A few more hours out of him moving this muck. No chance.

Still, he didn't seem to be giving up. Davie saw his supervisor darting over the mounds of trash, sending the scavenging gulls back to the sky to circle and squawk. He was still there, moving at speed.

The noise from the gulls and the quad bike, the revving of the engine and the crunching of the gears, all faded into oblivion as he stared through a gap in the fly splattered windscreen.

"What the hell is that?"

In the midst of the collected detritus of Ayrshire's landfill sat an unfamiliar object. Davie craned his neck to take in the sight before him.

"Wha — ?"

The sudden high-pitched din of the quad bike revving to a halt at his side broke the spell, but only for a moment.

"Davie, get out the way!"

He heard the call, but didn't register any interest.

"Davie!"

He sensed movement beside him, his supervisor gesticulating with his arms wide in the fly thick air. This moment was far more important than any bawling his boss was capable of delivering. Davie wasn't sure what it was that he was seeing — the shape was too indistinct — but he knew this much: it wasn't something you should see on a rubbish heap.

He let the bulldozer roll a few yards, clearing the now-established route through the wasteland, towards the shape. It seemed to be a collection of familiar objects, but none in the right order. There was a central pole, like a flagpole or a spike in the earth, but there was something attached, tethered.

"Stop!"

He rolled the bulldozer further forward. It was a tangle, like a tangle of limbs — arms and legs — was it a scarecrow? Had someone dumped a tailor's dummy?

"Davie, please!"

He depressed the brake and stilled the engine. The sun was high in the noon sky, a rare wide blue offering that filled the line of rooftops and stopped just shy of a shimmering yellow band of sunlight. Davie cupped his hand above his brows and stared front. No, it wasn't a dummy.

"Christ above."

At his side, Davie suddenly felt a whoosh of air as the cab door was swung open and his supervisor jerked a hand towards the dash to grab the keys from the ignition.

"What in the name of God are you playing at, Davie?"

The driver turned to face his interrogator; his lips parted and the lower of the two drooped.

"Is that?"

"Yes, it's a body!"

"A what?"

His supervisor's eyes widened; the red shine of exertion showed in their corners.

"A body! It's a dead man. Can't you see someone's put a bloody great spike through him?"

1

The antiquated-looking exercise bike in the corner of the gymnasium was about all Detective Inspector Bob Valentine of the Police Force Scotland could bring himself to tackle. There was a noisy game of five-a-side going on beyond the wall; the shouts and roars of rowdy recruits would once have proven too tempting an opportunity to go and knock off some arrogance, but those days were now over. Reluctantly, he stuck to the bike, the slow revolutions of the pedals emitting a whirring, hypnotic burr.

The DI's brow was moistening. It had been — what? — Ten minutes of low-impact cycling. The doctor had called for more, much more, but it didn't seem right to push himself. He didn't like getting out of breath, didn't like straining the muscle in the centre of his chest that was forced to do all the work. He knew his heart had been through enough. He watched as stiff arms attached to prominently knuckled hands gripped the handlebars. His hold was weaker, less sure than it had once been. He couldn't imagine hauling himself over the assault course, now, as he once had at The Scottish Police College.

"How you doing, Bob?" The voice seemed to come from nowhere, an eruption amidst the plains of his thought.

"All right, how's it going?" He drew the reply from a store of stock answers. The man"s face hadn't registered yet.

"You're still with us, then?"

Valentine had to search deeper for an answer to that question: did he mean at the training academy or did he mean in the land of the living?

"Yeah, for now."

He eased off the pedals and leaned back in the saddle of the bike. For some reason he found himself folding his arms over his chest as he took in the broad man in the red Adidas tracksuit. He looked older than himself, a bald head with short-trimmed grey hairs sat above jug-ears and eyes deep lined with creases. Fulton, his name was Fulton, he remembered now.

"Don't know what their plan is for me, long term."

The folds on Fulton's face deepened and he became jowly as he dropped his chin. "Right." He nodded.

What was he doing here? It was the incident, he knew that. The incident that he had been unable to alter, could do nothing to halt. Except, perhaps, to have been a little more lucky. But he had never been that.

"So, we could be keeping you, then?" said Fulton.

Valentine shrugged. "Who knows?"

A hand was extended, placed on the DI"s shoulder — it made Valentine flinch.

He got off the exercise bike. "Right, well, I better hit the showers."

Fulton smiled a wide rictus that made him look more of a fool than the PT instructor's garb. "Yeah, hit the showers." He leaned forward to slap the DI on the shoulder, but somehow inferred that it would be an intrusion on Valentine's space. He retreated a few steps, grinned again, then said, "Catch you later, Bob."

Valentine raised a hand and waved the instructor off. He watched him pace a few steps towards the door and waited to see if his suspicions would be proved right: they were. The man turned and put a stare on Valentine that he took as the last look of the utterly perplexed.

"See you, Fulton."

The DI had made the same impression on Fulton as he was having on everyone, lately: they thought he was losing it. Maybe he was. He shook his head and made for the changing room.

Tulliallan Academy was housed in a nineteenth-century castle, but it felt just like any other college or learning institution to Valentine. The sweep of the place, its history, was wasted on him. He didn't like the blonde-wood gymnasium and he didn't like the in-house Starbucks or the two trendy bars that would look more at home in some overpriced boutique hotel. He felt like a fraud just being there, but then he had no choice.

A door opened and a stream of noisy recruits gushed into the corridor, pinning Valentine where he stood. They seemed wholly oblivious to him as he held up his elbows and shrank into the wall, waiting for the crowd to pass.

He felt like he'd just stepped out of the path of a juggernaut, but he was overreacting. As he made a point of placing his hands in his pockets, Valentine gripped fists. He didn't want to carry on like this. He didn't want to be a shadow of his former self.

In the empty changing room, he rested his head on the locker door and sighed.

"Together, keep it together."

He repeated the chant to himself over and over until he heard the hinges of a door swinging open; he was no longer alone. He drew back his shoulders and retrieved the key from his shorts. The contents of the locker were neatly packed, his grey dogtooth sports coat on the hanger, his trousers beneath. He removed them one by one and then placed them on the bench behind him. Last to come out were his black shoes, Dr. Martens – he had got used to them on the beat. He placed them on the floor and then retrieved his cell phone from the locker. He'd missed a call.

The sound of showers running started as he checked his messages.

"Martin." He shook his head. "What the hell does she want?"

Chief Superintendent Marion Martin had been responsible for Valentine's secondment to Tulliallan. She had kept a close eye on him since the incident, but all his requests for a return to the detective's role had been rebuffed. A list of options, reasons why she might be calling, raced through his mind: being put out to grass at Tulliallan on a permanent basis topped the list.

Was this what his career had come to? Had the effort, the exertion, been worth it? Certainly, he would not chase the same dreams again. Ambition had been his flaw. The desire to make something of himself, measure his worth against others on the force, had filled his life, once. But life was too short for that, surely. Yet, Valentine still measured himself against the likes of Martin. Who was she? A careerist, an underwhelming police officer who had fashioned an overachiever's job. And what did she have that Valentine didn't, aside from the positive-discrimination policymakers on her side. She was merely acting like the chief superintendent that she imagined herself to be. The reality was not even a consideration for her.

Valentine grinned. Had he really once been so stupid? So naive? Yes, he conceded. He had been that stupid, once, and it had taken twenty more years of staring at the most blatant of life"s facts to realize it.

He held up the cell phone, looked at the screen, and then dialed Chief Superintendent Martin's number.

The sound of ringing filled the line.

A brusque voice. "Hello."

"Boss, its Bob."

A pause entered their exchange; he heard movement, the sound of clothes rustling.

"I called you nearly an hour ago, what the hell have you been doing down there? Not another bloody happy hour at the Cooper Lounge?"

Valentine held his tone in check. "I think that place only opens on a Sunday."

She bit. "Never mind that. I need you back at the station. How quickly can you get here?"

Valentine's pulse quickened. "The station — King Street?"

"I don't think they've moved it."

He lowered himself onto the bench. He was sitting on his coat, but he didn't care. "Is there something I should know about?"

The chief super's voice pitched up an octave. "I have Bryce, McVeigh and Collins either on annual leave or tied up on other cases, so you are back in business, as of today. Unless you"re going to tell me you're unfit or some such crap."

Valentine sensed a new thought forming. It lingered there for a moment — exactly the time it took him to realize that if he was returning to the fray, it was not for a good reason.

"What's the problem?"

A sigh. The sound of a telephone receiver being shifted between hands. "We have a body at the dump; good enough for you?"

Valentine's mouth dried over, the roof first, but then his tongue. "The dump?"

"Battered into next week, and just to put a cherry on top, impaled on a sharp bit of a 2 x 4, up the arse."

"That's horrific."

"If you wanted candy floss every day, Bob, you should have joined the bloody circus. Can I see you back here before close of play?"

His reply was on his lips before he realized the chief super had hung up.

"Yes, of course."

2

Valentine raised himself from the bench. As he turned, he noticed the crumpled mass of his sports coat and grimaced; it was then that he caught sight of his reflection in the tall, floor-to-ceiling mirror. He saw his face first, the dark hair above his temples — still thick, that was something to hold on to — and the smooth but clean-lined block of forehead. The tight grimace of his mouth subsided as he dropped his gaze onto, first, his neck and then to the expanse of white that sat between his shoulders. He had a broad chest, a barrel, some would have called it. His chest had always looked that way, except for the thick red-brown line that ran vertically through the center of the sternum, which was a recent addition.

Valentine let the lids of his eyes hang heavy as he tipped back his head. The Detective Inspector's focus was squarely on the ridge of unwelcome flesh that sat as thick as his index finger. The vertical line was more than a scar; the thinner white markings where the stitching had tightened the invasive hole could be called a scar. This was something more. A scar suggested an injury, a trauma, perhaps, but the object of Valentine's gaze said here was the point of a violent incursion, a message that this man was lucky to be alive.

A clamor of voices broke from the shower cubicles and a group of recruits, white towels circling their waists, burst into view. Valentine stood before them for a moment.

"Sir," said the first to see him.

He nodded back.

"Sir," the others followed.

The DI reached for his coat and started to shake it out. He was still in a state of disbelief, his thoughts swaying between his readiness to return to the station and the particulars of the murder that Marion Martin had relayed to him.

They called her Dino, after her namesake, but also because it was a dog's name, and she was of the type that station smart-arses loved to ridicule. As he amused himself, he glanced at the mirror — one of the recruits was nudging the other, drawing a line down the center of his chest with the tip of his finger. Valentine didn't need to second-guess what was passing between them.

"Want a better view, lads?" He turned and put his hand on his hips.

The recruits looked away; as the DI eyed them fully, he saw they were only young lads. Two big shots — chancers — and a "yes man." The type that's there to nod and gravely intone "yes, yes" while the others boasted and prattled about themselves.

"No, I was just . . ." said the nudging recruit.

"I saw you." Valentine stepped forward. "You were drawing attention to this." He pointed at the thick line of darkened flesh in the center of his chest.

The air in the changing rooms seemed to have altered. If there had been a pitch of bravado, it had been flattened by the steamroller Valentine was now driving over their egos.

"Don't for a second think this is some badge of honor."

"No, sir." The voices were weak. The three lads stared at the water dripping from them as it fell to the tiled floor beneath them.

Valentine raised his voice. "Look at this." He tapped his chest. "I'm not proud of it." He raised his voice, flitted looks between the three. When he felt sure he had their full attention, he spoke up again. "When I was first in uniform, an old sergeant of mine said your tongue's more useful than your baton. Just you remember that."

The DI kept a firm stare on them for a moment longer and then returned to his locker and began the slow ritual of dressing himself. He never felt comfortable bawling out those beneath him in rank, but he was an experienced enough police officer to know when a mind was receptive to a lesson that might make the job a little easier.

On his way out, the "yes man" turned his head away, but the two chancers painted on thin smiles and nodded like they had all now become friends. Valentine looked through them and continued to the door.

In the parking lot the sun was high in the sky, painting a hazy red wash over the day. As he started the car's engine his old preoccupation returned, and he tried to douse it with logic: he was entering into a murder investigation. He needed his attention to be on that, not the events of these last few months, not his self-doubts.

Leaving the parking lot, he turned his attention to the words the chief super had uttered: "You're back in business."

There was no denying the fact that he felt good about that. He needed to get back to what he was best at. He was a murder-squad detective and nothing that had happened changed that.

"No Bryce, McVeigh or Collins." He let his thoughts turn to words as he drove back to Ayr. "King Street must be as empty as the bloody ghost ship *Mary Celeste*."

It was good to be driving back to the station, to be back on the force — not messing around with wet-behind-the-ears recruits and has-beens. The likes of Bryce would be falling over themselves to get a case like this, so why was he filled with apprehension? He was going back to the place he knew best — the sharp end. The thought made his throat constrict slightly, but he brushed it aside: there was no place for doubts, now.

3

The road into Ayr was tightly packed with cars. It was that time of the evening, but then he remembered when the town's rush hour lasted only ten minutes. He had left the A77 to take the arterial road towards the airport and, after travelling only three car lengths, found his vehicle hemmed in by open fields on one side, all the way to the town of Troon, and by runways on the other, reaching to the outskirts of the village of Mossblown.

The traffic backup told him he was not getting to King Street station in time to meet with Chief Superintendent Marion Martin. The queue of cars nudged ahead a few inches and a horn sounded; Valentine shook himself into action and turned onto Heathfield Road. The wheel was slippery in his hands, now; he wiped a palm on his trouser-front, then repeated the action for the other hand. He was past the hospital and at the next set of lights before his thought-patterns turned.

Valentine made a reach for his cell phone and inserted it in the hands-free dock. As the phone rang, he counted — the call was answered on the fourth chime.

"King Street." It was Jim Prentice, the desk sergeant. Valentine recognized the voice at once.

"Hello, Jim, son. How's tricks?"

"Oh, it's yourself. To what do we owe the pleasure?"

"Later, Jim. Tell me, who's Dino got down at the dump site?"

A gruff clearing of the throat echoed down the line. "The dump ... oh, Christ, that was some caper. Got the fellow on a plank, I hear, up the bloody arse as well."

Valentine hoped the station foyer was empty. "Yeah, Jim, I've heard the details. Who's desking the bag-ups?"

"Hang on, what do you want that for?"

The car ahead started to move again. "I thought I was talking to the desk sergeant. If they've shunted you up to divvy commander in the time I've been away, Jim, I'm very sorry."

"Yeah, very good. Cheeky bloody swine." An audible smile crept into his voice. "I was only asking."

"It's my case, Jim. Dino gave me it today, so if you can tell me who's been chalking up the scores so far, I'd appreciate it."

Jim sighed, and the sound of a mouse clicking passed down the line. "Looks like Big Paulo's there just now. Christ, he'll not be selling many ice creams at the dump."

Chris Rossi was an Italian-Scot who had been fortunate, in Valentine's opinion, to have reached the rank of Detective Sergeant. He was not the only one on the force with that opinion, but the DS seemed to possess an extra layer of skin that helped him resist the endless jokes that had fallen under the politically correct brigade's radar.

Valentine knew better than to bite. "Is he on his own?"

"No. He's got three million flies with him." The desk sergeant found himself hilarious. "Jesus, a murder at the dump, eh? You've got to wonder about some folk."

Valentine nodded sagely. "What about herself, is she off?"

"Yeah, she'll not miss *EastEnders*, Bob."

The traffic suddenly opened; a full lane had been freed up in the wake of a bus moving off. Valentine raced through the gears on the way to the crime scene.

"Right, Jim, I'll catch you tomorrow morning. If Dino asks, I left a message for her an hour ago."

"You bloody chancer."

He hung up.

The entrance to Old Farm Road had been blocked off by two patrol cars, and uniform were already there behind a strip of blue and white tape that had twisted into a thin strand of rope with the wind. There were children patrolling the cordon on bicycles and a scattering of women stood, backs on walls, arms folded. They were all chattering, passing comment on the goings-on. Valentine knew that if the murder hadn't already made the television news, it would be blazoned in headlines across the morning papers. The gravity of the event of murder was never wasted on him, but a bolt twisting in his gut told him this one was going to test him.

Valentine wound down his window and nodded to the uniform at the roadside. The Police Constable seemed to do a double take when he caught sight of the DI. "Sir." He gulped the word, then steadied himself. "I wasn't expecting ... "

Valentine held up a hand. "Just lift the tape, son." He had no time for reunions.

As he drove towards the dump entrance, he spotted the "Scene of Crime Officers" white tent, the officers in their spacesuit livery, and the usual hubbub of hangers-on and dicks-in-the-wind.

"God almighty." He tried to locate Detective Sergeant Rossi, but the first to hove into view was the fiscal depute, then as he turned the car towards the crime scene, he caught sight of the DS talking to DC McAlister and DS Donnelly.

Valentine stilled the engine and removed his coat from the front seat beside him. As he exited the vehicle, he was approached by the public attorney.

"Bob." He put a raised inflection on the word that made him sound like an Australian schoolgirl.

"Indeed I am." Valentine walked past the public attorney, patting him on the shoulder. He muttered, "Later, Col, when I've spoken to my lads."

The first to approach the officer in charge was DS McAlister. He slitted his eyes, then took two firm steps in the direction of DI Valentine.

"I heard you were joining us, but I didn't want to believe it."

"Look, spare me the welcome party. What have we got?"

DS Rossi dismissed the white-suited crime scene officer and made for the newly formed enclave of officers gathering around Valentine.

McAlister spoke. "White male, late fifties and dead as dead gets."

"Is that a medical opinion, Ally?" said Valentine.

"You might say that." He tipped his head in the direction of the village. "The doc's been and gone, by the way."

"No surprise there, can't get a happy hour at the dump."

Valentine took hold of a small cardboard box being held out by one of the crime scene officers that contained clear-plastic gloves. He removed a pair and quickly snapped them, one after the other, onto his hands.

"I won't ask you to wear the blue slippers," said the officer. "Seems pointless in this mess."

Valentine nodded. "Right, lead the way."

Rossi was just arriving as they took off again. He called out, "Hello, sir."

The DI recalled Jim's ice cream remark. "Move it, Paulo!"

As the murder squad headed towards the white tent, the refuse crunched and squelched beneath their feet. An omnipresent hiss of flies followed with them. The group, almost in unison, raised their hands towards their mouths and noses as they walked.

"This is rank," said Valentine. "Almost makes you want one of those wee B&Q masks." He pointed to the officers up ahead.

"They're in short supply, apparently; we asked," said McAlister.

"You are kidding me."

"Wish I was."

Valentine stopped in his tracks and turned to survey the crest of the rubbish mound that they were standing on. He pointed to the edge of the site, to a concrete wall. "Where did our man come in?"

DS Donnelly spoke. "Over there, side of the wall, got blood and fibers from the squeeze."

"So what's that — a hundred meters?"

Donnelly flicked the pages of a spiral-bound notepad — the action shooed flies. "One-sixty-odd."

Valentine put himself between DS Donnelly and the view of the concrete wall; he widened his arms. "That's a path — as the crow flies — of about three meters wide, yes?"

The remark was greeted with nods.

"Right, Paulo, where are you?"

The DS pushed through the bodies. "Here, boss."

"Yeah, I see you." Valentine pointed to the wall. "From there, in a direct line to the tent, I want everything."

The team looked at each other, then back to the Valentine. McAlister spoke first. "Are you saying you want it bagged, boss?"

"Do I have to say it twice?"

"But it's rubbish — piles of crap."

Valentine shook his head; as the team stared at him, he pointed to the ground and stamped his foot. A cloud of grey dust erupted from beneath his shoe.

"Ally, this could be a goldmine of clues we're standing on, so get the lot of it bagged and stored and not another gripe out of you." He pointed at Rossi. "Paulo. You're the senior officer on here, why the hell have you not been bagging this?"

"Boss, the chief super will do her nut if she hears you've bagged that lot; do you know how much it'll cost? I mean in man-hours, never mind the storage."

Valentine smiled. "I couldn't care less about the cost." He edged forward and fronted up to the assembled group. "Do you know the only economics I care about?" He pointed to the tent. "I care why a group of paid civil servants are standing in the middle of the local dump with a white tent pitched over a dead man. That is all I care about."

Valentine made for the tent. "Come on, let's get a look at our victim."

4

There was nothing to indicate that the white tent, its sides fluttering like the sails of a pleasure boat, contained anything untoward. If the familiar comings and goings of men in white bodysuits had not been relayed on television screens a thousand times before, no one would have had cause to be in the least squeamish at the sight of it. The seagulls seemed to be the most interested in the movement that was underway. They circled overhead, swooping occasionally. They were arrogant birds, thought DI Bob Valentine, as he made to kick a king-sized one from his path. "Flying rats."

"They're bastards, aren't they?" said DS McAlister. "Should see them down the shore flats where I stay — think they run the place."

Valentine let the conversational gambit pass, but McAlister wasn't finished.

"See the roof of the baths, the Citadel, or whatever they're calling it these days, that's where they're nesting. If I was on the council, I'd be getting a squad of workies up there and burning them out."

"Burning them out?" said DS Donnelly.

"Too right I would."

Donnelly tipped back his head and laughed. "What with, flamethrowers?" He was still laughing as McAlister began his reply.

"Listen, mate, you don't have to live down there — the noise and the car covered in shit every morning — you can bloody well bet I'd be taking a flamethrower to them. I'd be bombing the bastards if I could."

The conversation had taken on a combative tone. Valentine knew there was a danger of the ante being increased; if he didn't intervene, the seagull topic would become a boxing match between the DS and the DC.

"Christ above, Ally, you truly regret missing out on 'Nam, don't you?" said Valentine.

Donnelly laughed and pointed at McAlister. "Fancies himself as Chuck Norris."

"More like Steven Seagull." Valentine's remark was greeted with an instant burst of cruel laughter. It took him by surprise — he never thought of himself as that amusing, that much of a joker. "All right, enough's enough." He asserted his authority. "Let's try and remember why we're here."

The squad had reached the entrance to the tent. The front flaps had been secured with a loose knot, which always struck Valentine as wholly insufficient: a light breeze might raise the flaps and expose the contents to those who didn't want to know what was inside, or worse, reveal something to prying eyes that shouldn't see inside.

The DI reached for the knot.

"It isn't pretty, sir," said McAlister.

Valentine peered over his shoulder. "When is it ever?"

As they walked into the tent the temperature was the first thing that the DI noticed; it was several degrees higher than he had expected, but at once he realized that the heat was compounded by the fetid air. The stench from the dump waste was intense inside the tent. Officers on the scene put up ultraviolet fly traps, but they were ineffective against the plague of insects.

"It's got worse in here," said Rossi.

"A statement of the bleedin' obvious," said McAlister.

It didn't strike Valentine as at-all unusual that not a single member of the squad had made any remark about the reason for them being there: the freshly mutilated corpse of a middle-aged man.

The DI was calm with the murder victim in sight. He couldn't explain this: for reasons he was utterly unable to fathom, the first sight of a body on his patch always intensified his obligation to the job.

"I'm thinking he's a child molester," said McAlister.

Valentine waited for another reaction from the squad; when none came, he put forward his own. "You think he's a pedophile because he's been impaled." He waved a hand towards the wooden shaft: "Like this."

"Yeah, up the arse."

The DI straightened his back. "Go on."

McAlister seemed less sure of himself when tested, rocking on the balls of his feet. "Well, from a motive point of view, if he was a pedophile, then a victim would want to, you know ... "

"Return the favor in kind," said Valentine.

 "Stick it up his hole, boss."

The DI let McAlister bask in his opinion for a moment, then dispossessed him of any illusion. "I think you're just giving your mind a treat, son." Valentine shook his head. "That's a reach; you have not one iota of a fact to back it up with. Pure conjecture. Now, if you'd told me you'd ID'd him and he had a record for fiddling with kiddies, I'd say you could be on to something, but a plank of wood up the crack does not a pedo make."

The squad fell into a lulled silence; the sound of swarming flies filled the air. Valentine knew the rest of the team would be reluctant to voice their opinions so freely now — if they were of the same caliber as McAlister's assumptions, then he was glad of that. He lowered himself onto his haunches and returned to the corpse before them. The mouth, its grey lips contorted, drew him; he removed a yellow pencil from his pocket, and with the eraser-end he pushed the lip towards the gumline. He stared for a moment and then extracted the pencil; the lip stayed in its new position with the gumline exposed. He shook the pencil like a doctor with a mercury thermometer and then began to fervently rub the eraser-end in the crook of his elbow.

"We have no ID, I take it?" he said.

Donnelly spoke. "No, boss, they've printed and swabbed, but they were hanging off on the dental cast."

Valentine cut in. "Why?"

"They were waiting on the OK to move him."

The DI shook his head. "I want that done now, not tomorrow morning. Now. And I've seen him, so you can get on that right away."

"Just hang fire, there, Bob." The fiscal depute was crouching under the tent flaps. "You can't move this corpse until I have a death confirmation; come on now, you know the rules." He applied a phony horseshoe smile to his face as he stared down Valentine.

McAlister and Donnelly turned to eyeball the DI, anticipating a reaction. DS Chris Rossi started to speak. "Colin, the ..."

Valentine flagged him down and took a step towards the fiscal. "Keep up, mate. Did you miss the episode of *Dr. Finlay's Casebook* shot at Ayr dump this afternoon?"

"What?"

"The doc's been and gone." Valentine turned to Rossi. "Paulo, get him a death cert' faxed over, eh."

"Yes, boss."

The fiscal was left standing in the middle of the tent as Valentine headed out, the other officers following behind him in a linear formation, trying to keep pace with the DI's quick step.

Valentine pointed the key at the car and the blinkers flickered; he was opening the driver's door as McAlister caught up.

"So, what's your guess, sir?"

"Haven't you learned a thing? I don't deal in guesses."

The DI removed his coat and placed it on the passenger's seat; he was putting the keys in the ignition when McAlister spoke up again. "OK, bad choice of wording. But you must have some ideas."

"It's a single perp, our victim isn't a big lad or in any way fit, so one mid-build male could have handled him. Two would have made a cleaner job of squeezing the body through the gap in the wall."

McAlister interrupted, passing over the collected case files. "So, he was killed somewhere else?"

"I'd say so. The pathologist will confirm the time of death, but I don't think our killer would have wanted to attract any more attention to himself when he already had the stake to hammer into the ground and the corpse to position on top of it."

Valentine started the engine and engaged first gear. "There's something else to consider: our victim's a married man, according to the ring on his finger, and he has some expensive-looking dental implants."

"So, he's well off."

"Well off, and in my experience that always means well-connected. People like that don't end up on a tip with a great spike up their backside unless they've made a very big mistake somewhere along the line, and somebody else wants the world to know all about it."

5

DI Bob Valentine knew that something wasn't sitting right with what he had just observed. It was a crime scene, a brutal murder, and nothing was supposed to sit right, but the information — the sights and sounds, even — were working on an altogether different part of him than usual. As he drove, a shrill chime started to emanate from the dashboard and he noticed the petrol gauge flashing. He had an instinct to curse, but the days of anger were over. He couldn't risk elevating his blood pressure or increasing his stress levels. Not now, Chief Superintendent Martin would be watching him so closely. Her opinions mattered little to him, but in one very important regard her views did matter: she had the ability to judge his future on the force.

Valentine had been questioning just that recently and had found himself wanting. The desire was still there, but he had his inner detractors: the little devils on his shoulders that poked fun at him, told him he'd lost his mettle. After the incident he wondered if he had, but more worryingly than that, he knew others — like Martin — worried also.

The car slowed as Valentine applied the brakes at the roundabout next to the old cattle market — it was a supermarket now, with a petrol station out front. He filled up and waited for a gap in the traffic to open up.

On the remainder of the road out to Maisonhill, the sun's fading light bounced off the rooftops and clouds began slow trails across the sky. The detective massaged the back of his neck as he worked the wheel with the other hand, but the action provided little benefit. Soon the window was wound down, and then to follow it, the radio turned on, then off again.

"Christ all-bloody-mighty."

He was allowing his thoughts to play tag. And he knew why.

As Valentine pulled into his driveway, he sat listening to the components cooling beneath the bonnet. He inhaled deep breaths but resisted a glance towards the front window. He became dimly aware of a figure in the front room, but he refused to acknowledge it.

The sound of the seatbelt being pulled into the inertia reel jolted the detective, pressed the fact that he was home – Chloe and Fiona would be in there, and also Clare. He opened the door of the car and eased himself out. It was still warm, perhaps even warmer outside than inside the car. Valentine tugged the knot of his tie free and loosened off the top button of his shirt as he moved to the back door of the vehicle to retrieve his case and folders. The dark patch on the back seat stared out at him as he lifted the items and for a moment it held his attention. He stared at the marked fabric, the blotch of ingrained staining that no scrubbing or chemical wonder-product had been able to shift. Surely it should have been removable. At least, by this time, shouldn't it have faded?

"Bob. Are you coming in?" It was Clare.

"Yes, of course. Just picking up a few files." He slammed the car door and directed the key ring, which locked the vehicle with one click.

"What are those?" Her tone was pitched higher.

As Valentine turned towards the house, he caught his wife's stare full on. There was no hiding the fact that he was carrying case notes; she recognized the familiar blue files Ally had given him earlier. He halted where he stood, brought the folders up to his chest and dipped his chin towards the edge.

"Well ... "

He didn't get any more words out. Clare turned from him. He watched her blonde hair flounce off her shoulders, catching a momentary tail of sunlight, and then she was gone. The front door of his home stood open wide and the long, carpeted corridor lay in darkness.

Inside the house, Clare sat on one of the kitchen's bar stools with a long cigarette in her fingers. She seemed content to ignore her husband, staring out into the garden through the open window as he walked in and placed his case and folders on the worktop. He watched her for a moment as she poked the inside of her cheek with the tip of her tongue — her angry gesture — and then he reached out for the cigarette.

"Come on, you don't need that."

Clare recoiled quickly. "Just bloody leave it!"

Valentine watched as his wife jerked away the cigarette and showered the distance between them with a trail of amber sparks from the burning tip.

"OK. It's only you I'm thinking about."

She huffed loudly, rolling her eyes towards the ceiling. "Is it really?"

It was quite a performance from Clare; he'd been deprived of the petulant turns of late and her sudden return to form was a shock. "I don't get it."

She rose. "No, you don't, that's for sure and certain."

Valentine recognized the fact that he had walked into one of Clare's ambushes now. It didn't matter what he said, or how he said it, almost certainly it would be the wrong thing. In their battles she had covered the entire house with lethal tripwires and he knew when he had sprung one. He didn't want to upset Clare either, he was grateful for how she had been these last few months, but the return to their familiar routine now felt like everything they had gone through was for nothing.

"Clare, I have a job to do."

She bit. "Not that job." She dangled the cigarette over the blue folders; her voice quivered above the jumble of words. "You said after what happened you'd be, what was it? Put out to grass."

Valentine watched his wife paint on a knowing smile. It was the look she wore when pointing out that she had outsmarted her husband, outmaneuvered him. It was the glib look of a smart-arse, the kind of expression that, outside of the immediate family, no one would contemplate trying on him.

"I do what I'm told, Clare." The reply was weak, and he regretted it the second it came out. What was worse, however, was that it was a blatant lie and he knew that Clare would see that.

She exhaled a long trail of smoke and started to stub the cigarette in the ashtray. Valentine waited for some kind of rebuttal, but none came, and that was worse. Clare knew when the situation had gone beyond words because the silence said so much more.

"Clare." As he spoke, the cell phone in Valentine's pocket started to ring. He ignored it for a moment. "Clare." His wife started to move away from him as he looked at the caller ID. "I'm sorry, I have to get this."

Clare steadied herself on the rim of the sink and looked out towards the garden. She bit down on her lower lip for a moment and then began to speak. "I was an idiot to think anything had changed."

Valentine watched his wife walk from the kitchen and close the door behind her; it bounced loudly off the jamb.

In a second or two, Chloe's head popped from the living room. She glanced at the blue folders. "Oh, back to work."

Valentine gave a weak wave to his daughter. He pressed a green button on his ringing phone and spoke. "Hello, boss."

"Well?" the chief super's voice came shrilly down the line.

"White male, middle to upper, with a serious grudge against him."

"ID?"

"No, not yet anyway."

She cut in. "Why no ID?"

"Well, I'd say it's in the post. Expensive dental that will be somebody's handiwork."

Valentine heard the chief super shuffle the phone into her other hand. A television set was blaring. He smiled to himself as he remembered Jim's *EastEnders* soap opera remark.

"Have you picked anything else up?"

"Yeah." He slapped the back of his neck for effect. "Enough fly bites to last me a lifetime."

"Stick to the case, Bob."

"I'll know more tomorrow, when we do the post-mortem."

Another interruption. "Christ's sake, why's that not being done tonight?"

"The usual reasons — personnel."

"Well, put your foot in that pathologist's bloody arse!"

"It's not the pathologist, it's his team. They won't be with us until first thing. After that we'll be rolling."

"Is there nothing sticking out?"

"Apart from the dirty great plank, you mean?" Valentine regretted the incursion into humor: CS Martin didn't possess a sense of humor.

"I'm glad you seem to be enjoying yourself so much since I've brought you back onto the squad, Bob. I think you and I should have a little chat before you start enjoying yourself a wee bit too much."

Valentine's facial muscles conspired to form a scowl. "Meaning?"

She snapped: "Meaning make your way to my office first light tomorrow morning before you do another bloody thing."

"But I have the post-mortem first thing, in Glasgow."

"Send Paulo. Be at my desk for nine."

"Yes, boss."

He said the words but no one heard them; she had hung up.

6

As Valentine walked around the mutilated corpse of the murder victim, he had the strangest feeling that he should be elsewhere. He remembered agreeing to meet the chief super, but the pressing urge to take one last look at the crime scene had supplanted that instruction. There was a heat inside his chest that shouldn't have been there, a pressure that sent his heart rate racing. For a moment he looked around for somewhere to rest, to take the strain off his body weight, but there was nowhere. The flies had gone now. He didn't know where, or care. It was dark, too. Night-time.

Valentine started to run fingers nervously through his hair. He heard his throat wheezing and then his state of self-absorption exploded. "Who the hell let the child into the crime scene?"

The detective pushed aside the assembled mass of milling bodies. He saw the child, a small girl of maybe five or six years old, in a bright red raincoat. She was blonde, that pale-to-white color like Fiona's and Chloe's had been. And she was dancing around inside the crime scene tent like it was a kiddies' playground.

"Paulo, who let the bloody kid in?"

No one seemed in the least bit bothered about the little girl. It made him wonder if they had been struck blind and dumb; was he alone in sensing the deeply inappropriate nature of the situation?

"Get her out of here! Get her away from that body!"

The child was laughing, smiling. She had been picking daisies and held a bunch of them in her hand. She was a sweet wee thing — a cutie, his wife would say — but she should have been away feeding the ducks or picking out a sweetie for herself; not here, not anywhere near here.

"Hey." He was being ignored. His indignation lit, his nostrils flared — he expected the reek of the dump's moldering refuse, but instead he smelled flowers, daisies. "What are you doing here?"

There were too many people, too many officers and uniform, too many crime scene people. They were all trespassing on his crime scene. He was the officer in charge, but his authority was being ignored. The detective lunged out, reached for the girl that no one else seemed to have even noticed. Valentine was caught by his arms and shoulders; he was held back.

"Get off me." He started to lash out. "Get your bloody hands off me."

The girl giggled. She watched the others holding Valentine back as he shouted out. He could still see her; she had bright-blue eyes that burned into him. Was she familiar to him? He didn't think so, but she seemed to recognize him. It was all a game to her.

"Get off me. Get the girl."

The little girl stood over the murder victim and for a moment Valentine caught her expression change. She looked unhappy now. He knew it was wrong; he didn't want the girl to see the dead body, the blood. He wanted to pick her up and take her away, back to her parents, but he couldn't move.

"Get away!" He lashed out with his arms. He just wanted to help the little girl. "Get away! Get away!"

He was flailing, his heart pounding hard against the inside of his ribcage.

"Bob."

Valentine heard his name called and the little girl slipped out of view. He saw her bunch of daisies resting on the corpse's chest, glowing like fairy lights, like the child had completed a bizarre ritual only she understood.

"Bob."

He recognized the voice now. When he saw Clare's face, the arms constricting him let go.

"Clare." He was at home, sitting upright in bed.

"You were screaming."

"What?" He felt lost.

Clare sat up and turned on the bedside lamp. "It must have been a dream."

"No, it wasn't a dream."

She touched his back. "You're absolutely soaking wet."

Valentine turned away, draped his legs over the side of the bed and lowered his head into his hands. His hair was stuck to his brow.

"I don't know what the hell that was, but it wasn't a dream."

"What was it, then? A nightmare?"

Valentine turned towards Clare. His mind was still full of the images of the little girl.

"It wasn't that, either. I was there. I was somewhere else."

Clare made a sly look towards her husband. "Get back to sleep, Bob."

"I'm not kidding you, Clare. There was this girl."

"Oh, yes."

"No, a little girl. Like, five or something. She had white hair, like our girls had at that age, and she was ... "

Clare started to rub at her bare shoulders. "She was what?"

"I – I don't know. Just, she had flowers and was putting them on my murder victim."

The mention of the case signaled a shift in Clare's attentiveness. She turned away from Valentine and reached for the lamp. "Get some sleep, Bob."

As the light went out, Valentine rose from the side of the bed and made his way towards the bathroom. The brightness of the main light hurt his eyes, but in a moment, he steadied himself against the cool tiles of the wall and drew deep breaths. His heart was returning to a normal rhythm now. As he opened his eyes, he saw himself in the bathroom mirror. His irises were lined in red; dark shadows sat in pockets beneath them. As he removed his sweat-soaked T-shirt, his eyes were drawn towards the thick ridge of scar tissue that sat in the center of his chest. He never liked to touch the mark — it didn't feel like a part of him — but he allowed his fingertips to dab at the edges of the fatty tissue that surrounded the scar.

"Oh, Jesus."

Valentine wondered what was happening to him. He felt like he had been given another chance at life, but he doubted whether he deserved it. Clare knew he was lucky to be alive and she didn't want to take the chance on losing him again.

Valentine started to run the cold tap and, slowly, to douse the back of his neck with water. The first splash made him shiver.

The bedroom was in blackness, only the orange fizz of the street lamps burned beyond the strips of blinds. He lowered himself down on the edge of the bed and placed a hand on Clare's bare back.

"Clare, I need to talk to you."

"Tomorrow. I need to sleep."

"It's important."

"Can't it wait?"

Valentine got into the bed and drew up the duvet. "I'm not doing this for me."

"Doing what?"

"Taking on this case. I can't explain it."

"Well, good. We can talk tomorrow."

Valentine reached over to turn on the bedside light; Clare grumbled and sat up.

"Right, you have my attention, can we get this over with?"

"About earlier, when you saw the case files, I knew you wouldn't be pleased."

She tutted. "And you knew why."

"Clare, please, I'm trying to explain. I feel like I've changed, been through some kind of life crisis."

"It was a crisis, all right, you nearly died, Bob. Jesus Christ, you nearly left me a widow and ... " She looked away.

Valentine's emotional-response signal flared. "And who'd have cleared your Visa bills then? Was that what you were going to say?"

He watched his wife raise a hand to her thinned lips. "That's not what I was going to say at all."

"I'm sorry. That was a low blow."

Clare looked towards the ceiling and shook her head.

Valentine sighed. "You just don't see where I'm coming from. I feel I have this new chance and that I should make a difference. I can't properly explain it, Clare, I feel like a different man."

Clare put her head in her hands. "Well, you're certainly that. You just look through me and the girls now." She met his gaze for a second but couldn't hold it. "Oh, just forget it. Forget everything." Clare reclined in the bed, turned over and switched off the light.

Valentine thought about reaching out and touching his wife's bare shoulder, saying sorry again and trying to talk. But he decided to lie down on the bed and close his eyes.

7

Valentine arrived at King Street station before the early shift had sorted itself out. He saw the youngish bloke who sometimes filled in for Jim behind the frosted glass, but he avoided eye contact. The bloke was one of those he didn't know but who would definitely know him, or of him. It was becoming tiresome, being a well-known face.

On the stairs, Valentine thought about the rest of the murder squad. They would now be heading up the A77 on their way to the morgue in Glasgow – to the dead place. Under normal circumstances, Valentine could take or leave a visit to the morgue but today he would have traded places with any one of them. Of course, he didn't like the accompaniments of the trip — the place seeped into the very fibre of your clothes and hair and colleagues came to sense it on you. A few liked to remark on the observation, but he could never understand the fascination that people who dealt with the dead every day had about an exaggerated storage facility. There were no souls stirring in the air; the dead did not sit up and speak or reveal their secrets.

In the canteen, Valentine paused with his finger over the button for black coffee, removed it, and selected white tea.

If he were being honest about his tastes the caffeine would have been more welcome, but he knew his nerves would soon be tested enough by Chief Superintendent Marion Martin. He took his tea, his case notes and briefcase, and made for the corner of the large, open room.

The detective's synapses were sparking with a familiar preoccupation now: his meeting with Dino would be a farce. It would play to a script because that's what the world dictated of such scenarios. The exchange that awaited him now would be no different. He was old enough and experienced enough to know that he was more likely to get the outcome he desired by playing dumb. Power liked dumb: it meant pliable and he was all for that — he would be as pliable as putty to get his way.

"Bob." His name came uttered under breath. As Valentine looked up, he saw the chief super stationed at the door with her coat slung over her shoulder, a broad flank and hip pointing in his direction.

"Oh, hello." He rose from behind the table and collected his possessions. A sliver of grey liquid evacuated from the rim of the white cup as he raised his tea.

"Leave it, Bob, I've some good stuff in my office." The wink she tailed off her remark with seemed wholly unnecessary to Valentine – unless the intention was to see him fetch up his last meal.

He smiled — deeply ironically — and followed in the chief super's wake.

"Shut the door, Bob," said the chief super. She walked over to the window. A jug kettle sat on top of a small filing cabinet. She raised the kettle, shook to test its water content, then pressed down the red button. "Coffee or tea?"

Valentine lowered his briefcase beside the chair in front of the chief super's desk. "Tea's good for me, thanks." He didn't really want a drink; he wanted the rigmarole over with. He wanted away from the cold, clinical office that didn't contain a breath of life between its walls. He wanted to stride down to his incident room and get to work on the case — to find out who the poor sod with the expensive dentistry and the large stick up his backside was. But he knew it was never going to be that simple. The chief super wanted to put him through the mill, she wanted to test his mettle — perhaps for no other reason than that she could and the simple act of the assessing would, as a direct consequence, assert her authority.

"So, how's Clare?" she said. It seemed a standard opener, a starter for ten.

"Fine, all good, thanks." His voice sounded like someone else's to him. His words were of the sort of slippery dinner-party chat that he despised.

"She'll be glad to have you in one piece, I suppose."

He smiled, reaching over to collect his cup of tea. The CS droned on, something about the girls — she didn't know their names — and how it must have been a terrible shock. She used the words "terrible shock" like their father receiving a cold blade in the heart had been no more than another day at the office.

"Fifty pints of blood." She jerked herself back in the chair, retrieved the note from the file she was reading and held it up. "That can't be right, surely?"

Valentine worried at the handle of his cup; it was hot, too hot for his fingertips. He placed the cup on the desk as he looked at the chief super. "It was fifty, yes."

"Jesus Christ. How many pints are in the human body?"

"Eight, I think."

She leaned forward, peering over the bridge of her nose as she spoke. Her voice was a shrill whine that echoed off the walls in ways that suggested she knew how to play the acoustics to their best effect.

"I can't believe they gave you fifty pints of blood, Bob. Fifty! There wouldn"t be any of your own blood left in you after that, then."

Valentine scratched behind his ear, shuffled in his seat uncomfortably. He had spent so long reliving the trauma that it had taken concerted effort to shift the images from his mind — but here they were again.

"What there was of my own blood ended up on the operating-room floor."

The chief super tipped her head cockily to the side. "Must have been black pudding on the menu that night, eh?"

She began a laugh that mounted a full-scale assault on Valentine's senses. He watched her meaty shoulders quaking under her already broad shoulder pads and something like pity for her lack of compassion entered his consciousness. He wanted to tell her that he had been stabbed in the heart, in the line of duty; it was not any source of amusement to him or his family. The pain of recall was nothing compared to the event, yet the prolonged agonies of its aftermath — the tears he had watched his wife and girls shed — were something he would never be greeting in even the remotest neighborhood of laughter.

She continued to read from the notes: "Left ventricle stab wound from below, through diaphragm. Angiography on arrival at A&E, followed by thoracotomy … Oh my God, this is just horrific reading, Bob

... Thick-walled ventricle contracted and closed the hole ... Heart-lung bypass for repair ..."

She put down the notes. "And how are you now?"

The detective raised his open palms and weighed the air. "Right as rain."

"Come on, don't play the bullshitter with me. You took a knife in the heart, on the job. You officially died, at least twice from what I can make out."

"I'm here now."

She picked up her cup of tea and sipped at it. The liquid vanished like rainwater in a gurgling gutter.

"I can see that. What I'm getting at is, how much of the old Bob have I got here in front of me?"

He cut in. "And how much was lost?" He leaned forward, balancing the point of his index finger on the rim of her desk. "And how much of the old Bob was left on the operating table, is that what you're getting at? None. Let me tell you that for once and for all. None. I am here in one piece and raring to go."

The chief super ran her tongue over the front of her teeth. Thoughts were queuing behind her green eyes. Valentine read the thoughts as easily as if they had been displayed in a PowerPoint presentation. She was going by the book, making sure she had done her due diligence. If there had been any other option available to her then he would still be at Tulliallan, teaching new recruits how to lace their shoes, and she wouldn't be worrying about the possibility of drafting in officers from another force to work her patch.

She rubbed at the bridge of her nose as she returned to the file in front of her. "It says here you had some psychotherapy."

"I was stabbed in the heart; they're not going to let me back on the force without looking at my head."

"It might be an idea to keep the therapy up for your return to active duty."

"I don't think it's necessary."

"I didn't ask if you thought it was, Bob. I'm telling you it's coming and you're going to jump at it with both hands if you want to take on this investigation."

Valentine had a reply on his lips, but he swallowed it.

"Good," said the chief super. "We'll see how you go with this. Any signs of stress, I want to know about it, do you hear me?"

"Yes, boss."

She closed the folder, put it back in the drawer and flagged Valentine towards the door.

"Get yourself into the incident room and brief your team."

"Most of them are at the post-mortem this morning, but I'll need to brief the others, and the press office."

She blinked her eyes towards the ceiling tiles. "Oh God, yes. I do not want to have the media jumping up and down about this today. Give them nothing. No, less than nothing."

"That's all we have at present."

Valentine reached out for the door handle, and as he grabbed it the chief super called out.

"Oh, Bob, what did he get for the stabbing? Young Darren Hainey, wasn't it?"

"What do you think he got? A slap on the wrist with a feather."

8

Detective Inspector Bob Valentine's jaw tightened as he walked from the chief super's office; his teeth would be grinding next. He knew there were good reasons for him not to play up the emotions he was feeling — the strain it placed on his heart, that hard-pressed, overused and badly damaged muscle, was one good reason — but he also knew he had never been very good at containing his anger. Dealing with Chief Superintendent Marion Martin suddenly felt like an unnecessary and unwelcome weight to add to the load he was pushing uphill. Throwing him under the watch of a psychotherapist was a low blow, anyone in his position would have objected to that.

Valentine halted mid-stride and checked his watch, tapped the face. He tried to clear his thoughts and assess what he needed to do — more than bemoan his boss. One of the civilian staffers passed by and glanced his way; he felt his skin prickling as he made a poor attempt at a smile. He gripped tight to the handle of his briefcase and walked on.

The incident room was bare. Valentine strolled between the rows of tables towards the broad window that looked out onto the town of Ayr. He didn't know how long he'd been staring out the window, hands in pockets, just contemplating the day and his duties, when the heavy doors clattered off the top wall and two female PCs giggled their way into view.

The two young officers seemed wholly unaware of his presence at the other end of the room. Valentine felt invisible as he watched them dislodging photographs from the blue folders in their arms.

He approached the table and started to leaf through the photographs from the crime scene. The first one to strike him was of the victim's face

— the expression he wore looked different from how the detective remembered him. It was strange, he seemed almost contented, but it was the camera playing tricks. The next picture was a close-up of the main entry wound — it would take a perverse mind to be contented by a wooden spike inserted where the sun didn't shine.

DC McAlister was the first of the officers to show, sauntering through the door and nodding to Valentine. "Morning, sir." He moved towards the table and picked up a paper cup. "Coffee, nice one."

Valentine turned back to the board and started to loosen off his collar. "What are your thoughts today, Ally?"

The DC laughed. "Oh, no. Caught me with that already. Not making any guesses."

Valentine smirked. "How's the sweep-up going?"

"They got the lion's share of the garbage bagged last night, take a wee while for them to sift through it. You know Dino's going to lose her nut when she hears about that."

"Leave her to me." Valentine picked up a cup. "I'm the one calling the shots. How many uniforms have you got sifting through the rubbish?

"Plenty, about twenty at least."

"Double it."

What?

The DI tilted his head towards McAlister. "You're not going to make me ask you twice, are you?"

"No, sir." He placed the paper cup on the table and reached for the telephone. As he spoke into the receiver, Valentine returned to the folder containing the photographs and looked for the accompanying paperwork.

There was a list of items that the photographer had seen fit to draw attention to: scrapes on the wall of the dump; red markings that may have been blood on a sheet of corrugated iron; a fresh splinter of wood that had detached from the wooden stake. He matched the list to the pictures and tacked them to the wall.

McAlister raised the paper cup to his lips and nodded approvingly. "That blood splatter's in for testing.

"Know it's blood, do you?"

"Looks like it." He took another swig from the coffee cup, then altered his voice to a more matter-of-fact tone. "Right, that's for the dump's team."

Valentine smirked. "Tell me about the door-to-door last night."

McAlister sighed. "Well, it didn't turn up much. There was a white van in the locus around 9 p.m. and ... " He put down his cup again and removed a spiral-bound notepad from his jacket pocket. "Yeah, around 9 p.m., and it was seen again about 9.30-ish. It could have been a delivery — y'know, no one in and he's leaving it with a neighbor."

Valentine scrunched his brows. "At 9 p.m., working late for a delivery man. Did anyone get a license plate number?"

McAlister shook his head.

"Nobody ever does," said Valentine. "Check it out, see if anyone on the street got anything delivered, or a tradesman called between 9 and 9.30. You know the drill."

Way ahead of you, sir. Got uniform on that this morning. Got the whole area gridded off and being checked."

"Good." Valentine knew they were searching for the slightest lead, anything. A chance encounter, a strange-looking maneuver in the street, just something that stuck out as unusual and could be examined more closely. This was the vital time: the chances of solving the case depended on the information that came in during the first forty-eight hours. After that, clues withered, got washed away, and singularly human traits like memory and waning interest came into play.

Valentine and McAlister were returning to the folders when there was a thud on the swing doors of the incident room and a rush of movement sent a gale to upend the paperwork.

"Do you want the good news or the bad?" It was the chief super, marching towards them as the doors passed each other in an out-of-sync motion.

Valentine sensed McAlister turning towards him, but he looked away at the quick-stepping chief super.

"What do you mean?" he said.

"ID on your corpse from the tip." She spat the information in a staccato burst. "Oh, and you'll love this as well, he's a banker!"

Valentine let himself pause for breath to digest the sudden turn of events. As he watched the chief super draw up to within inches of his stance, he became aware of her heady perfume. "And the bad news?"

She reached out and flicked Valentine's tie. "You'll need to smarten yourself up. The news hounds are on the sniff."

9

As he rolled over his thoughts, Valentine had an urge to laugh out. He resisted, but only because he knew the joke was on him. He was bemused by his repeated indignation at the world's injustice.

"When was it never thus?" he said.

"What's that, sir?" DC McAlister glanced over from the driver's side of the car.

"Nothing. Just thinking aloud." Valentine closed the blue folder that was sitting on his knee and rested his elbow on the window's edge. The road out to Alloway was quiet, only the odd 4x4 on the way back from the school run. He remembered when the girls were younger, how he would catch them counting the Ayr number plates whenever they were on the road out to Alloway. The scenery certainly changed, the closer you got to the big houses.

"Did you catch the look on Dino's face when she came in with the news? Thought she'd nabbed a bone."

Valentine removed his face from the breeze blowing in from the window. Outside, the sun was a dull copper penny being bullied from the sky by bulky rain clouds. "That'll be short-lived, knowing her."

McAlister stole a glance at the DI. "Yeah, she's rarely pleased for long."

"I mean, if you think this is going to be an open-and-shut case, you're deluded. It's never simple where the moneyed classes are involved."

McAlister rounded the bend at Alloway Church and depressed the clutch as he took a lower gear. "At least we have an ID."

Valentine sneered over the brim of his nose. "We've a report of a missing person who fits the bill — let's wait and see if family formally identifies him."

McAlister over-revved the engine and then managed to grind the gears; he was shamed enough to look embarrassed. "Sorry, boss."

"Don't worry about it, I think we've already drawn enough attention to ourselves driving around in a cheap model Vauxhall."

"Yeah, it's Beemer country."

The normal procedure of planning regulations seemed to have been abandoned, with red-brick mansions sitting next to slope-roofed nods to modernism. Valentine knew he was entering another world to the one he inhabited, and the discomfort he carried about the case started to make itself known again. He rolled up the window and returned to the blue folder to read the notes that had been hurriedly printed off before he left the station. If this were their victim, then he was called James Urquhart and had been a former head of a stockbroker's that had been bought out by the Bank of Scotland before the financial crash of 2008. He hadn't hung about to get cozy with the new company, but had opted for early retirement. The notes didn't say much more, but the grainy photograph that had been taken from the Internet was a definite likeness for the corpse Valentine had seen at the tip.

The car started to decelerate as they turned into Monument Road.

"Right, I think this is us, sir."

The driveway was gated, and as the car slowed to a halt McAlister leaned out from his window to press the intercom button — but the gates were already in motion.

"Bingo, we're in," he said.

The car's tires scrunched over the gravel as they rolled up the long drive towards the mansion house.

"Looks like they gave him a hefty payout," said Valentine.

"Come again?"

"Urquhart was the boss of a stockbroker's that was bought out three months before the crash."

"Lucky timing."

"Yeah, very."

As they reached the end of the driveway, a youth in jeans and a T-shirt waved them to a side entrance. The pair parked up behind a Range Rover that looked to have been abandoned after braking heavily in the loose chippings.

Valentine was first from the police vehicle; he strode round the front of the car and nodded to the young man. The detective watched the youth dig his hands into his pockets and raise his shoulders awkwardly. He didn't make eye contact, but Valentine was close enough to see the pitted declivities that bordered his hairline in a sad echo of once-rampant acne.

"Hello, I'm Detective Inspector Bob Valentine and this is my colleague, Detective Constable McAlister."

The pair were greeted with a nod but no introduction.

Valentine went for the direct approach. "And you would be?"

"Adrian." He removed his hands from his pockets.

"Urquhart?"

He nodded. "My mum's inside."

Valentine raised a hand towards the door and started to walk. The wind was picking up and thin, dark rain clouds cut the sky. The home was airy; some muddy footprints that looked like they had come from Wellington boots covered the floor, but everywhere else was neat and tidy. Adrian ushered the police officers through to the lounge and directed them towards his mother, who was sitting next to a ruddy-cheeked man with his arm around her shoulder. As the officers were introduced to the man called Ronnie, he removed his arm and leaned back in the sofa.

Valentine approached the pair, which prompted Ronnie to distance himself further. "I'll leave you be," he said, rising and turning to face Mrs. Urquhart. "I'll drop in again later. Just to see how you are."

She nodded and sucked in her lower lip.

Valentine kept his eyes on Ronnie; he thought about engaging with him but decided it wasn't the time or place. As the neighbor hurried out the door, Mrs. Urquhart made to stand, but her balance didn't seem to be functioning — she flounced onto the sofa's arm and Adrian ran to her side to support her.

"It's OK, there's no need to get up, Mrs. Urquhart," said Valentine. He watched her steady herself on the couch once more: her face was gloomy, the droop of heavy eyelids accentuated by dark hollows above the cheekbones. As she took in Valentine, he felt her searching stare: it was a look that spoke to you without words; it was such a knowing look that Valentine wondered if his own thoughts were as readable as the pages of a book to her.

He shifted himself sideways, sat down on the adjacent seat and crossed his legs. "Hello, Mrs. Urquhart. I believe you called the station."

She nodded. "Yes."

"Can you tell me when you first became aware that your husband was missing?"

Adrian squeezed his mother's hand. "I think it must have been sometime yesterday afternoon."

"I take it Mr. Urquhart has never been missing like this before?"

"No. Never."

Valentine cast a glance at McAlister, who was walking around the room. "You will be aware of the television news bulletin."

Mrs. Urquhart nodded again, she scrunched up her eyes as she spoke. "Yes."

Valentine shuffled uneasily on the chair, the woman was in no fit state for questioning, but it was one of those moments where the demands of the job overrode etiquette. He lowered his voice. "I have to ask you, are you capable of making an identification?"

She looked towards her son and buried her head in his chest.

Adrian spoke. "Can I do that?"

Valentine's mouth widened, but he didn't have time to answer.

"No. I'll do it, detective," said Mrs. Urquhart.

Valentine rose from the chair and beckoned to McAlister. It was pointless pressing her: very little of any value could be obtained from someone in such a state. There was a thought pressing itself upon Valentine's mind, though: most murder victims knew their killers. She might indeed be in shock, but her gut reactions would be difficult to fake.

"Mrs. Urquhart, if I may ask just one question before we progress." The DI paused for a moment. "Can you think of anyone who would have cause to harm your husband?"

Mrs. Urquhart looked to her son and then turned on the detectives. "No, no one." Her cut-glass vowels seemed even sharper now. "Why would anyone want to do such a thing?"

10

On his return to King Street station, Valentine collected a stack of notes from the front desk and retreated to the glass-partitioned end of the incident room. He was haunted by the look on Mrs. Urquhart's face as she had taken in the growing realization that her husband was not coming home. No matter how many times Valentine saw the look, he could not get used to it. He remembered what it had been like to see his mother on her deathbed.

To see someone he loved dying, to know they were going to leave him forever, had marked death as permanent in his own existence for the first time. Valentine sensed the cold shift immediately. He never wanted death to be a personal matter again, because it was all too personal as it was.

The detective turned over the cover of the blue folder that he had positioned in the middle of his desk and stared at the first page. The post-mortem report was not a big document — it always surprised him how little information the ending of a life seemed to generate. Valentine turned the pages and scanned to the section where conclusions, of a sort, were made. He had tried to prejudge the pathologist's outcome because in his gut he felt the victim had been killed a certain way, but Valentine knew better than to jump to conclusions.

The first term to attract his attention was "traumatic brain injury." There had been a depressed skull fracture, the result of blunt force. More detail was given: acute subdural hematoma, cerebral contusions, dramatically increased intracranial pressure. They were all terms familiar to the DI, jargon he classed as necessary evils, but they all mounted up to the same thing in his book: James Urquhart had been hit on the head by someone who wanted him dead.

Valentine was hunched at his desk, poring over the pathology report, when the hinges on the door called out and DS Rossi and DS Donnelly walked in.

"Sir." Donnelly was the first to acknowledge the officer in charge.

"Come in, lads." He turned over the final page of the report and closed the blue folder. "Just going over the post-mortem."

Rossi nodded. "Hammer or a crowbar, something like that."

"Well, it was pretty clear it wasn't done out at the tip. There wasn't enough blood, or anyone picking up on a struggle on the boundary street."

"He wasn't alive when he was squeezed through that fence, that's for sure," said Donnelly.

Valentine placed his fingers on the rim of the desk and slowly pushed the wheels of his chair back. He was talking as he rose and walked over to the window. "There's no evidence of a struggle, not so much as a fingernail scraping."

"Not one, no battle scars at all, sir." Rossi kept his eyes on the DI. "So, he's been whacked and then moved. But why to the tip?"

Donnelly folded his arms, then quickly removed one to illustrate his speech with wild, looping gestures. "That's a message for somebody right there, Rossi. The tip's where the rubbish goes; he's been dumped there because someone wants the world to know exactly what they thought of James Urquhart."

Valentine's thoughts were building to a fog inside his head. He had been content to sift through the facts in the report, to analyze and to draw his own conclusions. He felt now like he was being side-tracked by the officers — it was as if he had set out for a leisurely stroll and the sudden incursion into his office had resulted in a cross-country run.

"OK. Let's keep the party clean. We don't know the first thing about this victim yet, we can't be jumping to the conclusion that the place we found him is a marker to his murderer's state of mind."

Donnelly flared up. "But it's an option, boss."

Valentine nodded, allowed a slight indicator of doubt to play on his face, and then delivered a puncture to the DS's ego. "Our killer might have thought the worst about Urquhart, or the best, or any one of a million other perceptions you could list. Just because you can put options on a list, it doesn't validate a single bloody one of them."

Donnelly rubbed at the stubble on his chin. He didn't seem to have any more to add to the debate at present.

Valentine spoke. "You're right about one thing though, Phil." Donnelly's head lifted as he eyed the DI. "We need to keep our options open. At this stage, all ideas are worth investigating."

The remark seemed to be enough balm to cover Donnelly's pride. "Yes, sir."

"Right, I think it's time we put our heads together," said Valentine. "Paulo, get Ally and the team together round the board. I want to talk to them in ten minutes."

DS Rossi pinched his cheeks. "I think Ally's upstairs at the press office, there was something said about a statement." He shrugged his shoulders and levelled a palm at Donnelly.

"Search me," said DS Donnelly. "That boy's a law unto himself."

Valentine circled his ear with an index finger. "If he thinks he's going to be standing in front of a camera this afternoon, he's dreaming. You can tell him from me, if he's any ambitions on that front then he better be preparing to streak down King Street."

DS Rossi and DS Donnelly took their cue to laugh up their colleague as they exited the DI's office.

Valentine drew back into the moment, removed himself from the claustrophobia of thought, and immediately turned his gaze on the two fingers he was rubbing against the shirt pocket on his chest. Was he checking his heartbeat? Trying to massage sympathy into the damaged muscle? As soon as he became aware of his actions the detective jerked his hand away.

"Christ above." He knew he was coming close to losing focus, and that worried him.

He looked out towards the incident room: the team were gathering.

11

As Valentine closed the door on the partitioned office in the corner of the incident room, he saw the doors at the far end swing open. There was a flourish of long dark hair and a thudding of high heels. As the detective stared at Chief Superintendent Marion Martin, he observed a numbness in his throat that he knew was caused by the automatic locking of his jaws. She stomped through the mass of bodies with all the grace of a bulldozer and made straight towards the noticeboard, where Donnelly stood with a photograph in hand. As the chief super halted, she dropped her barely perceptible chin onto her fleshy neck and swiped the picture from Donnelly's outstretched fingers. She started to speak as she waved the photo like a baby's rattle in the DS's face. Valentine had seen the chief super carry on like this before; she came into investigations and stood in the corner like a headmistress who'd come to oversee a less experienced teacher.

It was off!

He pressed his tongue on the roof of his mouth and tried to release his locked jaws. He could sense the familiar copper taste that precipitated anger; it was enough to alert him to the off switch. As he walked, he put his hands in his pockets and tried to remind himself that he had a bigger aim than playing office politics with Dino.

"Right, everybody." He made sure his voice was heard. "Can I have your undivided attention?"

There was a rustle of paper; a filing cabinet drawer was closed loudly and a ringing telephone cut off by dumping the receiver on a desktop.

"Well, I'm not shouting to the four corners of the station, so you can gather round here."

As the squad started to assemble, the detective leaned towards DC McAlister and laid a hand on his shoulder. He kept his voice low. "Ally, what did uniform turn up on the delivery van?"

McAlister shook his head from side to side. "Not good, boss. No deliveries in the locus and no tradesmen uncovered on the door-to-door."

Valentine huffed. "So, we can rule out white van man."

"Unless we turn up another lead, I can't see how the van's useful to us." McAlister turned his gaze towards the board. "Might have been nothing, sir."

Valentine patted the DC on the back and moved with the rest of the room's occupants as they gravitated towards its center. The chief super was left out on the periphery of the group, by the noticeboard, holding the photograph she had snatched from DS Donnelly.

"OK, you'll all have seen the pictures and the crime scene officers' reports — for what they're worth — by now. The post-mortem report is on my desk through there and you can have a look at that if you haven't already. I'm not going to try to prejudge anyone's opinion at this stage; what I want is to make sure we're all singing from the same hymn sheet."

Together: "Yes, sir."

"Good," said Valentine, edging himself onto the side of a desk, taking the collected gaze of the squad with him. "So, what are we looking at? A brutal, almost ritualistic murder on public ground — if not carried out there, certainly the intention was to make people think so. And of a figure who might be described as privileged, perhaps, extremely wealthy, certainly." He halted, drew breath. "A point in fact: our victim's social status will be a bone of contention with the media — bear that in mind."

A hand went up in the middle of the crowd. "Are you approaching this from a financial perspective, sir?"

The DI shrugged. "We don't have a motive at this stage, but am I willing to explore blackmail or a monetary grudge, maybe even resentment or jealousy? Yes, of course, I want everyone to keep their minds open. This is not the time to be jumping to conclusions, but it's also not the time to be ruling anything out."

DC McAlister leaned forward in his seat and held up a pencil. "If it's related to cash, then why the impaling, boss? Seems a bit unusual."

Valentine smiled at McAlister. "Good point. It's unusual, all right, unless it's a distraction. Make it look like a psycho-killing because you want to draw attention from the fact that the motive is money."

"They could be linked, though," said DS Donnelly. "I mean, say the motive is money, but also a grudge."

"You mean murder's not enough to settle a grudge?" said the DI.

"What I mean is, say our killer wanted to do more than settle a score, say they wanted to pour shame on the victim."

"Or their memory, or the entire family for that matter. Good point, Phil."

Valentine felt like the focus of the team's attention; he could tell by the way they sat forward in their seats, on the edges of desks, that they were as engrossed in the task as he was. In contrast, the chief super seemed to be uninterested. She stood leaning on the wall, arms still folded and long earrings swaying in time with her shifting eyes. She seemed to have had enough.

"Right, I don't think I need to be around for this."

Valentine drew his eyeline level with hers. "Come again?"

She pushed herself away from the wall and stood square footed. "I'm off." She turned for the door. "But I'll see you in my office when you're done, Bob."

The DI followed the line of her steps for a few seconds, then returned to the group, without answering the chief super.

"OK, I'm glad you're keeping your minds open. Let's recap, then: a ritualistic impaling, on public ground, of a wealthy banker. Where do we start? A grudge, maybe. Given the nature of the victim, possibly financial. Given the nature of the execution, possibly sexual or an attempt to make it look that way. I want you all to start thinking about James Urquhart in three-dimensional terms. Who was he? What did others think of him? And what had he done?"

DS Rossi lifted a blue folder. "Boss, the firm he worked for was the subject of a buyout, we should be looking into that."

Valentine nodded. "You take that, Paulo. Let me know what it turns up. I want to know who was for it, who was against it. If there was a significant benefactor or, more importantly, a significant loser, I want to know their inside-leg measurement."

"Yes, sir."

"And, Phil, I want you to dig even deeper into Urquhart's business history: was there an affair? A disgruntled partner, maybe? If there was bad blood between an employee or a client or a bloody delivery boy that didn't like the look of him, I want to know what they had for breakfast the day Urquhart copped it."

"OK, boss."

Valentine pressed his palms together. "Ally, you and I will talk to the victim's next of kin; we've already made contact so they know our faces, but I want you to go beyond that: find out what Urquhart did with himself. Did he belong to any clubs? Play cards on a Saturday night or go out on the pish? Was he passionate about anything?"

"Maybe he was in a cult, sir?" said DS McAlister. "One that put spikes up your arse."

A low hum of laughter passed around the room.

Valentine kept his face firm and pointed at the DS. "You're joking, Ally, but you never know. Check him out, thoroughly. And talk to his neighbors, all of them. Not just the ones he lives beside now, but if he lived anywhere else. And talk to his colleagues, are there any that he's kept in touch with? All of them, Ally."

"Yes, sir."

Valentine caught the wave of spreading energy and turned towards the group.

"Right, get on with it. Anything that you turn up, I want to see it straight away. However insignificant you think it is, I want to know. If you can't get hold of me, then go to Ally or Phil, or in emergencies, Paulo! Though you'd have to be bloody desperate to do that."

Ally aimed a weak punch at DS Rossi's arm.

"Only messing, Chris," said Valentine. He clapped his hands together. "Right, get to work."

12

Valentine smiled to himself as he went over the markers that the chief super dropped about her state of mind. None of her solar flares could be avoided. The workplace was always a forced union of opposites, a crucible for the embittered, and he knew he had to be on guard lest the collective malaise enveloped him.

He clattered his knuckles off the wooden door, just shy of the brass nameplate, and walked in. "You wanted to see me?"

The chief super was sitting behind her desk, the chair in full recline, her stockinged feet balanced on the brim of a blue folder. In her hands was a copy of a paperback book – Valentine couldn't be sure, because she quickly buried the book in her lap, but it looked like Fifty Shades of Grey.

"What the bloody hell are you doing barging in here, leaving Desperate Dan shapes in my door?" She swung her feet down from the edge of the desk and lunged forward. The sound of the book landing on the floor was unmistakable, but she ignored it.

Valentine's stomach fluttered. "If it's not a good time."

She was rattled, her mouth cinching into a tight little knot. "Shut up and sit down." She raked her fingers through her hair and then grabbed at the edges of her scalp and started to rock her head to and fro.

Valentine casually withdrew the seat in front of the desk and sat down. He crossed his legs and made a point of straightening the crease of his trouser leg. He let his eyes rove around the room while the chief super clawed a blue folder towards her.

"I can come back if you'd prefer," he said. The remark was a prod for her.

She pointed to the chair he sat in. "Stay put." As she turned the pages in the blue folder, her index finger bounced on the table. Valentine noticed how scalloped and short her fingernails were. They'd been bitten to the flesh in a manner normally reserved for adolescents. "Right, here we are." She seemed to be calculating something; he imagined she normally counted on her fingers, but was trying to appear wise before him. "Perhaps you can tell me why I have a lab chit here requesting I facilitate storage for half a ton of bloody rubbish?"

Valentine held firm, he kept his eyes locked with the chief super's. "I'm investigating a murder scene."

CS Martin turned over the folder and slapped the desk. "You put forty uniforms on this, Bob? Forty?"

"I didn't count the exact number, but if you say so."

She pushed herself away from the desk and the castors of her chair sung out. "Oh, I do say so. Forty officers bagging Mars bar wrappers and empty Persil packets on time-and-a-half — does that sound like a good spend of budget, Bob?"

He brought his fist up to his mouth and cleared his throat into it. "Like I said, I'm investigating — "

He was cut off. "Yes, I heard you the first time." The chief super tipped back her neck, stared at the ceiling for a moment and then swung forward. She was pointing at Valentine as she spoke. "You better hope some vital piece of evidence emerges from this midden that we're creating downstairs, Bob, because if not I'll be calling you on a very grave error of judgement."

Valentine folded his hands and started to play with his wedding ring. He would continue to carry out his duties in the same manner; carpeting over the costs of preserving a high-profile murder scene was as pointless as it was embarrassing.

"Is that everything?" he said.

"No, it's bloody not." She reached out for the blue folder again, raked it towards her and started to turn pages over. "I'm warning you now, Bob, don't think about testing my patience. You won't win and your coat's already hung on a slack hook, remember that." As she spoke, she scanned the contents of the page she had alighted upon. Her tone seemed to harden as she changed tack. "Right, what does the name Cameron Sinclair say to you?"

The detective raised his eyebrows. "Bit pretentious, giving a kid two surnames."

Her eyes burned. "Does it ring any bells, Bob?"

"Should it?"

She sat back in her chair. "He's a hack, works for the Glasgow-Sun."

"Not one I've run across before."

"Yeah, well, I'd like you to run across the bastard now."

"What's he done?"

"It's not that he's done anything, but if you can find something, that'd be bloody useful." She seemed to regret revealing her inner thoughts. "Cameron Sinclair has been badgering the press office about our latest stiff."

"Well, I haven't released any information yet and neither has anyone on the squad."

"Well, he's been calling a few people, and a few people have been calling me."

"Like who?"

"People, Bob, people." She let the implication of her words hang in the air between them.

"The murder scene is on the edge of the tip, there's public housing a street away, and we've got a team of crime scene officers with a white tent pitched out there — "

She cut in. "All right, no need to draw me a bloody picture. I don't care if this Sinclair character has got a lead from Joe Public, what I'm more concerned about is if he has an inside track."

Valentine closed his mouth and breathed out slowly through his nostrils. He resented the implication that she was making, but it was just the kind of thing he'd come to expect of the chief super. He watched her crease her eyes at him and knew that his own stare was a notch above threatening, but didn't bother to alter it.

"Be it on the squad, or elsewhere." She had to add the "elsewhere" to get herself out of the bind she'd created.

"I'm not responsible for the entire west coast of Scotland, but no one on my squad talks to the press without my authority and at this stage no one has been given authority."

"All right, Bob, don't give yourself a heart attack."

It was a low blow, but she was all about the low blows.

"If the cat's out the bag, I think we should call a press conference," said Valentine.

"Oh, you do, do you?"

"It would seem the smart thing to do, don't you think?"

Her mouth shut like a zipper, then sprang open again. "As ever, Bob, I'm one step ahead of you. I've called a press briefing and you're fronting it up," — she looked at her wristwatch — "in forty-five minutes."

The response the chief super would have expected, Valentine knew, was complaint.

"Brilliant," he said. "I'll tie in with the media department, then."

In the hallway he started grinding his teeth — it wasn't that he resented being spoken to like a third-rate moron, or the ridiculous assumption that Martin was in possession of superhuman policing prowess, it was the grim realization that this was, in fact, his situation. Valentine understood that he was the officer of last resort — she hadn't wanted to give the case to him — but he now saw that she clearly thought he would live up to her expectations.

As he walked back into the incident room, Valentine wanted to prove the chief super wrong, but more than that he wanted to prove to himself that she was wrong. The case wasn't only about him finding a killer, now; it was about finding the strength inside him to restore his wounded pride.

As he entered the incident room, the detective scanned the rows of desks for a familiar face. He raised a finger and beckoned. "Ally, get yourself over here."

DC McAlister closed the cover on a blue folder and eased himself out of his seat. As he rose, Valentine noticed the squint tie and the hanging shirt tails.

"Can you not smarten yourself up a bit?"

McAlister's mouth drooped; he looked down at his tie and grabbed the knot. "I'm only reading reports, sir."

"I can see that, Ally." He shook his head. "I don't expect you'll ever be heading up Paris Fashion Week, but I want you looking at least presentable if you're going to be standing beside me at the press conference."

"The telly?" said the DC.

"Don't get excited, son, I don't expect you'll be getting introduced to Pamela Anderson."

The room's attention had focused on the conversation now. A ripple of muted laughter spread around the place as the pair turned back for the door. Valentine sensed the shift in the axis and stopped in his tracks. "We're only going to deliver a statement." He homed in on Donnelly and Rossi. "So, you can put the petted lips away. I need your lot here, holding the fort."

The media manager was standing over a table, reading what looked like the prepared statement.

"Hello, Coreen," said Valentine.

"Oh, it's yourself. How's the, eh?" She ran a finger up and down the length of her breastbone.

"Just fine. Is that the statement?"

"Yes, I thought it was best to keep it as general as possible at this stage."

"Are they in situ?"

"More or less." She turned away to the young girl who seemed to be her assistant this month — they changed with the weather. "Is there anyone else coming, Debbie?"

The girl shook her head. "I think they're all in."

Valentine nodded. "Right, let's get this bloody thing over with."

The officers settled themselves behind the desk and Valentine adjusted the microphone. He watched McAlister fiddle with the water carafe and put out a glass for each of them.

"OK, ladies and gentlemen, if I can have your attention please," said the DI. The room fell into silence. "At the Ayr municipal refuse site yesterday morning, a member of the public raised the alarm with police about a possible deceased white male."

A few of the reporters started to rustle notebooks; others adjusted recording equipment.

Valentine continued: "After investigation and having fully secured the site, officers from King Street station confirmed the presence of a white male in his late fifties who had been left at the dump. As a result of that initial investigation, a post-mortem was carried out, which confirmed officers' suspicions that we are dealing with a murder inquiry."

One of the reporters leaned forward in his chair. "Can we have a name?"

Valentine started to shuffle the papers in front of him. "As I said, this is a murder investigation and we would appreciate your patience with regard to what information we can release at this stage."

The reporter called out again. "Is there any truth in the fact that the deceased is a stockbroker called James Urquhart?"

Valentine stood up and pointed to the reporter. "Are you Cameron Sinclair?"

The reporter tapped the ID badge on a lanyard round his neck. "Of the Glasgow-Sun, yes."

Valentine collected up his notes and cut the air with the blue folder. "That's the end of the press conference, everyone. I'm not taking questions, so if you'd like to make your way to the door, please."

He moved out from the desk, took brisk strides towards the front row of reporters and laid a firm hand on Sinclair's shoulder. "I think I'd like to turn the tables and ask you a few questions, Mr. Sinclair."

13

Leanne Dunn woke with a humming in her head and a dull, persistent ache in her stomach. As she eased herself off the edge of the bed, she felt her cold foot touch the bare floorboard and jerked it back. At once, she knew this was a mistake, as it started the bed shaking and sent waves of nausea coursing through her already delicate digestive system. She tried to right herself, placing her body weight on her elbow, and vomited onto the bedspread. The sight of the dark bile made her retch again and more fluid escaped her mouth. As she rocked on the bed's edge, sharp pains pressed into her clenched stomach. She leaned forward, arms gripping shins, and watched as the floor swayed beneath her.

Leanne felt worse than she had in a while, but that was coming to an end because Gillon was due to collect the night's takings. He always brought a few wraps — and she'd had a good night, scoring a ton-fifty — so she'd be clear of the withdrawal symptoms, soon.

Leanne found the strength to attempt another rise from the bed. She looked down at her thin, bruised legs; they were as pale and white as her feet, the only indicators of color being the blackness between her toes. Gillon would yell at her for that: he didn't like his girls looking like street trash. She knew she had to wash before he arrived or he'd remind her of the rules or, worse, withhold the precious wraps.

Leanne managed to stand, but soon started to sway. The sound of Leanne's bony frame landing on the bare boards was a pathetic thud, like shopping spilling from a burst bag. An hour or so after Leanne passed out, she awoke, shivering again, with a thin line of drool tethering her mouth to the filthy floor.

As she curled in the base of the shower cubicle, she began to feel like a return to the real world was possible. She was cold and shivery, but there was no place to hide. Gillon would be arriving soon. She ran her fingers through her wet hair and tried to focus on her face in the mirror. Around her eye the skin had started to yellow after connecting with the boards earlier, but she could cover that with make-up; it would be another day or so before the actual shiner showed and Gillon had anything to complain about.

Leanne felt her body's functions returning. She poured herself a glass of water and turned on the portable television that sat on the kitchen worktop. She didn't know why the news had her attention until she realized that she was staring at a familiar scene — the town of Ayr.

"Shit."

Leanne moved closer to the screen and turned up the volume.

"Police have confirmed the recovery of a body from Ayr's dump and that they are dealing with a murder investigation."

The reporter sounded so formal, not like the people Leanne knew. There were some people she spoke to — punters — who could speak posh, but they tended to keep their mouths shut.

The journalist continued with the report: "Police have refused to confirm the victim's name until family members have formally identified him, but a number of unofficial sources have claimed the victim is a local man, believed to work in the banking industry."

Leanne jumped away from the sink as a loud knock sounded on her front door.

"Leanne, open up!"

She heard more knocking on the door.

"Leanne."

She recognized the voice, but it wasn't Gillon's. She had expected Gillon, but this voice was a shock. She made her way to the front door.

"You need to go away, Danny's coming and he doesn't like you here."

"Leanne, if you don't open this bloody door, I'll knock it down and I'll go through Danny Gillon next!"

Leanne's hands were trembling as she removed the chain from the door and turned the key. There was a sudden gust of stale air from the close as Duncan Knox pushed in.

"You've seen it, then?" He was roaring, his voice pitched high and bursting with emotion.

As Leanne entered the kitchen, she saw Knox standing in front of the television screen with his hands pressed tight to his face. Knox grabbed her, and the dressing gown she was wearing opened up and exposed her scrawny breasts. She shrieked out as he pulled her towards him.

"Haven't you seen what's going on?"

As Leanne turned to look at the screen once more, she retraced her earlier viewing before the knock at the door and pieced the two ends of the report together. It was a murder investigation in their hometown, that much was certain.

"What's that got to do with me?" she said?

Knox pushed her away and stamped his feet towards the other end of the kitchen. "What's it got to do with you — are you kidding?"

"I don't understand."

The man in her kitchen seemed beside himself. He slapped his palm off the side of his face and then ran it over his stubbly chin. He kept walking, pacing, as he spoke. "Don't you know who that is?"

"No."

Knox halted. "It's James Urquhart."

The name took a moment to register on Leanne's memory. "James... It's ..."

"Yes." Knox's voice was thundering now. He crossed the floor towards Leanne and grabbed her by the shoulders. He was shaking her to and fro as he bellowed into her face. "And you better pretend you never laid eyes on him! Do you hear me? Do you hear me?"

Leanne had no words. She was frozen, her body rigid.

"Leanne, do you hear me?" Knox shook her shoulders, and her head lolled on her neck. "You never knew James Urquhart. I mean it: you better keep your hole shut about him. You better, or we've all had it!"

14

Valentine had watched over the years as his wife regaled herself with glossy magazines that portrayed a lifestyle truly alien to her — an alternative reality where the beautiful people frolicked under holiday-brochure blue skies. The inference to be taken was always that an Amex with unlimited credit would deliver you from the woes of reality. It was a myth. The world Clare aspired to didn't exist outside of an ad man's imagination.

It disturbed Valentine that his wife's inner life had become so unhealthy. There was no spiritual side to Clare, no real depth. She possessed no desire, it seemed, to expand her life"s reach beyond accumulating material possessions. She was like a woman who had been shelled out and her innards supplanted with a robotic desire to consume. When she became stressed, like she was now, the obsession intensified. Problems with the girls, or his job, became submerged under mounds of packing foam, crumpled paper, carrier bags and clipped labels.

As Valentine sat down to dinner, he watched Clare fussing about the kitchen. The dress she wore was new, but the time when he would make a comment on a new item of clothing worn by his wife had passed — now, any remark would be met by recriminations. He stored the fact of the dress away, though; if Clare was seeking solace in shopping then it was good to be forearmed with the knowledge.

She placed his food down in front of him and pulled out her chair.

"What's this?" said Valentine.

"It's dinner," said Clare. She sat down beside him and began to pick at the food on her plate.

"Salad, I recognize. This looks like chicken or pork, but it's neither."

"It's tofu."

"And what the hell's that when it's at home?"

"It's good for you, is what it is — eat it!"

Valentine stared at the contents of his plate and turned over a few pieces of tofu. He raised some on his fork and began to chew. He didn't like the taste. "This is pretending to be something that it's not."

Clare shifted her gaze towards the wall and then turned on her husband. "No, it's not. Now eat it."

Valentine took a few more desultory mouthfuls and then began to roll the fork around his plate. "I saw a pig's head in the butcher's once."

"Really?"

"It was plastic."

Clare sighed. "That's nice."

"Is that what we've got here?"

His wife dropped her cutlery on the plate; the clatter was ear-splitting. She lowered her head onto her chest and then pushed out her chair and left the room.

"Clare." Valentine called to her. "I'm only having a joke with you. I'll eat it."

She turned on her heels in the kitchen and stomped back into the dining room. "I bought it because it is good for you, lower fat, healthier, better for your heart. Perhaps I shouldn't have bloody well bothered." She left the room again and closed the door behind her.

Valentine dropped his own knife and fork and stared out into the garden. He could see his neighbor's sprinkler spraying a wide arc of lawn. For a moment the scene felt calm and familiar, and then the realization of recent events hit him. Valentine was filled with a strange kind of sadness. It was the type of feeling he'd had when watching the girls grow up: a pride tinged with loss, the realization that each day they were getting further away from him. There would be no more first birthdays, no more first steps; so many good times had passed. He knew Clare was not dealing well with his return to active policing; she was handling the situation in her usual way, and he knew what that might mean.

The detective removed his cell phone from his trouser pocket and scrolled the contacts for DS Rossi's number.

"Hello, sir."

"Paulo, I've been waiting for the update on what happened with Mrs. Urquhart."

"Oh, yes, sorry boss."

Valentine cut in. "Well?"

"I was having my tea."

"Well, you can get back to your bloody spaghetti in a minute."

The sound of shuffling and the creaking of a door came down the line. "It's a positive ID, sir. Mrs. Urquhart picked him out at the morgue."

"She did, and what was her response like?"

Rossi cleared his throat before speaking. "She seemed a bit stony-faced."

"Not emotional?"

"Well, there was some dabbing at the eyes with a hankie, if that's what you mean."

Valentine tried to spool the image in his mind: it seemed to fit with what he had come to expect of Mrs. Urquhart. She was too high up the social ladder to put on any outward display of emotion in public.

"And the son, Adrian, how did he appear?"

Rossi's regular tone returned. "He wasn't there, sir. It was the neighbor." The pause in his speech was filled with the sound of pages turning in a notebook. "Ronnie Bell's his name."

"I know who he is. What I want to know is what he was doing running Mrs. Urquhart up to the morgue when her own son was on hand and there's no shortage of luxury motors sitting in the driveway?"

"Erm, well."

"It didn't strike you as just a wee bit odd?"

"Now you mention it, sir, I suppose the boy would have been the likely one to go and hold his mother's hand."

"Right, I want you to start a file on this Ronnie Bell character, and in that file, I want to see everything, including his preference for Ys or budgie-smugglers, and it better be all there the first time I pick the file up. Am I making myself clear?"

"Yes, sir."

"Good. And in future, Paulo, the second anything comes in, you pick up the phone, do you hear me? I don't care if you've got a mouthful of spaghetti, you let me know what you know right away."

"Yes, sir. I'm sorry about that."

Valentine hung up. He could feel the throbbing of his vocal cords from when his rant had reached a rasp.

He scrolled down his contacts of his phone again and found DC McAlister.

"Yes, boss."

"Ally, we have our ID."

"She picked him, then?"

"Yes, it's officially James Urquhart. I don't see any point in keeping it from the press when this Sinclair hack has so much information."

"What was his explanation?"

"He said he got an anonymous tip-off from someone claiming to be an ex-employee of Urquhart."

McAlister made a dismissive huff. "I don't know. Sounds like one from the hack's rulebook to me."

Valentine felt the skin tightening on the back of his neck. "We'll see. I don't think there's any point going in too hard on Sinclair at this stage. It might just be one lucky bit of information that fell into his lap. If he starts sprouting them on a regular basis, we might need to look a bit more closely."

"Understood, sir." McAlister paused. "You don't suspect anyone on the squad, do you, sir?"

Valentine's response to the same question by the chief super had been swift and decisive, but after talking to Sinclair and seeing the whites of his eyes he wasn't so sure of himself.

"I suspect everyone, Ally. Always do. One thing's for sure and certain, though: if we have a mole on the team feeding cookies to Sinclair, then I'll be feeding them into a mincer."

McAlister's voice rose. "For what it's worth, sir, I'd be stunned if anyone was that stupid."

"Ally there's no shortage of idiots in this world." He cut the conversation off at the knees. The point had been made and he could rely on Ally to circulate the salient facts. "Anyway, get in touch with Coreen in the morning and tell her to give the victim's name to the press pack at close of play tomorrow — not before. I want a clear day for us to get our ducks in a row before we have to start answering press queries again. But, at the very least, we'll be raining on Sinclair's parade."

McAlister bit. "What do you mean?"

"I asked him not to release the name in tomorrow's paper for fear of prejudicing the investigation."

"And he agreed?"

"Ally, if he's smart, he'll play fair by us."

"I don't know, boss, like you say, there's a lot of idiots in the world."

15

Valentine awoke from an uneasy sleep, and troubling dreams, to an empty bed. Clare had been there when he'd decided to slink upstairs the night before, but she had slept with her back to him. He reached out to her side of the bed and touched the linen sheet: it was cold. For a moment Valentine stared at the ceiling, allowing his thoughts to swirl around, but then he started to feel them gather there like dark clouds above the bed.

Valentine lay for only a second or two longer and then flattened his palms either side of him and pushed away from the mattress. He knew it was becoming difficult to avoid dark thoughts about Clare, even though he tried to fend them off. When he thought about her issues, they seemed so ridiculously trite compared with the issues he dealt with in his working life — but he understood they were very real to her.

The DI dressed quickly and took himself downstairs. Clare was in the kitchen reading the newspaper and smoking a cigarette when he appeared.

"Good morning."

Clare turned towards her husband and plucked the filter tip from her mouth. "Morning."

Valentine watched the blue stream of smoke spiral upwards and declined to comment. He filled the kettle with water, instead; he was removing the coffee jar when Clare spoke again.

"Isn't this what you're working on?" She held up the newspaper: it was the Glasgow-Sun.

Valentine squinted towards the page — along the top, not quite a page-lead, was the story of the Urquhart killing. He read a few words from the first deck of headlines and then his brain started to hum.

"I don't believe it." He reached out and snatched the paper from his wife.

"What is it?"

Valentine stood over the newspaper, shaking his head. The kettle started to roar and steam beside him. "This bastard's only went and released the name of my victim!"

"Who?"

Valentine was gripping the paper, scrunching it in his hands. "Cameron bloody Sinclair."

"And who's he?"

"A reporter, or likes to think he is. I told him not to print this name and he's only gone and done it."

Clare pinched her cheeks. She seemed to be searching for the right words, but pouring oil on troubled waters had never been one of her strengths. "Maybe it just popped out, like a mistake or something."

"What?" He couldn't believe what he was hearing. "Are you trying to be funny?"

"No, I'm just ... "

"Well, just don't."

Valentine balled the paper in his hands; he was wringing it like a rag as he stomped from the kitchen and collected his coat and case. The chief super would soon be on the hunt for someone to blame, if she wasn't already. He checked his phone as he got in the car to see if he'd missed any calls from her: he hadn't. He threw the mobile on the dash and groaned audibly as he sat, resting his forehead on the rim of the wheel.

"Bloody Sinclair. I'll string the bastard up."

He turned the key and pulled out of the drive.

This wasn't about the actions of an over-ambitious journalist; it was a blatant swipe at his authority. Valentine had lost the first skirmish, and the fact that he wasn't going to be able to usurp Sinclair by releasing the victim's name to the rest of the press later was another blow that had been landed without any effort.

At King Street station, Valentine locked the Vectra and walked towards the door. There was some heat in the morning air now and the dew on the grass by the sides of the road was evaporating.

Jim Prentice was on the desk when Valentine walked through the door. He wore a grave expression as he tapped the buttons on a telephone. "Oh, just about to give you a ring." He put the receiver down. "Herself is up and about early this morning."

Valentine maneuvered towards the desk, raised up his briefcase and attuned himself to Jim's frequency. "What's up?"

The sergeant inverted a smile. "A paddock out at the track, something going on there."

Valentine shrugged. "What are you saying to me, Jim?"

He played with the lobe of his ear as he spoke. "I'm not saying anything because I've been told nothing." He leaned forward and let his gaze thin. "But if you were asking me to guess — from the way she's acting — it's not bloody pretty. Got uniform on the way out there, now."

Valentine eased himself from the desk, retrieved his briefcase and made for the stairs. On the first rung, he spun and called to Jim. "Anything comes on that radio — you shout me."

As Valentine bounded up the steps, his pulse quickened. He had started the morning with a shock, but if his worst fears about Jim's announcement were realized, then the newspaper issue would be overtaken. On the top landing, the DI loosened his tie. He was removing his coat as the chief super's door opened and she stood in the frame. He wondered if she'd been listening for his footsteps.

"Bob – in here, now."

He watched her turn away from him and return to the office. She had a look that unsettled him. Martin was usually so full of her own self-importance, but she seemed to be on edge in a way that indicated panic.

She spoke again as he entered. "Close the door."

Valentine took a few steps towards her desk and lowered his briefcase onto the floor. He was laying his coat on the back of the chair when she caught his attention by slapping her palm off the desk.

"What's the worst possible nightmare you can imagine?" Her voice bled anxiety.

Valentine held himself together; it was a trait he was adopting more and more at the sight of rising tensions. "Are you looking for a list?"

The chief super turned away from him and dropped into her chair.

She slumped for a moment and then leaned forward. Valentine removed the chair in front of him and sat down. Martin was grimacing as she spoke.

"We had a call from the racecourse about half an hour ago." She brought her hands together and looked as if she was about to start praying. "It was from one of the maintenance blokes. He reckons there's a white male impaled on a stake in the middle of the track."

Valentine studied the chief super's face for more information, but it was clear she had none.

"Are you sure?"

"No, Bob, I'm making it up for a laugh." A dark glare entered her eyes. "I've got uniform out there taking a look now, but it sounds genuine, so you'd better get yourself prepared for a day and a half."

It seemed like a good time to bury bad news. Valentine made to rise; his chair legs scraped on the carpet tiles as he stood. "By the way, in case you haven't seen the paper," — he retrieved his case and coat — "our man Sinclair shafted us well and truly."

"What?"

Valentine was at the door when he replied. "Gave our victim's name away. When the hacks get wind of today's turn of events, I think they'll be having a day and a half as well."

16

There had been a moment at the outset of his career when Valentine thought that he was doing some good. But, somewhere along the line, he'd realized that the task was a thankless one: he was merely working to keep the prison service supplied. He didn't want to be a social worker, picking up the mess from political failings: "an instrument of the state" was the term his father had used to galling effect.

Valentine knew he remained a police officer for two reasons: because it kept his attention after all these years, and because he had passed the point where there was any other option on offer.

The DI stood in front of the whiteboard in the incident room and pressed the flat of his hand on the blank area to the left of the photograph of James Urquhart. He drummed his fingers momentarily and then he removed the red marker pen from the shelf and circled the picture. When he was finished, he drew a thick horizontal line leading from the circled area and ended the task with a question mark. As he stood staring, he contemplated what was likely to cover the question mark and approached the board again, circling the area in heavy red ink. He was placing the cap back on the marker pen when the telephone started to ring.

"Yes, Valentine."

It was Jim Prentice on the desk. "That's the call from the track. It's a body. White male, same MO as the dump."

Valentine felt a chill. "You sure?"

"Certain."

The DI was still digesting the information when the chief super walked in. Valentine lowered the telephone receiver and turned to face Martin.

"I take it that's the bongo drums?" she said.

Valentine blinked; it seemed to prompt him back to life. "We have another one, then."

Martin positioned herself on the rim of the desk and folded her arms across her chest. For a moment she seemed to be thinking, tapping the leg of the desk with the heel of her shoe.

"The press is going to have a field day," she said.

"Well, that was already on the cards. Look, I should get out there now."

The doors to the incident room opened once more as Valentine spoke; DC McAlister stood in the doorway and stared at the chief super — he seemed to intuit something. "What's going on?"

"Ally, don't take your jacket off. We've got another body out at the track."

"What?"

The chief super raised herself from the desk. "The crime scene team is on the way. I'd suggest you get out there now and start to make yourself useful."

McAlister nodded. "Yes, boss."

As he turned back towards the door, Valentine called out. "Can you give Paulo and Phil a holler?"

"Yeah, sure. You want them out there?"

The DI scratched behind his ear. "Just Phil. Keep Paulo back here, I want someone looking after the phones."

As McAlister left the room, Valentine felt the chief super's stare burning him. "Are you OK, Bob?"

"What do you mean?" He dropped his hand. "No need to worry about me."

"We both know I've every need. Don't think just because the workload has doubled you can skip out of the therapy sessions. I need you on the ball, Bob, more than ever now."

"Like I say, you've no reason to worry about me."

The chief super turned away, flagging the detective off with the back of her hand as she went. He watched her leave, listened to the doors' batting motion and snatched his coat from the back of the chair.

On the road out to the racetrack, Valentine felt stiff and tense behind the wheel, gripping the gearstick in his left hand like it was a cudgel.

Outside, the street was weary, a row of houses that had lost all charm since the giant supermarket had relocated just up the road. The detective rowed the gears back and forth as he passed through the traffic lights. He could see the racetrack on the right, but turned away to check the clock on the dash. He tried to keep his mind open, but assumptions about a double murder on his patch pressed themselves again and again like mosquito bites.

Valentine parked the Vectra outside the track and made his way towards the collection of uniforms. He was ahead of the crime scene team, but the site had already been cordoned off by the first on the scene. His gaze roved the surrounding area and caught sight of DC McAlister, walking towards him. Clouds crossed the sky above and dim sun rays fell like ticker tape on the stand, before slipping towards the track lanes.

"It's the same as the last one, sir," said McAlister.

Valentine gave the DC a look, then walked past him and made for the crime scene. When he got behind the cordon, his shoulders tensed. He took a few steps closer and then walked around the victim. The man was heavier than James Urquhart, a bigger individual all round. He had a sports top pushed up around his neck, exposing a prominent stomach. The skin was pale, verging on chalk white, and streaked with dark-red blood. Below his abdomen, a wooden stake poked skywards, streaked in blood that covered the genitals and the ground beneath.

Valentine walked towards the uniforms. "What's the word from the track staff?"

"No idea who he is, sir. Groundsman found him just as you see him now."

The detective beckoned McAlister towards him and stepped away from the uniforms. As he took a few steps further, he hooked his hands below the tails of his sports coat and gripped the edges of the pockets with his thumbs. "What do you think?"

The DC turned towards the victim. "He's bigger than Urquhart, but I think it could still be one man that moved him."

Valentine nodded. "There's no fence, no wall, no obstacles from here to the parking lot, so it's possible."

"He doesn't look like a banker."

"The tattoos and the fingers."

McAlister tilted his head. "Fingers?"

"Yellowed with nicotine: I'd say he rolled his own smokes."

"I don't see the number one crop being a good look in the board room either."

Valentine unhooked his thumbs and folded his arms. "There's got to be some connection, though, someone has executed the pair of them in an identical fashion."

"We might know better when the crime scene officers get here. Certainly, if we get an ID we can explore links."

Valentine scratched beneath his chin. He started to shake his head as he spoke. "Why, though? Why put them up on a spike like this?"

"It's obvious: to send a message."

"But why draw so much attention to yourself? If you want to kill someone, you hide the body, give yourself a chance of getting away with it. This is insanity."

"You're not kidding. We're obviously dealing with a psycho."

"Or somebody who wants to get caught."

"Or somebody who thinks he's too smart to get caught."

The DI spotted the first of the crime scene vans to arrive; the fiscal and the pathologist would be next. "Ally, I want you to stay put. Anything crops up, get on the phone."

"Yes, sir."

"I want the time of death and how long he's been out in the cold as soon as you get it." Valentine removed his car keys from his pocket. "I want swabs and prints, and, if we have him on file, I want to know right away."

"Sir."

17

On the road back to the station Valentine sensed his spirit collapsing inside him. He couldn't think clearly — the whole situation had the unreality of dreams. His mind wandered back to the vision he'd had when he saw the little girl with the white-blonde hair and the red coat laying flowers round the corpse of James Urquhart. He thought of the girls, Fiona and Chloe: they had been that size once. Chloe had been most like the girl in the vision — she had been a chatty child, though, and this girl had seemed so withdrawn. When Chloe was very young, she would stay in her room and hold conversations with imaginary friends, always happy, always benign. But, when asked who she was talking to, she would go quiet and cross her lips with fingers as if forbidden to say. It puzzled Valentine then and it made him think about the situation again now: children possessed something special at that age, almost preternatural, which was lost in adulthood.

As Valentine drove towards the station, a thought lodged in his mind. He was being bothered by this case in a way he hadn't been before — he felt it more, but the feelings the case triggered were not ones he had ever encountered.

As he pulled up and killed the engine, Valentine sat drumming his fingers on the dash for a moment. The sight of the latest murder victim had lit a fuse in him. Valentine had allowed his intuition to play a part in the job before, but this was something altogether different: he felt as if he were being led by outside forces rather than by his own knowledge and experience. He rolled up the window and let his breathing still as he tried to focus.

He slapped a palm off the wheel and opened the car door. On the way into the station he nodded to Jim on the desk and then made straight for the incident room. The first person to catch his attention was Paulo, who had his back to him and was speaking into a telephone.

"Yeah, put that on and give me another two hundred on the nose."

Valentine moved in front of the DS and stood with his hands in his pockets, making it perfectly clear that he had caught the gist of the conversation.

"Got to go," said Paulo. "Sorry, boss."

"That wasn't what I think it was, because if it were, then you'd have my foot in your arse and a new role mopping out the kennels for the dog handlers, Paulo."

He daubed a contrite look on his face. "Yes, sir."

Valentine let his indignation burn into the DS for a moment and then he called out to the room. "Right, can I have all of you round the board, please."

There was a shuffle of chair legs and some muttering as the squad made their way towards the whiteboard. Valentine picked up a pen and removed the cap; he was writing a description of the latest victim as he began to speak. "White male, middle aged, blue-collar worker and spiked through the backside with a sharpened plank of wood."

"It's the same MO, then," said DS Donnelly.

"Ah, Phil, you're here."

"I was just on my way out to the scene, sir."

"Ally can handle that lot, you'll be more use to me here if they get an ID." The DI put the cap back on the marker pen and walked in front of the board. "There are obviously striking similarities to the murder of James Urquhart, so I'd be expecting to uncover links between the two victims. What those links will be at this stage we can only guess."

Paulo asserted himself. "They must have known each other."

Valentine tapped the board at the description of the latest victim. "Do they look like the kind of people to be friends? See James Urquhart going for a game of darts with our latest victim?"

"Maybe casual acquaintances: he could have been a gardener or tradesman, odd-job man?" said Donnelly.

"Get on that, Phil. Anyone get anything on James Urquhart's movements yet?"

DS Donnelly spoke again. "He was a member of the Rotary Club, but not a regular by any means, and there was a model-railway club that, according to their website, meets on a Wednesday night in the town."

"Check it out with the club, and with his wife. See if they tie up."

"Yes, sir."

"Anyone got anything else to report at this stage?"

DS Rossi raised a hand. "I looked into the neighbor, Ronnie Bell."

"Oh, yeah."

"Well, on paper anyway, he's clean."

"Most folk are, Paulo. I'm not interested in his parking tickets. Pay him a visit, get under his skin. How friendly was he with Urquhart? And how friendly is he with his wife?"

"Yes, sir."

Valentine clapped his hands together. "Right, that's it for now. Get back to work and let me know the second anything comes up."

The DI returned to the board and stood with his hands on his hips, taking in the details that had been put up. They had little to go on. He looked at the photographs that showed James Urquhart's brutal injuries, and he thought of the latest victim and the pictures of his injuries that would soon be added to the board. He wondered how long it was going to be before the chief super started to goad him with the possibility of turning the case over to the Glasgow Murder Squad. He closed his eyes in an effort to summon inspiration, but the process was immediately drowned out by the ringing of a telephone.

"Hello, Valentine."

It was DC McAlister. "Sir, you're not going to like this, but they've ID'd our stiff."

"They have?" He paused. "And why wouldn't I like it, Ally?"

"Well, for starters he's known to us."

"Go on."

"Sir, he's a child molester."

"Convicted?"

"Yes, hes a convicted pedophile, sir. Name's Duncan Knox."

The name didn't register with Valentine. "I take it you've run him through the system."

"Yeah, and it's a list of convictions as long as your arm. If you were looking at a revenge killing, you could be pulling potentials from all over the country. I'd say he's spent more time inside than out."

Valentine eased himself down into a chair. Pressure was building in his chest and he started to rub the palm of his hand down the front of his shirt. As he looked up, he noticed the chief super walking into the room, eyeing him cautiously.

"OK, Ally, get yourself back to the station when you're ready."

18

Leanne Dunn pressed her head against the wall and started to moan. She turned over on the floor and laid the palms of her hands in front of her. As she knelt, her head drooped. She was slipping, falling into a stupor that threatened to engulf her, when her head was violently jerked backwards.

"I told you I didn't want that child molester round here!" Danny Gillon roared directly into Leanne's ear. He held her hair in a clump.

"I–I never ... "

Gillon pushed her towards the wall, pressed her face into the plaster and roared again. "How many times? Eh? How many times have you got to be told?"

"But he wasn't ..." Gillon was too strong for her. Leanne wanted to collapse in a heap on the floor and let him tire himself out yelling, like he usually did, but this wasn't the usual situation.

"You let that child molester in here again, though. Was he paying?"

"No, he wasn't here."

"Was he after a freebie, like the old days?"

"No." Leanne felt her hair freed from Gillon's grasp; she sat upright, pushing herself away from him. "I didn't."

"Don't you lie to me, Leanne. Don't even think about that, because I'll burst your face wide open if you're lying to me."

Her hands shot up to protect herself. "Don't."

The pimp took two steps back and stood watching Leanne where she sat on the floor. She was cowering, her knees locked together and her shoulders trembling. He withdrew a packet of cigarettes from his pocket. As he lit up, he called out to her, "Right, c'mon, on your feet."

"Why? Where are we going?"

He flicked his lank fringe. "C'mon, into the kitchen. Have a seat."

He seemed to have changed his tone, but Leanne wasn't fooled. He offered her the cigarette; Leanne took it and pressed it to her thin lips.

"There, see, we can be friends when we want, eh?" said Gillon.

Leanne nodded and followed him through to the kitchen. She watched Gillon filling the kettle with water. "You hold onto that smoke, doll." He dipped into his pocket and produced the pack again. "I'll fire up a new one for myself." Gillon clearly wanted something from her, but she didn't know what it was.

"There you go." He placed the cup down in front of her. "Nice cup of chai."

Leanne watched the steam rising from the liquid. She couldn't bring herself to drink the tea.

"OK, Leanne, I can see you're wondering why I'm so curious about that big fat pedophile," said Gillon. He leaned back in his seat. "See, I know you had him round here the other day, because I know you."

"What do you mean?"

Gillon formed a mean smirk that showed the yellowed teeth in his mouth. "See, every time that pedo's round here you become a bag of nerves. It's like you're a wee lassie again."

Leanne looked away. She was reminded of that part of her, the place deep inside, that had died. She watched cars hissing by the window on the street below. There were people walking on the pavements, birds swooping in the sky. It always felt strange to know that there was a world of ordinary people and ordinary goings-on and yet Duncan Knox existed within that same sphere. "He came 'round."

Gillon withdrew his cigarette and pinned back his lips. "There, see, wasn't so bad, was it?" He flicked his ash on the floor. "Now, what did he want?"

Leanne kept her gaze on the street. "Why? What does it matter what he wanted?"

Gillon's voice rose. "It just does. Look, Leanne, tell me what he wanted."

She turned her head and caught sight of Gillon's anger growing behind his eyes again. "He told me someone had died."

"Who?"

"Nobody really, just someone I used to know."

"And why did he tell you? Why did he come 'round here?"

Leanne shrugged. "I don't know."

"Tell me the name of the person who died, Leanne."

Her throat constricted; the words wouldn't pass. She wanted to say them, to get the name out in the open to show that he meant nothing to her. He couldn't harm her: he was dead. "James Urquhart."

Gillon pushed the chair back, the legs scraped loudly on the floor. In a second, he was on his feet pacing the kitchen. "That's him, the man on the telly."

Leanne watched her pimp, flapping his arms and walking the length of the room again and again. "Gillon, he's dead, what's the matter?"

He stopped still, moved towards Leanne and planted his hands on the table. "He's dead all right, and so's our fat pedo friend."

"What?"

"Knox copped it out at the track. Place is heaving with filth, right now."

Leanne felt a tingling sensation inside. "Dead?"

"Yes, Leanne. Both your wee pals have been knocked off, what do you make of that, then?"

She watched the ash fall from her cigarette — the tobacco had burned nearly all the way to the filter tip. She raised the cigarette to her lips and drew deep. She tasted a burning sensation that chimed with the heat building inside her. "The police. They'll want to speak to me."

"Why?" said Gillon. "How are they going to know anything about you?"

Leanne touched her face. "The police will want to know who killed them. He was just here, Knox was here."

Gillon closed down the space between them and threw his arms onto Leanne's shoulders. He was shaking her as he spoke. "You just stay away from the police. You hear me? I'll tell you how to play this. I've got other ideas and they don't involve the police."

19

DI Valentine ruminated on the latest victim's identity for a moment and found his train of thought suddenly hijacked. The death of a pedophile — what was really so bad about that? He caught himself just before the notion became a more solid philosophy; he knew it was the act of murder he needed to focus on, not the murdered. He had been thinking about death a lot lately, but he recalled a time when death was no more a cause for thought than sleep. In life, there was no escape, no release. Knox had been released from it all.

From the corner of his eye Valentine caught sight of the chief super approaching. He turned to face her and flagged her towards the glassed-off office at the end of the incident room. As he went, he felt as though a heavy burden was weighing on him, as if he were dragging the contents of the incident room along with him. He knew, of course, it was a fallacy, but he knew also that there would be a new tone to the conversations he would now have with CS Martin.

Valentine held open the door and watched the chief super walk through. She avoided eye contact, but once behind the closed door, she fixed him with her gaze.

"Well?"

He spoke slowly. "We have an ID for the victim out at the track: Duncan Knox."

She shrugged. "Who?"

"He's a pedophile, long list of convictions, mostly time-served. I haven't pulled the file yet; I just took the call."

The chief super folded her arms, the look was practiced: she was battling her true reaction. "And it's the same MO?"

"Almost identical."

She unfolded her arms and started to pace the confines of the small room. "What the bloody hell's going to tie him to Urquhart?"

Valentine had the chief super in his sights as he spoke. "If there's a link, we'll find it."

She looked out to the incident room — her gaze seemed to fall on Paulo – and shook her head. "You"re not exactly blessed with a full complement of detective genius out there."

Valentine's first instinct was to react with a rebuttal, but his second instinct was to say nothing and let the burn of her criticism be felt in his silence. She spoke again: "I think it might be time to talk to Glasgow about the case."

The DI knew the last thing Martin wanted was another area's officers on her patch — it would be humbling, just shy of humiliating, and the chief super liked to be able to strut around her territory.

"Let's not be too hasty, we haven't even cracked the seal on this Knox death yet. Who knows what the next twenty-four hours will hand us? It would be a shame to serve everything up on a platter for Glasgow."

The chief super halted her pacing and stood tapping the toe of her shoe on the ground.

"All right, Bob, I'll give you the benefit of the doubt, but if you're telling me you can handle this with the team you have, then there better be something more than white space to look at on that board the next time I come in here." She removed her gaze from the detective and walked past him on the way to the door. "And tomorrow, Bob, first thing, you have a therapy session. Hope you can fit it around your workload."

The muscles in Valentine's arms tensed as he watched the chief super walk into the incident room. He held himself in check for a moment longer, until she was out of sight, and then he reached for the door handle.

"Paulo, get your coat." The growl startled even himself.

DS Rossi rose from his desk. "Are we going somewhere, sir?"

"Out to see the Urquharts."

Rossi looked perplexed. "Shouldn't Ally be going with you, then?"

"Ally's at the scene, so I'm making do." He started to walk towards the door, and the police officers in the room dropped their heads to avoid eye contact. "And anything comes in, I want to be informed straight away — call!"

There was no reply, but the message was received. DS Rossi wrestled himself into his jacket as he caught up with Valentine on the stairs. "So, are we running the Knox killing past them, boss?"

The sound of the DS's voice had started to grate on Valentine already. "What do you think, Paulo?"

He shrugged as he pulled his collar down. "Will I drive, sir?"

The DI nodded. "Well, I didn't bring you for your repartee, son."

By the time they got to the parking lot Valentine was several strides ahead of DS Rossi, who depressed the remote locking. As he got inside, Valentine had to tip a pile of folders onto the floor. He picked up a cell phone that rested on the seat and noticed there was a missed-call notification. Valentine registered the caller's ID just as DS Rossi opened the driver's door. "Is this your phone, Paulo?"

The DS looked at the phone in Valentine's hand and seemed to clam up. "Erm . . ."

"Simple question: is it or isn't it?"

Rossi nodded. "Yes, sir."

"Then you better take it. Was sitting on the seat, lucky it wasn't nicked." Valentine kept a stare on the young detective. For a moment there was an uneasy silence in the car, and then Rossi turned towards the windscreen and started the engine.

On the road out to Alloway, Valentine allowed himself a few snatched glances at Rossi; he knew he had something on the DS now and that he would have to act on the information. For some unknown reason, Valentine felt the need to observe Rossi: his own temper was too hot to take any action. Valentine closed down his thoughts and stared ahead. By the Maybole Road, the atmosphere in the car seemed to have lost its stressed air, but then entering the well-heeled streets of this part of town always made Valentine ease a little further back in his seat. It was as if the meandering driveways dictated it; this was where people came to enjoy the rewards of a good life.

"How the other half live, eh?" said DS Rossi — his voice faltered a little on the conversational gambit.

"You can always dream, Paulo." Valentine returned the glance. "So long as you know it's just a dream."

They had reached the Urquharts" home. Rossi made an elaborate turn of the wheel and changed direction from the main road. In the driveway, he pulled up behind Mrs. Urquhart"s Range Rover and stilled the engine.

The moment he stepped outside the car Valentine was assailed by a wind that sent a shiver through him.

"Everything OK, boss?" said Rossi.

"Yes, why shouldn't it be?"

Rossi raised his brows. "You're as white as a sheet."

Valentine dropped his tense shoulders and turned back towards the door; he was pressing the doorbell as he spoke. "No need to worry about me."

In a few moments the door was opened by Adrian Urquhart. He released no words until Valentine introduced himself.

"Would you like to come in?" he said.

As Valentine stepped into the vestibule, his eyes took in the home: he knew more about the former occupant than he had on his last visit and the knowledge dredged up James Urquhart"s spirit for him. The banker was suddenly everywhere he looked. The rug on the floor, the paint on the walls, the ornamental lamp on the side table — they all bore his signature.

Mrs. Urquhart was standing in the middle of the lounge when the detectives entered the room. "Hello, gentlemen."

Valentine nodded and accepted the offer of a seat. "I hope you don't mind us calling round like this. It's just we've had some developments."

"Oh." She lowered herself into the armchair. Adrian followed at her side.

For a moment Valentine toyed with the idea of slowly building up to the revelation of Duncan Knox's murder, but as he eyed the Urquharts sitting before him, perfectly calm, there seemed no need for soft-soaping.

"There's been another killing, in much the same fashion as before."

The pair looked unmoved. Valentine checked them for a flinch, the gripping of hands perhaps, but nothing came. He turned his eyes towards

DS Rossi, who was looking at the Urquharts with a perplexed expression playing on his face.

Valentine spoke again. "I have to ask: does the name Duncan Knox mean anything to you?"

This time there was a reaction. Mrs. Urquhart rose from the chair and stood behind her son, then she placed her hands on his shoulders and gripped tightly. "No, why should it?"

Valentine registered how she snatched her words. "You seem very sure."

"Certain."

"Is there something you'd like to tell me, Mrs. Urquhart. This isn't the reaction I was expecting to the news that your husband's death has been mimicked."

Adrian walked towards the middle of the room. "I wasn't aware there was a grieving widow's handbook that my mother was supposed to be reading from."

"That's enough, Adrian." Mrs. Urquhart walked round beside her son. Mr. Valentine, we are still in deep shock."

"I appreciate that."

"Then why on earth are you questioning us when you could be out hunting a killer?"

Valentine caught sight of DS Rossi rising from his chair; in the space of a few minutes the cordial atmosphere had turned nasty. "It's very important that we ascertain any links between your husband and the latest victim, you must be able to see how that could assist us."

"What makes you think there are any links?" said Mrs. Urquhart.

"Well, if there aren't, then it's important that we eliminate that line of inquiry."

Mrs. Urquhart's glass-smooth skin reflected the light from the window where she stood; she looked pale and fraught as she spoke to her son. "I don't know this Duncan Knox, do you, Adrian?"

Adrian Urquhart shook his head. "No."

A frown settled on Mrs. Urquhart's face and then she touched the seam of her blouse nervously. "Well, there, that seems to be an end to it, doesn't it now, Mr. Valentine?"

DI Valentine's words came bluntly. "I suppose it does."

"Good. Then I'll show you both out." She turned to the door and stood holding the handle.

At the door Valentine halted. "Thank you for your time."

"You're welcome."

The detectives followed the hall into the vestibule, before being shown out the front door. As they stood in the driveway, buttoning their coats, Valentine spoke. "I'm afraid, Mrs. Urquhart, there are one or two other formalities that I'll have to address with you."

"Formalities?"

"Regarding the investigation. I'll be back in touch." Valentine made for the car; as he went, he could sense angry eyes burning into his back, but his attention fixed on the sight of Ronnie Bell peering over the neighboring wall. The detective turned to see if Mrs. Urquhart had registered Bell, but she was already heading indoors.

"More neighbor concern, or was it the sight of the police that brought him out snooping around?" said Valentine.

Inside the car, DS Rossi started to shake his head and curse. "What the hell was that all about? Couldn't wait to get us out of there, you'd think we were the ones that murdered him."

Valentine waited until they had left the Urquharts' driveway and crossed the first of the broad Alloway streets before he spoke. "Don't you concern yourself with that, Paulo, you've got other things to be worried about."

The DS jerked the wheel. "What do you mean?"

Valentine raised his arm and made a show of exposing the watch face on his wrist. "By my guess, it'll take you about nine minutes to get back to the station. That's as long as you have to explain why your phone was showing a call from Cameron Sinclair when I got in this car."

20

DS Chris Rossi played the bluff card because it was instinctual: a remnant from a childhood when pleading ignorance to gullible parents had once paid dividends. Valentine didn't buy the dummy, though, and was vaguely aggrieved by the insult to his intelligence, until he realized who he was dealing with.

"And you can take that stupid look off your chops, son," he yelled. "It's not going to get you out of this hole."

Rossi closed his mouth and his Adam's apple rode up and down in this throat. "I'm sorry."

"I don't much like apologies either — the damage has always been done by the time they come out."

Valentine took his eyes from the detective and watched the road ahead for a suitable place to stop; he selected a calm stretch where the road tapered off into a bus lane. "Just pull up there."

Rossi looked in the mirror and put on the blinkers, even his driving had become more cautious now.

"What do you want me to say?"

"You can say what you like, Paulo, at this stage it's unlikely to make a blind bit of difference."

Rossi slapped at the wheel: it was a petulant gesture. "You know what it's like."

"Do I?" He had no idea what Rossi was implying: that they were all blokes together, perhaps? Or, that he should sympathize with a fellow officer who had been tempted in ways he had never been and never would be?

Rossi exhaled a long breath. "Look, do you mind if I smoke?"

"Yes, I do." Valentine placed a hand on the dash and tapped gently. "You have until I tap here again to say something that might help you or mitigate the fact that you are in some serious bother. If I like what I hear, I'll do all I can for you. If I don't, you're on your own."

The DS"s complexion settled on a shade just shy of grey, though his eye sockets were dark and sunken. He was sweating, his brow damp and his top lip glistening. "Look, sir, you know I've had some financial problems and I'm not about to use that as an excuse, but ... "

Valentine turned in his chair to face him. "Go on."

"I have a family and it's tough on a cop's wage."

"I've got a family too, son. But I've never been tempted to put my fingers in the till."

Rossi wiped his brow and then fingered the edges of his mouth. "I've never done anything like this before. I got into debt. The money was put out there and ... "

"You took it?"

Rossi nodded, then clamped his mouth shut.

"Tell me, I need to know: did Cameron Sinclair make you an offer or did you go to him?"

The DS kept his eyes fixed on the middle distance but didn't answer. He'd told Valentine all he needed to know.

"You bloody idiot, Paulo."

On the way back to the station, the pair sat in silence until Rossi parked up in the King Street lot.

"Go home," said Valentine.

"What?"

"You heard me. You"re off the case and almost certainly suspended. When I relay this to the chief super there'll be an investigation, a tribunal likely, and you'll get a chance to explain yourself. But my advice to you, Paulo, would be to use the break to start polishing up your CV."

Valentine got out the car and slammed the door. He didn't look back as he headed for the station and climbed the stairs all the way to the chief super's office.

The detective's thoughts collided as he stood facing the brassy nameplate, and then he knocked twice on the door and walked in. Chief Superintendent Marion Martin was sitting at her desk eyeing the contents of a tuna-fish sandwich as he appeared.

"I found our mole," he said.

The tone of his voice was so matter-of-fact and the content of his words so at odds that he seemed to confuse the chief super. "Come again?"

"Chris Rossi tipped off Cameron Sinclair. He's up to his neck in debt. I caught him on the phone to his bookies earlier — he tried it on with Sinclair for a few quid."

"Is this a joke?"

"Do I look like I'm laughing? I've sent him home while we get the suspension proceedings going."

"What?" CS Martin shook her head and touched her temples with her fingertips as if testing whether the perception was real. "Couldn't you have let me know sooner? At least given me some kind of warning."

Valentine turned away from her, towards the door he had just walked through. "I just found out myself. Look, what was my option, put him in a cell?"

"What if he goes back to Sinclair?"

"My next call's to the editor of the Glasgow-Sun. I think Sinclair will be joining Paulo in the unemployment line before long."

"Unless they stand by him."

"After bribing a police officer? He'll get his marching orders and we'll be shed of him. I could almost thank Paulo, it's his greatest contribution to the whole investigation."

Martin stood up, shaking her head as she spoke. "Bob, get real, if the Sun punts Sinclair he'll just go freelance and chase us, but with an axe to grind this time. And what about the squad? It was bare bones before you shunted Paulo out the door."

Valentine reached for the handle and jerked the door open. His voice was rising, too, he knew it wouldn't be long until they were upping the volume even more. "I think we'll get by without Robocop, don't you?" He walked through the open door and yanked the handle firmly behind him — the door hit the jamb like a full stop on the end of the conversation. In the hallway, Valentine's neck tensed and a firm pulse began to beat beneath his collar. He started to loosen his tie as he walked back to the incident room to break the news that not only had he no idea how

Duncan Knox and James Urquhart were connected, but the squad was now a man down, too. He knew the impact on morale would be severe. Valentine didn't want the group to suffer for DS Rossi's sins, though. He had been on the receiving end of harsh treatment for others' mistakes in the past and knew the resentment it caused. If there were to be a way forward for the team, it would be by maintaining focus on solving the case.

He opened the door of the incident room and stepped inside. "Right, listen up, everyone."

The place seemed to still, like a low-voltage shock had been passed through the furniture, and then suddenly everyone regained composure and started to mill towards the inspector.

"Something up, boss?" DC McAlister had returned from the crime scene at the track.

"Yes, you could say that." Valentine's voice signaled another jolt to come. "I'm just back from talking with the chief superintendent and have some bad news for you, I'm afraid." Valentine's gaze was on one of the PCs: she held a blue folder tight to her chest, as if looking to put a barrier between her and what was about to come. "Detective Sergeant Rossi has been relieved of all duties as of today."

A low barrage of muttering buffeted Valentine. "That's enough. The DS is suspended pending a review of his actions of late and, in the meantime, I'm raising DC McAlister to the post of acting detective sergeant."

McAlister's eyes widened for a moment and then his face cracked into a grin. "Thanks, sir."

"Don't get overexcited, Ally. I'll be wanting my pound of flesh from you — you'll be taking on Paulo's workload, so that's looking at the buyout and Ronnie Bell to add to your duties."

DS Donnelly crossed the floor to pat McAlister on the back and shake his hand.

Valentine spoke up. "Right, I haven't heard my phone ring once since I was out, so I'm presuming there's nothing to report."

Silence settled in the room and was punctured by a woman's voice. "There was a call from your wife, sir. I left a message on your desk. It wasn't to do with the case."

Valentine looked at the officer and nodded, then turned back to the others and clapped his hands together. "OK, back to work. Come on, move it!" As he walked through the shifting bodies Valentine called out to Donnelly and McAlister. "You pair — in my office, now."

The detectives looked at each other and set off in the wake of Valentine's heavy footfalls. At the office door, he reached out for the handle and ushered the others through. He let them get inside and then closed the door firmly and headed towards his desk to retrieve the telephone message from his wife. It was a short note in looping, large handwriting that reminded him of his daughters'; the contents were, however, all his wife's. He lowered the note onto the desk, then quickly retrieved it before crushing his fist around the thin paper and dropping it towards the wastebasket beneath his desk.

"More good news?" said McAlister.

Valentine set eyes on the newly appointed DS and held his mouth tightly shut. He straightened his back, pressing his hands onto his hips, and then removed his chair from below the desk and sat down. Donnelly and McAlister followed his lead.

"I'm presuming neither of you knew about Paulo's addiction?" He spat the last word like it had left a bad taste.

The detectives looked at each other. Donnelly spoke. "Well, I wouldn't say we never knew, exactly."

Valentine raised a hand and cut him off. "You misunderstand me. I'm not asking you, I'm telling you. I know neither of you are so bloody stupid as to jeopardize your careers like that, but ... " He leaned forward on the desk and pointed his index finger back towards the chief super's office. "Some people will be asking just those questions and you better have your answers ready. Do you understand me?"

"Yes, sir."

"Good. Paulo's been a clown, every circus needs one, but no more than that." The DI shook his head. "He's dug his own grave, but if either of you let on you had suspicions, that might be looked at as tacit approval. Am I painting a clear enough picture?"

"Yes, sir."

Valentine was growing tired of the staccato responses, he felt like a teacher admonishing the behavior of errant pupils. He eased back in the chair and the castors squeaked beneath him.

McAlister spoke. "Can I ask about the shape of the squad, boss? We're a man down now, and ... "

"I know. And Dion's been threatening to bring in some Glasgow boys since day one."

"We don't want them coming down here and big-footing the lot of us. It would be just like them to steal the show."

Valentine replied: "It's bad enough on Glasgow Fair having them down for an ice cream."

"We'll be seeing a few more of them if Rangers ever claw their way to a promotion," said McAlister.

The three men laughed, but it was short-lived. Valentine's grave expression signaled the true nature of the situation.

"If she brings in Glasgow, we're in the shit. But at least we know the territory." Valentine sat forward again, picked up the receiver from the telephone on his desk and started to search his blotter for the number he'd written down earlier. He nodded the others towards the door. When he was alone in the room, he drummed his fingers on the keypad of the phone for a moment — the call to the editor of the Glasgow-Sun with the Sinclair allegations would have to wait a few minutes longer. He dialed another number.

"Hello, Clare."

His wife sounded stressed on the other end of the line. He surmised she had been busy juggling her shopping addiction with the housework.

"Oh, you got back to me then," she said, her tone smothered in sarcasm.

"I'm sorry, love. I've had a lot going on. What's this about my dad?"

Clare sighed down the line. "I gave him a call today, just checking in."

"Yes, and ... "

"Well, he didn't answer at first." She shuffled the receiver. "I thought he might have been out in the garden or something, but then I called back and he was still in bed."

"He's retired, he's entitled to a long-lie."

"It was eleven o'clock, your father never sleeps that late. Anyway, he didn't sound himself is what I'm trying to say. I was concerned enough to call you at the station."

Valentine stepped in. "OK, leave it with me."

"What does that mean?"

"It means I"ll look into it."

"Will you go 'round?"

Valentine's eyes roved towards the ceiling in exasperation. He had far too much on to be entertaining his wife's insecurities, even if they were well-intentioned. "If I've got time."

Clair sparked up. "Look, I would go myself, but he's never keen to have a woman fussing over him, you know how he is, and he's your father, Bob."

"OK, Clare, I'll pay him a visit."

"Today?"

"Yes, Clare, today."

As he put down the receiver, he glanced towards the clock on the wall and sighed. He still had time to make the call to the editor of the Glasgow-Sun. He reached out for the telephone and tapped in the number he had written down beside the name Jack Gallagher. As the line began to ring, he knew it was a call that wasn't going to make him any friends.

21

Valentine lowered the car's momentum by dropping gears on the way into Cumnock. When the vehicle in front's tail lights glowed red, he applied the brakes and brought the Vectra to a standstill. He put down his window and the touch of rain revived him. The town was his father's home: not his, it had never been his, even when he lived there. Cumnock was one of those stations where no new recruits wanted to be posted. It was a rough place: in Ayrshire they called it Dodge City – a nod to the number of its inhabitants that were on the dole. Cumnock, and much of Ayrshire, was increasingly growing to look like Zombieland, its inhabitants guided by full-time carers who were there to tell them how to put their trousers on, how to feed themselves, how to swallow their methadone, to shut up and slump back into stupor so the rest of us could get on with life.

The curtains were drawn as Valentine pulled up outside his father's home on Keir Hardie Hill. He wound up the window and felt the stirring in the depths of his chest that occurred each time he came back. He collected the small carrier bag he'd filled with goods from the convenience store and opened the car door. Valentine stood in the street for a moment, watching the rain clouds looming over the rooftops. A cold wind rattled down the road and whipped at his bare throat; he turned up his collar as he walked towards the house. The gate screeched like an early warning of his approach, but as he raised his head to take in the window once again, the curtains remained still. He returned the hasp and headed towards the doorstep, knocked twice and reached for the handle. The door was open.

"Hello." Valentine called out as he stood in the hallway. The carpet was faded and worn beneath his feet — he remembered the day when it had been taken up and turned around to allow the less worn end to bear the brunt of the front-door traffic.

"Dad, are you in?" His voice echoed off the walls; the place was cold, damp and musty. He opened a window and made his way to the living room. As he went through the door, he heard some stirring in the next room. The noise of feet on boards and a wracking cough brought him a deep sense of relief. He made his way through to the kitchen, deposited the bag of groceries on the table, and started to fill the kettle; it was beginning to whistle as the thin frame of his father appeared, haunting the doorway like a ghost.

"Hello, old boy."

"To what do I owe the pleasure?" His father seemed several pounds lighter than the last time he had seen him.

"I brought you some rolls and bacon. Thought I'd do you a bit of tea."

His father started to tighten the belt of his dressing gown as he watched the goings-on in the kitchen. He seemed to be in possession of a stoop now — shrinking his frame to boyish dimensions. "You've been talking to that wife of yours."

Valentine placed a mug of coffee in front of his father. "Yeah, well, we do exchange words now and again."

"I don't need looking after." He raised a bony, gnarled finger and wagged it in front of him. "Never taken a handout in my life, not even in the strike!"

Valentine's will to challenge withered and died. He lowered his shoulders and turned towards his father with the frying pan in hand. "Don't start about the bloody strike again." He lifted the frying pan: "Or you'll get this!"

His father pinched his gaunt face and the white bristles on his chin pointed towards his son. "Wouldn't be the first clout I'd got from a policeman."

Valentine turned back to the stove and sparked up the gas.

He ignored his father's goading; experience had taught him that ignoring him was the fastest route from conflict.

His father sipped the coffee and continued. "Summer of '84, after

Thatcher had stockpiled enough coal, that's when I first faced down a policeman on a horse. Shields and sticks, they had. They were all pally with us before that, joking and laughing away, but it got nasty quick enough. Did I ever tell you they used to come down and wave five-pound notes at us?"

"Once or twice, Dad."

"Aye, well." He eased back in the chair and looked out of the window. "Bloody coal board took full-page ads in the paper; said we were blocking essential supplies of coal to the hospitals and the schools and the old folks' home." He made a spitting sound, and sighed. "Utter rubbish. I went up on the hills, hawking coal for the wee wifey who lived next door. Never saw anyone go short."

Valentine turned around and presented his father with the bacon roll he had prepared. The plate clattered on the tabletop as he put it down. "You want any sauce on that?"

He shook his head. "I'm all out."

"I could nip down the shops."

"No. Be cold by time you got back."

The pair sat in silence as the old man ate his bacon roll. Valentine watched his father raising his thin arms and thinner fingers towards his mouth as he ate and wondered what had ever become of him. The slow masticating of his father's thin jaws and brittle teeth looked like such a trial to him.

"How have you been keeping?"

His father moved his head from side to side in lieu of a shrug. "So, so."

"Clare worries about you. The girls are asking for you."

The mention of his granddaughters brought a smile to the old man's face; his eyes lit up. "There's no need to worry about me. I've never died a winter yet."

It struck Valentine that the optimum word was "yet." "Well, is there anything you need?"

"Not fussing, anyway."

"Dad, please."

"I'll be fine with some peace and quiet, get back to that wife and those daughters of yours and fuss over them."

Valentine felt his father's gaze burrowing into him and for a moment he was a small child once again. He had never managed to understand his father's complete rejection of all affection shown to him, but he knew it sprang from the same source as his own overweening pride. He couldn't criticize him for it, but he wondered if he could target some censure at himself for perpetuating the fault. He turned away from him, catching sight of a pile of library books in the corner of the room as he did. "Do they need to go back?"

"Aye, they do."

Valentine picked up the books: two detective novels by William McIlvanney sat on the top. "What's this, are you reading up on the police now?"

"He's a Kilmarnock laddie, the writer."

"I know, I read the books years ago. Set in Glasgow, mind you."

His father slouched forward in his chair and spoke with his finger tapping out his main points on the table. "But it would take an Ayrshire man to make sense of that place, you realize."

Valentine smiled. "The son of a miner, no doubt."

"Are you making assumptions?"

"Me, Dad? No, never." He picked up the other books and turned for the door. "I'll get these back. Do you want me to pick up some others?"

The old man nodded. "Aye, you can get me the third one in the series: *Strange Loyalties*."

"The police again?"

"They make good reading."

It was the closest Valentine had ever heard his father come to a compliment.

22

DI Bob Valentine spent the night in fitful sleep. There were some familiar figures in his visions, while others were mere phantoms. The small girl with the white-blonde hair was there once again, as was his late mother. It made the detective feel uneasy to see visions of the dead; they somehow came alive once more.

As he made coffee, said goodbye to his family and drove to the station, Valentine tried to downplay the significance of the night before. By the King Street roundabout, he had put the entire situation down to the stress of the case: his unconscious mind wrestling by night with the problems he couldn't find solutions to by day.

"Morning, Jim," he said as he entered the front door of the station.

"Oh, it's yourself." The desk sergeant leaned over conspiratorially and beckoned Valentine with a nod. "Big Dino's in already, I see."

Valentine approached the counter and lowered his briefcase to the floor. "Starting early, isn't she?"

"Yeah, and that's not the all of it." Jim looked back towards the staircase as if to set the scene for his next announcement. "She's got some new blood up there with her now."

"New blood?"

"Young one, twenties, never seen her before, but she's police, got it written all over her."

Valentine didn't know who the young police officer was, but he had his suspicions already. "Did you catch an accent?"

Jim frowned, the creases in his brow making his skin look even more like old leather. "No, afraid not. What're you thinking?"

If Valentine had learned one thing in his time at King Street station, it was to keep what you were thinking to yourself. "Who knows, with Dino. Could be my replacement." He let the implication hang, then struck again: "Or yours, pal."

On the stairs, Valentine felt Jim's eyes on his back. He knew he'd set the cogs turning in Jim's mind and that he'd be paying close attention to their every revolution until something like thought ignited. The detective knew if there was any hope of the new officer's identity being revealed in a hurry then the desk sergeant would be the first to know; with any luck, Valentine thought, he would be the second.

In the incident room, he hung up his coat and carried his briefcase to his office. He allowed himself a glance towards the whiteboard to discern any new information, but spotted little, save a few additional jottings about the Urquhart post-mortem report in red marker pen. Before he had closed the door, the telephone on his desk was ringing.

"Hello, Valentine."

"Morning, Bob." It was Chief Superintendent Marion Martin, her voice high and chipper — too cheery by far. It unsettled him.

"Yes, Chief, what can I do for you?"

"Anything to report since yesterday?"

"I need to get an update from the squad before I can brief you; I had them on a number of specifics so I'd be hoping to be edging closer today."

"Closer to what, Bob, the door?"

It was a glib remark and he ignored it.

"Anyway, I'd like to see you in my office when you have a moment."

"Oh, yes."

"Yes, Bob. In fact, right away." The line clicked off.

Valentine held his hand in mid-air for a moment, staring at the receiver. He couldn't quite believe that he had reached his time of life and was still susceptible to the taunts of so-called superiors.

He booted up his computer, waited for the Windows icon to appear and sat in his chair; its back creaked behind him as he twiddled frustratedly with the mouse in his right hand.

"Right away." He repeated the words, but couldn't quite take in that she had said them. She had taunted him like a new recruit who needed to be shown the lie of the land. He reached for the telephone receiver and pressed the speed-dial for the press office — the line was answered promptly.

"Hello, media relations." It was Coreen's assistant. Valentine struggled to remember her name, but then it came back to him.

"Debbie, I was after your boss, is she about?"

"Who's speaking?" She sounded aloof, and there were officers who would have been offended — served her arse in parsley for questioning — but Valentine guessed it was Coreen's training coming to the fore: the girl had obviously made the mistake of handing over stray calls once, but she wouldn't do it again.

"It's Bob Valentine from CID, detective inspector."

A rummaging on the other end of the line was greeted with a sharp intake of breath, then a gap stretched out that had Valentine tapping his fingertips on a pile of blue folders.

"Bob." It was Coreen.

"Good morning."

"And what can I do you for?"

Valentine leaned forward and rested on the desk. "Have you heard anything about our man, Sinclair?"

Coreen cleared her throat. "I thought that's what you might be interested in. Yes, suspended on full pay, I hear."

"Nice one."

"I wouldn't put out the bunting quite yet."

"Oh, no?"

"Definitely not. By all accounts he went ballistic."

"So what? Paulo's on the record with the finger pointed squarely at Sinclair."

Coreen sniggered. It was a fake laugh, more for effect than anything. "If I know Cameron Sinclair, he'll have a bloody great hard-on for all of us now, Bob. Don't expect we've heard the last of him."

"Just you let me know the second he comes anywhere near you with that hard-on. You hear me?"

As Valentine lowered the phone, the computer screen lit up and little icons formed themselves into neat rows on his desktop. He clicked on Internet Explorer. When the search engine appeared, Valentine dragged the drop-down menu to select his daughter's Facebook account and waited for the page to appear. The network was slow, but he conceded that might have something to do with the number of pictures on Chloe's timeline. His daughter was sixteen and not quite an adult, but seemed to be living a kind of sophisticated social life that he couldn't comprehend. He justified the intrusion into her life as a necessary evil in today's world. Valentine no more wanted to snoop on his daughter than anyone else, but it was a means to an end: the conclusion of a nagging feeling that something wasn't altogether right with her.

He checked her posts, all innocuous enough: pictures of puppies with pop-philosophising captions, links to music videos, adumbrations on the week's highlights to come. Only one remark struck him as worthy of closer scrutiny: "Daddy's becoming a popular man." A hyperlink followed. Valentine clicked on it and was brought to the website of the Glasgow-Sun. As he scrolled down he quickly identified Cameron Sinclair's byline on the article his own name featured in.

"What the hell is this?" He couldn't understand why anyone would post the link on his daughter's timeline, but conceded much teenage behavior was inscrutable to him. Then a thought struck him. He returned to his daughter's stream and checked for the post's author. As he read the same name he'd seen on the byline only a few seconds ago, his hand constricted tightly round the mouse.

"You've crossed a line, Sinclair."

The DI closed down the webpage and rose from the chair. He surmised that the Facebook post was some kind of mocking taunt: parents were good value on the embarrassment scale for youngsters. It was a move meant to embarrass his daughter and create some tension at home for him. But Sinclair was sailing close to the wind assuming he wouldn't check his daughter's web usage. Either that, or he was a more reckless idiot than he had previously given him credit for.

Valentine knocked on the door, twice, and took firm hold of the handle as he stepped into the chief super's office. Dino was standing by the window with a coffee cup in hand; in her other hand was the elbow of a young woman who she seemed to be keen to impress. She threw back her hair and laughed as if the scene merited a kind of cocktail-party bonhomie.

Valentine took two steps and coughed into his fist. "Good morning."

"Ah, Bob. Thought you'd lost your way."

"You wanted to see me?" He found his gaze shifting towards the young woman, who turned to face him and nodded. It was a polite nod, almost conspiratorial in its suggestion that she had the chief super in hand.

"Oh, yes indeed, Bob, I want to see you." CS Martin motioned the young woman to the front of her desk and walked round the other side herself. "I'd like to introduce you to Sylvia McCormack, if I may."

Valentine put out his hand. The woman reached out and shook it enthusiastically, a wide smile filling her face. "Hello, sir."

Dino stepped between them and made her way towards the coffee pot for a refill. As she poured, she spoke loudly. "Sylvia is one of Glasgow's finest young detective sergeants." She continued on, but by the time Valentine had heard the words "Glasgow" and "detective sergeant" he knew exactly what was afoot.

He cut in. "Am I to assume Sylvia has been seconded to Ayr?"

The chief super turned around, held up her coffee cup and dipped her head towards it. "You assume correctly, detective."

Valentine's pulse jolted and the familiar taste of a bitter pill being swallowed passed down his throat. Martin had gone behind his back; she hadn't consulted him. He knew it was her right to do so, but he also knew better people would have played it straight. He ran a finger down the crease of his shirtsleeve as he tried to find his response.

"The investigation is at a crucial stage. I'm not quite sure how an officer from another force will improve the dynamic," said Valentine.

The young woman stepped forward. "I've been brought up to speed." She snatched a blue folder from the desk and opened it up. "I've sketched out a profile on the kind of individual that might ... "

Valentine cut in. "That might impale a man through his arse with a piece of 2 x 4?" He had tried to ruffle her, but was unsuccessful.

"I have profiling experience, and I've worked a number of similar cases in the Central Belt."

"Similar?" His intonation suggested the idea was ludicrous.

"By that, I mean serial mutilation." The young woman lowered her head and stepped back. It was a retreat that signaled she thought Valentine's truculence was insurmountable.

The chief super pitched in. "Bob, I think Sylvia is trying to say that her experience might be useful to the team. A fresh pair of eyes and an outside perspective may pay dividends."

"This is not a serial killer we're dealing with here: there's no trophy taking, there's no mutilation, sexual interference or anything else to suggest we're dealing with an abnormal psychology. This is calculated and precise, yes, but it's not a pattern killer, and I'll stake my reputation on that."

CS Martin fanned the lapel of her jacket in an animated manner. She turned to DS McCormack and made a lullaby of her voice. "Perhaps you'd like to go and acquaint yourself with the incident room, Sylvia."

The young woman's grey eyes flashed. "Yes, of course."

The DI felt a pang of guilt: she was an unwitting pawn in Martin's game and he'd been harsh on the DS, but life was harsh, and life on the force as harsh as it got.

"What the hell are you playing at, Bob?" Her sweet tone evaporated as quickly as a morning mist.

"I'm not sure I know what you mean."

"Don't act it with me, pal, I'll give you your head in your hands to play with if you start that patter in here." She pointed to the floor as if it indicated a marker of her territory.

"If you're referring to the fact that you've parachuted a new DS into my team with no prior notice then I'll put my hand up to not being overly chuffed about it."

"I gave you plenty of notice: how many times did I tell you, now let me see?" She walked over to her desk and opened her diary. She was hiding behind the rulebook, a favorite tactic of all bureaucrats.

Valentine turned. "I'm referring to specific discussions, not veiled threats to pull the rug out from under me."

The chief super's eyes narrowed, and then her lips formed themselves into a thin pout that precipitated a gale-force blast to come.

Two loud knocks on the door shattered the momentary silence.

The officers turned to hear the hinges creaking and saw Jim from the front desk bounding in like a tired marathon runner. "I think you should see this." He held out a copy of the Glasgow-Sun. "It's hot off the presses."

23

Leanne Dunn eased her hands beneath the tabletop and fixed her stare on Danny Gillon. As their eyes met, the pimp smiled, and then the action seemed to prompt a hacking cough that ended with him reaching for a cigarette. When he brought the filter tip to his mouth, Leanne seized the moment and leapt from her seat. The sound of the chair's back clattering off the wall startled her, she shot her arms towards her ears, but her mind was set and she ran from the kitchen with wailing, frightened screams. As she moved, her vision started to blur; she was light-headed and nauseous and each barefoot step on the floorboards sent a shot of pain through her ankles that fled all the way up her leg to her hip bone. She was unsteady and nervous, and when she looked back to see Gillon jumping into the hallway, her balance deserted her. Leanne fell to the floor, her knees taking the brunt of the impact before she crashed onto her front and smacked her head off the wall with a solid thud.

Gillon halted where he stood and laughed. "Oh, dear, Leanne."

Her position on the floor beneath Gillon made her feel even more vulnerable, but the stinging pain that had begun deep in her brow was somehow working its way into her stomach. She raised herself on one arm, but as the weak limb buckled beneath her there was a turn in her intestines and she vomited.

"Oh, man." Gillon was laughing harder now. He walked towards her and grabbed a handful of Leanne's lank hair. "Going somewhere?"

A long trail of bile spooled from her mouth; she tried to speak, but her words were in competition with the vomit and the blood evacuating from a burst lip. "No, Danny."

"What? What you saying?" He leaned forward, made a show of

bringing his ear towards her mouth.

Leanne tried to speak again, only one word came: "No."

"No? I'll give you fucking no. You don't say no to me." Gillon yanked Leanne from the ground. Another scream bounced off the narrow confines of the hallway and Gillon brought a fist up to her face. "Are you going to make me belt you, Leanne. Is that it? You want a belt, want reminding who you're dealing with?"

Leanne's eyes followed her pump's fist. "Please, Danny."

The fist disappeared from her line of view and was buried in her stomach. The pain didn't seem to matter when she saw what was coming. As Gillon threw her on the bed she tried to curl over, even though it was a futile gesture: there was no escape, no avoiding the inevitable.

"Get on your back," he roared.

Leanne was too weak to move, holding her stomach where the blow had toppled her.

"On your back!" Gillon grabbed her and slapped her twice across the face. Leanne felt her legs rising. She bent her knees and tried to kick out, but he was too strong for her, pinning her legs down to the bed and ripping open her dressing gown.

"You've got scrawnier than I remember," said Gillon as he stood unbuckling his belt. "Have to get a few burgers into you. Nobody likes a scrawny whore." He rolled down his jeans and underwear and eased himself over Leanne. "Not heard that the bigger the cushion, the better the pushing?"

Leanne shut her eyes and felt her throat constricting as Gillon raped her. She was frozen, unmoving, like someone tied to the bed. She imagined herself as another person, as if she weren't Leanne anymore, as if she had somehow left her body and were standing in the corner watching Gillon thrust himself into someone else. She heard his guttural heaving, the shortness of his breath, the belt buckle banging off the bed frame and the floorboards with a dull rhythm. She felt the dampness of his sweaty brow on her cheek and the tightness of her lungs as he laid himself heavily into her, but she wasn't there. Leanne had long ago learnt to disengage herself from the physical act, the violence, the pain. If she didn't acknowledge it to herself, then it didn't happen. She had told herself that as a child — it could be blocked out. Everything could be blocked out if you tried hard enough.

When Gillon raised his jeans and belt, sweat hung from his brow and eyelashes. He ran the back of his hand over his face and smiled towards Leanne where she curled up on the bed. He pointed towards her as he spoke. "You need to get your act together."

She didn't reply, just moved herself to the edge of the bed and fastened her dressing gown.

"You hear me? You need to start paying attention to your punters. I wouldn't pay for a ride like that." He shook his head as he fastened his belt. "No way would I pay for that. You need to start thinking a bit more about the punter and a bit less about scoring."

Leanne stared out the window; the gloom of the early evening sky had settled above the flat rooftops and a small white moon sat low and stark in the sky.

"You hearing me?"

"What?" She turned towards Gillon, who had his hand out to her, as if offering to help her from the bed.

"Come on, get yourself dressed," he said, nodding towards the door.

"Why?"

"We're going out."

Leanne rose from the bed and tightened the dressing gown around her waist. "Going out?"

"So, you're not deaf then." Gillon clapped his hands together. "Come on, move it!" He pulled her towards him by the shoulders, then spun her to face the wardrobe in the corner of the room; the dressing gown was yanked clean from Leanne's back as she took her first step.

Gillon laughed. "Christ almighty, need to put some meat on those bones." A faint gleam entered his eyes as he made for the door. "Going for a smoke, be dressed and ready by the time I've finished or I'll drag you out in the buff and show the world that skanky arse!" He was still laughing as he made his way to the kitchen.

Leanne's eyes studied the wardrobe; she reached out and began to dress for Gillon.

In the hallway, Leanne leaned against the wall and listened to her pimp stubbing his cigarette; the ashtray clattered off the tabletop as he dug the butt into the glass. When he was finished, he started whistling: his mood was bright, and Leanne knew that was something to hold on to — she didn't want to be around him when his mood was dark. If she could keep him this way then Leanne knew that she would likely avoid any more conflict. She was a tart, Gillon's tart, and when she forgot that she felt pain. It was better not to think about those things, though.

"Right, you set?" said Gillon.

"Where are we going?"

"To see a man."

Leanne's pulse raced. "Who?"

"Are you questioning me?" His bottom row of teeth was bared. "Eh?" He reached out and grabbed Leanne's face in his hand and squeezed it. "Is that it, you're questioning me?"

"No."

He pushed her head away and she stumbled.

"Good. Just keep it that way."

Gillon went for the door and Leanne trailed behind him. He held out his hand and grabbed Leanne's arm when she came into reach. "Move it."

Gillon's van was parked on the other side of the road, she recognized it at once. As they headed for the van, she wondered if she was going to be forced to turn tricks in there; he had made her do that before.

They drove to Ayr Road and over Tam's Brig before heading out to Prestwick shore, at the end of the esplanade, where the walkway ran into an expansive parking area. There was a car on the other side of the van, about forty or fifty meters away. Gillon turned and wound down his window, waving to the man in the car.

"What's going on?" said Leanne. She peered past Gillon's shoulder towards the approaching man.

"This is a mate of mine," said Gillon. "I want you to have a word with him."

"What about?"

Gillon spun round to face her. "Whatever he wants to know, you tell him."

"I don't know anything."

His eyes widened; she sensed a threat. "Look, don't mess me about,

I want you to tell him about that fat pedo and your other pal."

"What other pal?"

The man approached the window and smiled. He nodded to Gillon, then waved a hand towards his passenger. "You must be Leanne?"

She watched Gillon reach for the door handle and step outside, and as he did so, the man leaned forward and extended his hand. "I'm Cameron Sinclair and Danny here's told me a lot about you."

24

Detective Inspector Bob Valentine didn't realize his posture was so stiff, his demeanor so harsh, until he crossed his legs and caught sight of the rigid angle his foot made to his ankle. He stared at his shoe, pointing upwards towards the desk, and wondered if it might snap off, it looked so brittle, like it was the frozen branch of a tree that threatened to fall.

"Is everything all right, Inspector?" said Carole-Anne. Her voice was a low, flat monotone that never contained any inflection: a professional contrivance, no doubt.

"No, everything's just fine."

The therapist's eyes seemed to be measuring him. "Perhaps you could tell me what it's like being back to normal duties?"

Normal duties — what were they? Was it normal to find a member of the public had been impaled on a wooden spike at the communal tip? Was it normal to find a repeat sex offender — one who had never expressed an ounce of remorse for the children he abused — executed in similar fashion? Oh, yes, it was all another day at the office. He let his gaze shift through the woman who was perhaps young enough to be his own daughter.

"Inspector, are you uncomfortable speaking to me?" She started to fan the yellow pencil in her fingers; the rubber tip became a blur.

Valentine knew he was in a no-win situation. CS Martin had made it clear the therapy sessions were to be a trade-off: a return to the training academy at Tulliallan was the alternative. If that happened, he knew also that the case would be turned over to Glasgow CID.

"I don't want to appear uncooperative."

"But?" She presented the one-word interruption like an uppercut.

"I really do feel that your experience could be put to better use elsewhere. I'm fine, I told Marion Martin as much."

Carole-Anne put down the pencil and eased herself back in her chair; a reporter's notebook that sat in her lap followed the pencil. "Bob – you don't mind if I call you Bob, do you?"

Valentine shook his head.

She continued. "We have to get something straight. I'm doing a job. I know you know how to do yours, but you need to appreciate that you've been referred here by a senior officer with, it must be said, good cause."

"I understand that." Valentine paused; he could see there was no point in parrying her questions. "What would you like to know?"

"Why don't you tell me how you feel about what happened to you?"

"You mean how I felt about being stabbed in the heart? You can say it, y'know."

She pressed out a smile, a weak one; no words followed.

Valentine continued. "The physical aspects are impossible to describe. I mean, you can appreciate, I'm sure, what it feels like to have a piece of cold metal thrust into your chest cavity, but the shock almost cancels that out. I remember the blood, the sight of the knife sticking out my chest — they say your whole life flashes before you, by Christ it does."

The therapist shifted uneasily in her seat; her face seemed to slacken and her mouth dipped downwards. "Perhaps not the physical aspects, I was alluding more to the way you were affected psychologically — that's what I'm here for."

She was there to make notes in her little book, to tote up the pros and cons of keeping him on the force. He suddenly felt an almighty enmity towards her, but it seemed to wash over him and disappear as quickly as it had appeared. She wasn't a bad person — that much he knew — she was just, as she had said, doing her job.

"I thought I wasn't going to see my children again, or my wife."

"You have two children, Bob, is that right?" She reached over to retrieve a stack of notes from her desk.

"Two girls."

"It must have been hard for them, and your wife."

He had officially died and been revived; he was a man risen from the dead — how real could that story be? And yet he knew it was him, even if he wasn't the same Bob Valentine after being stabbed in the heart with a nine-inch blade.

"I'd sooner not talk about my family," said Valentine.

Carole-Anne's cheeks flushed. "Of course, we don't need to discuss them if you don't want to."

The detective felt a pang of guilt; they had only just thawed the room. "Maybe next time."

A car passed by the window outside, its headlamps washing over the battleship grey walls. "It's later than I thought, perhaps that's enough for a first session."

Valentine felt relieved, as if he had been released from a straitjacket. As he headed to the door, Carole-Anne was waiting for him with her hand outstretched.

"Thank you, Bob."

In the corridor, Valentine caught sight of the cleaners wheeling a Henry hoover towards the main incident room and the image brought him back to reality with a shudder.

"No, you're all right there, love." He started to jog towards the cleaner, who dipped back her head and eyed him from beneath her heavy glasses. He grabbed the door from her. "Maybe leave this one till last, eh, got a couple of things to tidy up in here myself."

"If you're tidying up, son, I'll give you the trolley and the dusters!"

Valentine smiled, but the cleaner pressed out a frown, which suggested she wasn't joking.

"I'll only be half an hour, if you don't mind."

She retreated a few steps and made for the chief super's office, shaking her head and trailing the vacuum cleaner like it was a badly-behaved child.

When Valentine got inside the room the light outside was dimming. He reached out for the row of switches by the door and pressed them down. The strip bulbs buzzed. He was about to walk towards the glassed-off office at the other end when some movement caught his eye.

"You're working late, aren't you?" he said.

DS Sylvia McCormack sat behind a pile of case notes. She patted the top folder and peered over. "Maybe not for much longer."

Valentine approached her. "What are you doing, anyway?"

She shrugged. "Oh, good question."

He walked towards the desk and picked up a file. "Knox. You"re going over his record?"

"I'm sorry, I don't mean to be stepping on any toes; if someone else has this in hand . . . It's just . . ." She cut herself off.

Valentine returned the folder. He had a twinge in his back; he'd been in the office too long and needed to find some time to release the tensions. He wondered how it felt for DS McCormack on her first day in the post. "No, you're all right. I was going to give this to Phil or Ally, but they've both got pretty heavy paper rounds as it is. And what with this morning's press kerfuffle."

The DS nodded. "Yes, sir."

He knew when he had hit a raw nerve — the press situation was a bigger embarrassment than he thought, if the squad's newest member already had the good grace to look ashamed at the mention.

"I should probably get off." The DS reached out to retrieve her handbag from the back of the chair and eased past the detective.

"Hang on. "It's just – what?"

She stopped. "Sorry?"

"The files." Valentine turned towards Knox's case notes and tapped the top. "You had something to say about these."

"Oh, right." The strap of her handbag worked its way off her shoulder, but she caught the bag before it hit the floor. "Yes, the name Knox. It rings a bell. I don't know from what, though."

Valentine took two steps towards the DS. "The name Knox rings a bell with you. What do you mean?"

"I don't know, I just thought I'd come across it before."

"Where – Glasgow?"

She started to play with the buckle on the outside of her handbag. "I don't know, sir. It might be nothing."

Valentine saw his hopes, at once raised so high, now dropping back below the horizon. "It's a pretty rare name, you'd think you'd remember the case."

The DS shrugged her shoulders again. Valentine felt a twinge of anger and locked it away — it had been a long day. "Right, get off home."

"Yes, sir."

"But before you go." He turned towards the desk with the large pile of blue files and picked them up. "Here, take these with you. If there's something in there that jogs your memory, you can tell me about it in the morning."

"Yes, sir."

"Oh, and this is your personal obsession while you're in Ayrshire – get to know Duncan Knox inside out. I want all there is on him — if he traded a jelly trifle for a bag of snout in Peterhead, I want to know who with." He placed the pile of files in her arms and held the door open for her.

"Yes, sir." She collected the files on her way through the door. "Thank you, sir."

As the door's hinges let out a sigh, Valentine sat down on the top of the desk. Where he had removed the files sat a copy of the Glasgow-Sun that seemed to have passed through the hands of the entire murder squad. He picked up the newspaper and turned to the story Jim Prentice had brought to their attention at first dawn. The paper was dog-eared and tatty, beyond any doctor's surgery or barber's shop waiting-room offer. There were smudges of ketchup and the ringed remnants of coffee cups everywhere, but none of it altered the contents or the headline:

AYRSHIRE POLICE HUNT DOUBLE MURDERER

"Bastard." Valentine felt like spitting on the paper, but he resisted. The article's subheading had drawn his attention away:

KNOWN PAEDOPHILE FOUND AT RACECOURSE

He had read the article already, but he passed his eyes over it again: if nothing else, it would reassure him that he hadn't imagined it — the newspaper had, indeed, identified Duncan Knox as the murder victim.

"That's twice they've shafted me now."

Valentine scrunched up the paper and threw it into the wastebasket.

25

Valentine had called the squad to gather at 9:15 a.m. By 9:20 there was still no sign of DS Sylvia McCormack and the mumble of judgmental voices around the incident room was steadily on the rise. Valentine stood by the board and drew a line down the side of the crime-scene pictures of Duncan Knox's corpse; beside the line he made a list of bullet points that he copied from the post-mortem report. When he was finished, he picked up the red marker pen and circled the words "depressed skull fracture," drawing a line to the matching words under the image of James Urquhart.

"Right, listen up, everyone." Valentine returned the top to the marker pen and clasped it in his hand. "As you can, see there's a distinct correlation between the two post-mortem reports."

DS McAlister spoke. "We're looking for the same man, obviously."

"It would seem that way, Ally. The MOs are almost identical, though we probably didn't need the pathologist to tell us that." He paced the front of the board and the squad followed him with its collective gaze. "Brutal, ritualistic murder on public ground — carried out twice, if not at the locus then with the intention to make us think so — one victim a privileged figure and the other the exact opposite. Right, what have we got?"

As he turned to face the squad, the door at the other end of the room opened. DS Sylvia McCormack entered with her jacket on the crook of her arm and proceeded to the coat stand.

"Sorry I'm late — traffic."

A few tuts followed her explanation and then everyone returned to the DI.

"OK, Phil, so we're all on the same page, what have you got for us on James Urquhart's history?" Valentine eased himself onto the edge of the desk and gave DS Donnelly the floor.

"Right, thanks, boss. Well, I've spoken to the bank and the staff he took with him after the buyout, and I have to say there's no sign of any ill will. This is a man who seems to have made few enemies. Certainly, in his professional life, there were very few dissenters." The DS turned over a page in his notebook. "One of the former partners, Carter, thought they should have held off before selling, but he admits he did very well out of the buyout and I don't think there was any bad blood between them, far from it, actually. That's the picture I got across the board, really."

Valentine folded his arms and fixed the DS in his stare. "What about clients, employees?"

"Yeah, very little to go on there. The phrase "kept himself to himself" cropped up a lot. I got the impression that he held his social life and his family life totally separate from his business affairs, but again, no troubles bubbling up to the surface. Sounded like a decent enough boss, really."

"Well, he pissed someone off, Phil. Are you forgetting how he met his end?" Valentine shook his head and scanned the crowd. "Right, Ally, you're up — the buyout, you took that from Paulo, yeah?"

DS McAlister frowned and shook his head. "Eh, no, Phil took that since he was looking at the employers and employees."

"Jesus Christ, is that it? We've even less to go on than I thought." Valentine pushed himself off the desk and stood with his hands empty in the air. "Well, what have we got?"

McAlister spoke. "I took the neighbor from Paulo – Ronnie Bell."

"Yes, what did you unearth?"

The DS opened a blue folder and turned it over. "Well, he's retired, had a string of pound stores but sold them off."

"A pound a shop, eh?" said Valentine.

A smile. "Er, no, bit more than that, quite a few million, as it happens. He's certainly not short of cash, and he did invest some money with Urquhart's brokers before the buyout."

"Tell me he lost his hat."

"No, seems to be quite the opposite, actually."

"Money goes to money." Valentine had a knot of tension building in his chest.

He turned back to the squad. "So, that's a blank on the work colleagues and the neighbor. Any more good news?"

DS McAlister hoisted up his belt and spoke. His voice was quieter than it had been before, the timbre more drawn out, almost a drawl. "Well, it might be nothing, but I checked out the Rotary Club and one or two other things."

Valentine's eyes widened. "Go on."

"Urquhart was not a regular at the Rotary: he'd show for a Burns' Supper and a couple of other high points in the year, but that was it." McAlister found his stride and started to punctuate his words with hand gestures. "He did attend a regular bridge night and Mrs. Urquhart mentioned a weekly model enthusiasts' club that he went to, he was into trains and the like."

The DI raised his arm. "Ally, is this going somewhere?"

McAlister fixed his stare, his face looked solemn. "No, this is my point, sir. The model-railway club was a weekly thing, met on a Wednesday night."

"Don't tell me, like clockwork!" said DS Donnelly.

McAlister started to look nervy, as the room erupted into more laughter. "No, listen, what I'm getting at is, Mrs. Urquhart said her husband went to the model club every week without fail, but when I spoke to the bloke in charge ... " he started to turn pages rapidly in his spiral-bound notebook. "Yeah, Mr. Forgan, he told me he'd only seen Urquhart a handful of times in the last three years."

Valentine's thoughts started to swirl in his mind. As he looked at DS McAlister fingering the edges of his notebook, he noted he had the pleased look of a dog that had just retrieved a stick for his master.

"Ally, are you saying Urquhart was AWOL every Wednesday night?" said the DI.

He nodded. "More or less."

Valentine folded an arm across his stomach and rested his chin on the knuckles of his fist. As he fastened his eyes on the squad, tight radial lines appeared at their edges. He made a half-smile, not because he was happy, but because he couldn't help it. "Right, listen up, all of you: I want to know where our murder victim was on all those Wednesday nights. I want bank cards, visas, gas receipts checked and mapped. If we can pinpoint his whereabouts, I want uniform door to door with photographs and dates. I want CCTV footage taken from shops, garage forecourts and bloody eye-in-the-sky traffic reports, if necessary. I want his car circulated, and registration, and I want all of this yesterday. If there's something unusual, anything — be it a trip to a toy store or a hotel that charges by the hour – I want it on that board!"

The team moved away from the whiteboard and the room filled once again with the familiar sounds of chair legs scraping the floor, telephones being raised and filing cabinets opening and closing.

Valentine looked out the window towards the cloud-crossed sky and saw weak sun rays patting the rooftops. He knew he needed something solid, something that would link Urquhart to Knox and unlock the investigation, but he felt a long way off. When he turned back to the desk to retrieve his notes, DS McCormack was standing there.

"Sylvia, glad you could join us." It was sarcasm, and he almost regretted it.

"Sorry, sir. I had a late night, last night, with the Knox files."

"Oh, yes, did you remember the case you thought he was linked to?"

The sun's glare crept up and a pair of drowsy eyes flickered. The chatter and fuss of the busy office seemed to subside as she spoke. "That's what I wanted to see you about."

26

Valentine waited in his office at the end of the incident room for DS McCormack to retrieve the paperwork she wanted to show him.

"Right, what have you got for me?" he said.

DS McCormack tapped two fingers on her cheekbone before bursting into speech. "Right, you remember I told you that I thought I knew the name Knox."

"And do you remember I told you I wanted a complete case file on him, not just chasing rainbows?"

"You have it." She rummaged in the pile of notes and presented the DI with a blue folder.

He took the folder and opened it up; he was scanning the contents as McCormack started to talk again. She seemed animated, keen. He liked to see that in his squad, but he knew enthusiasm was no substitute for groundwork, she would need to impress him with her police work over any desire to shine.

"Knox has spent more time inside than out in the last thirty years, some hard yards, as well," she said.

"Took a shiv in the back in Peterhead, I see."

"Yeah, it was a sharpened chicken bone, I believe. He did the rest of his stretch in isolation, but still managed to get his top row of teeth knocked out."

"Popular bloke. Can't say I'm welling up with sympathy, mind you. This record's horrific. I'd have knocked his teeth out myself."

"Never expressed remorse once, never submitted fully to any treatment. I think it's fair to say Knox was a serial pedophile without contrition for his crimes."

"He was bloody well committed to it. He was a beast, nothing more."

The DS nodded. "There are psych reports in there, but they don't make for pretty reading." Her eyes darted. "Sir, if you don't mind, I'd like to make a point about Knox's time in custody."

Valentine closed the folder, leaned back and laced his fingers across his stomach. "Go on, then."

"I listed the times Knox was inside and plotted his known whereabouts when he was at liberty. Not always easy, because a few times he managed to slip under the radar, but in the main, save a period of about six months I couldn't account for, when I think he was in the north, he stayed in and around greater Glasgow."

The DI edged forward in his seat, placing his fingertips on the rim of the desk. "Are you going to tell me you remembered the case?"

"Better than that, sir." A gleam entered her eyes as she reached for another folder. The desk was becoming messy. "I found the case by cross-referencing all of Knox's offences with all of those of a similar nature stretching back through his period of offending."

"Thirty-plus years — you trailed that last night?"

"Not exactly. I subtracted the times he was inside and only looked at what was left, which cut it down by a massive amount."

"Sylvia, I'm guessing you still had quite a few cases to wade through."

"Yes, sir."

She took her hand away from the blue folder and stepped back from the desk. She was pacing as she spoke, finding the exact words clearly a struggle for her. "There was a case in Partick and a case in Shawlands, so two cases with the same MO, and Knox was living in a bedsit on Jamaica Street at the time of both." She paused. "Boss, Urquhart was in Glasgow then, too. This is the only time outside of their recent past in Ayr that I can pinpoint them in the same locality."

"And years later, they both turn up on wooden spikes in my patch."

The DS nodded. "This could be the link."

"Tell me they took him in?"

She sighed. "Not for the Partick one."

"Glasgow questioned Duncan Knox for Shawlands?"

"Yes. I checked just five minutes ago, sir, the Partick case was closed anyway, but the one they quizzed Knox on is still open."

Valentine got up from the desk and put his hands in his pockets. He walked towards the window and stared out at the grey sky.

"Give me the details."

The DS reached for one of the folders and removed a single sheaf of paper. "A missing Shawlands schoolgirl, Janie Cooper."

The girl's name made Valentine reel. He had never heard the name before and his reaction puzzled him. A lightness in his head sent his balance askew and he reached out to steady himself on the filing cabinet. He felt like the air had been sucked out of his lungs. It was a strange feeling of weightlessness, of being a soul separate from the physical body.

"Is everything OK, sir?"

He nodded and heard the blood pounding in his eardrums. "Yes, go on."

"She was only six, a pretty wee thing by all accounts."

"Do we have a picture?" He didn't know why he had asked. He was drawn to Janie Cooper's plight.

"No, not a hard copy, I'll print one up. It was twelve years ago she disappeared."

"He did it, Knox."

"What?"

Valentine moved away from the filing cabinet and placed the flat of his back on the bare wall. "Don't ask me how I know, I just know."

DS McCormack looked away. "Erm, Glasgow questioned Knox, but he was released soon after."

"He did it."

McCormack closed the folder over and started to tidy the notes on the desk into their respective piles. She tried not to look at the DI as she spoke. "I know at least one of the officers is still on the force, sir. I could arrange a meeting."

"What about Janie's parents?"

"I don't know. I could find out."

Valentine nodded. "Yes, do that. I want to meet them."

"Is that a good idea, sir?" The DS seemed to be overwhelmed by the reaction the information had generated in the detective. "I mean, won't that be like building their hopes up?"

Valentine pushed himself off the wall. The room felt suddenly small and insufficient for the knowledge he carried inside him. "It's twelve years, Sylvia, did they ever find a body?"

"No, sir. The remains of Janie Cooper were never recovered."

Valentine crossed the distance to the door and opened it. He felt detached from the reality he knew. He yelled out to the room, "Ally, get in here!"

McCormack looked panicked as she picked up the files and headed for the door. "I'll get onto Glasgow, get images."

"Get onto the parents, as soon as possible."

27

Since his stabbing, Valentine had become aware of a distant, almost imperceptible, ticking. There was a clock on him now. He had never thought of it before, even at forty, which may have been the logical time to detect its presence. At forty, you may safely look back, then count the years forward to assume — bearing in mind some luck of genetics — you have lived longer than you have left to go. Valentine's father would not see out his sixties, his grandfather had gone in his fifties; how long did he have left?

His previous decade — his thirties — had passed in a blur. He could remember turning thirty clearly, as it was the time of the millennium celebrations, but had it really been so long ago? He couldn't believe all those years — all that time — had really passed. What had he done with it? The incidents of memory were few: his daughters' birthdays, a couple of holidays, the surgery. In the main, it had been a period of drudge, of paying his way in the world, playing to a set of rules he had nothing to do with establishing.

The living room door eased open and Clare appeared with a glass of wine in her hand. "You look deep in thought. Penny for them."

Valentine eyed his own glass; the ice was melting over the Scotch. "Yeah, you could say that."

Clare sat down in front of him. "What's wrong, Bob?"

She seemed calm, wearing her concerned face. There were no neuroses on show, none of the nervy gestures of late, like tucking hair behind her ear over and over again. He eased deeper into the chair and tapped a fingertip off the glass he held. Before he realized it, he'd removed a photograph from his shirt pocket and passed it to Clare.

"Who's this?" She turned the picture over as if hoping to find the answer to her question written on the back.

"Her name's Janie Cooper."

"She's a pretty little thing."

"Was."

Clare's eyes widened. He thought she might throw the picture at him and storm out of the room, she didn't like hearing about his cases. "This little one's dead?" She seemed saddened. "It's an old picture, must be a few years ago now."

"Twelve years."

"Why are you carrying her picture around?" She placed the photograph on the arm of her chair, where the wineglass had been resting a moment ago.

Valentine didn't think he had the right words to explain what he was doing with a photograph of a murder victim who may not even be related to his ongoing investigation.

"Do you remember a few nights ago I woke you, wanting to talk?"

Clare glanced at the photograph on the arm of the chair. "Yes, I remember, you'd had a turn."

"It was a vision, or something … "

"Hang on, you said you'd seen a girl with hair like ... " She retrieved the picture. "You said she had hair like Chloe and Fiona, at that age."

"She does remind me of the girls at that age. They were like little angels." Valentine caught himself smiling into the past.

"Bob, what is going on with you?"

The reverie was broken. "What do you mean?"

Clare leaned forward in her chair. "You"re under too much stress with this case."

"No, you don't understand."

Clare pressed her temples with the tips of her nails. "Is this about you feeling different, about having changed?" She dropped her hands and stood up; the empty wine glass fell over. "No, don't answer, I don't want to know."

"Clare, please."

His wife left the room before Valentine had a chance to explain himself. He raised the whisky glass to his lips and drained it. What he had wanted to tell her, to make her understand, was that he hadn't seen the photograph of Janie Cooper until today. The fact that he already had seen her in a vision was a mystery to him; he couldn't explain it. But there she was, or had been, laying flowers on the dead corpse of James Urquhart, dancing round him at the scene of his murder with fairy lights in her hands. The image caused a shiver to pass across his shoulders and he tensed as if caught in a shrill breeze. None of it made any sense, it was all a mystery to him. The detective wondered what had become of his life, of his perceptions; he questioned his sanity. He knew he should relieve himself of his duties, tell the chief super that he was not fit for purpose.

He rose from his chair and placed the empty tumbler on the coffee table. He walked towards the door, put out the lights and carried on to the staircase. As he ascended the stairs to bed there was a lightness in his head that he put down to the whisky; the room was in darkness and only a few stray glints of light emanated from the edges of the heavy curtains. He had enough vision to see his wife lying in the bed, her back to him.

"Clare, look, you need to bear with me on this one."

She remained silent for a moment, then turned to face him.

"This isn't working. We're dysfunctional."

The word sounded ridiculous to him, like a term from a self-help manual. He let a laugh emerge that, at once, he knew he should have suppressed. "Oh, come on."

She looked at him, and the whites of her round eyes shone in the darkness of the enclosed space.

"Go to hell, Bob, just bloody well go to hell."

28

DI Bob Valentine woke from cautious sleep with aching bones and the scent of whisky on his breath. He removed his hand from the duvet and collected up the alarm clock — the exposed flesh of his arm told him at once that there was colder weather in store. He took time to focus on the burn of the digital clock's message; when it registered, he let out a yawn and padded towards the bathroom. Clare had risen early; her side of the bed was empty. He ran the taps, letting the sink fill up and then cautiously splashed warm water on his face.

When he was dressed, the DI took himself downstairs, collected a cup of coffee from the pot and greeted his wife with a cordial, "Good morning." There was a package waiting for him on the kitchen counter and the outside of the brown envelope indicated view the contents at once.

"What have you been getting now?" said Clare. It seemed a strange remark, as if he was the one who was continually running up the credit card bills.

"It's something for my dad." Valentine opened the package from Amazon and removed the worn copy of McIlvanney's Strange Loyalties. "He's been reading detective novels. Can you believe it?"

Clare collected the book from the counter and creased her nose. "Couldn't you have got him a new one?"

"It's been out of print, I had to shop around for this."

"I'm surprised you had the time." It was a calculated remark, and one that Valentine had no reply for.

He sipped his coffee and watched his wife return to the morning newspaper and her glass of orange juice. "Could you drop it off later today, Clare? He's just sitting up there on his own, I think he'd appreciate it."

She turned and put widened eyes on him. "Well, you'd think he'd appreciate a visit from his son, then."

Valentine put down his coffee cup and raised his briefcase; he wasn't prepared to pick up where he had left off the night before. "I'm off to work."

Clare had returned to reading the newspaper as he closed the kitchen door and headed towards the car in his shirtsleeves. The air outside was sharp as he flung his coat on the backseat; it covered the haunting dark patch.

The town was a hoard of bodies, all shuffling, eyes down. DS Sylvia McCormack was staying at the Caledonian Hotel. It had changed its name several times over the years, but to Valentine it would always be the Caly. He pulled up outside and waited for his colleague to appear.

The car door was soon opened. "Hello, boss."

Valentine nodded towards DS McCormack. "Glasgow, here we come."

She smiled back at him, and what he thought had been a cruel mouth gave way to an otherwise pretty face.

"It's grey out," she said.

"Yeah, well, that'll be the summer by with." He indicated on his way through the roundabout and onto Barns Street. He could already see the Sandgate clogged with cars. "When are they expecting us?"

DS McCormack was shimmying out of her raincoat. "Any time after ten. That's what Mrs. Cooper said when I called."

Valentine noticed how tense her face had become. "How did she seem, Mrs. Cooper?"

The officer sat in silence for a moment and appeared to be considering her response. She said: "Empty."

Valentine repeated the word. "Empty."

"It's the best I can come up with to describe the woman. It was like talking to a shadow on the phone, once I mentioned Janie."

Valentine stored the response away; he didn't want to give too much importance to the DS's observation, though he knew it was likely to be accurate. "What did you tell the Coopers?"

"That we were investigating a murder."

"Did you mention Knox?"

"No, I didn't think that would serve any particular purpose at this point."

"Good. If we bring the Knox angle into play, I'd like to see their reaction."

DS McCormack squinted. "What are you hoping to gain from this meeting, sir?"

Valentine was pulling onto the main arterial road to Glasgow; the stretch of single carriageway was busy but allowed him to reach 50 mph. "If I knew that, Sylvia, I'd send you and save myself the bother. Trust me, if there's a link to Knox and Urquhart, I'll find it. Of that I've no bloody doubt."

"You seem very sure of this lead."

"Knox was questioned at the time Janie Cooper went missing and the bank's confirmed that Urquhart was living and working in Glasgow at the exact same time. Call me an optimist, but I'm betting this is our link."

The Ayrshire countryside stretched out on either side of the road; green fields washed in buckets of rain. A few cows, Friesians, made a lazy trail towards a copse of trees. A grey half-moon still sat in the morning sky; there was no sign of the sun.

"You think they knew each other, Knox and Urquhart, don't you?" said DS McCormack.

"Think? I know."

"But how can you know?"

He had never dealt in what-ifs — he reasoned and made use of the facts. "Do you doubt me?"

McCormack frowned. "That's not an answer, that's a question."

"OK, then, ask me once we've seen the Coopers. You'll have your answer then. Knox knew Urquhart and they both ended up dead because of that association. I don't know how they came to know each other yet, or how they came to know Janie Cooper, but I know someone else on the force took a similar line of reasoning twelve years ago when that little girl went missing. Knox was in the frame then and I doubt he's blameless now. Urquhart might have slipped under the radar at the time, but whatever went on has well and truly caught up with them."

29

DS Sylvia McCormack appeared clutching two paper cups filled with coffee. She smiled towards her boss as she placed the cups down on the Formica tabletop. The liquid let off a slow flare into the brisk air that signaled its unsuitability for drinking.

"Watch, it's hot," said McCormack.

"I see that."

"Yeah, well, I felt it when I was stupid enough to take a sip."

"It'll not be long cooling down. I swear, Glasgow is the coldest place on the planet. Vladivostok doesn't get a look in."

Valentine watched the DS huddle her hands around the paper cup like it was a mini-brazier she had acquired for the purpose. There was a lot of people around, just milling about — old men and youths alike. Valentine wondered where they came from and why they seemed to lack all sense of purpose in where they were going.

"Like the land of the living dead around here," he said, glancing over McCormack's shoulder.

She took her cue from the DI and ran her gaze over the scene. "The homeless brigade. You get used to it."

He knew she was right. He could remember a time when there was one tramp — they called them tramps, then — in Ayr and one in Kilmarnock. They were well-known faces; the towns had complete genealogical records on them, knew their previous lives and ultimate falls from grace as the stuff of legend. Not now, though. Valentine couldn't keep pace with the number of the fallen in Ayrshire.

The DI ventured a sip of coffee. It wasn't as warm as it looked or as inviting as the idea suggested — the greasy rainbow swirling on top made his nostrils flare.

"Pretty dire, isn't it?" said McCormack.

Valentine stuck out his tongue. "Did you buy it from a mechanic?"

She smiled. "No, I did not. You saw me going over to the counter."

"Maybe they do oil changes as well." He stood up and fastened the button of his coat.

"Are we off, boss?"

He nodded. "Come on, you can bring your coffee with you. Might run into an AA man you can give it to."

The officers left the car in a side street between a kirkyard and playing fields and made their way to Pollokshaws Road. Janie Cooper's school was a short walk from the car. An imposing stone building, it reminded Valentine of the way schools used to be made. It looked like Ayr Academy, not some prefabricated box that had been flung up in five minutes.

On the other side of the road sat a tacky, flat-roofed oblong of flats that looked to have been built in the Seventies. They now housed a children's play center below and balconies with peeling paint and plastic furniture above.

"So, this is where she ... " Valentine couldn't bring himself to say the words, to complete the sentence. They both knew where they were and what had happened to Janie Cooper that day, twelve years ago, when she never made it home from school.

"The Coopers still stay in Bertram Street." DS McCormack indicated the direction of the route the young girl must have walked.

"Hardly any distance at all," said Valentine. He paced himself as he walked, taking in the scene of utter simplicity — an anywhere road in any town in Scotland. He knew why the Coopers had never moved: where could they go that would not remind them of the utter mundanity of the place?

As they reached the corner of Bertram Street, the detective stopped in his tracks. They stood beside a low verge and boxy hedgerows that edged the communal gardens of tenement flats. He was overwhelmed by the singular feeling that he had been there before.

"How many streets are there just like this?" he said.

McCormack pulled a stray hair from her mouth; the wind was picking up. "At least a million, we could be anywhere. Edinburgh, Inverness, the

Borders."

"We could even be in Ayr."

The DS nodded. "That we could, sir."

They progressed down the street and made their way to the front door of the Coopers" tenement. As they stared at the rows of buttons on the outside wall, Valentine paused.

"I've a very strange feeling about this." The words were out before he realized what he had said, and the DI made a sudden and sharp intake of breath. He wished he could have swallowed his last utterance.

"Sir, what do you mean?" McCormack's stood granite-firm on the path beside her boss and stared into him.

Valentine shook off the enquiry and reached forward to depress the buzzer in front of them. "Nothing, just thinking aloud."

"Is there something you want to tell me?"

He shrugged and turned back towards the door. "Like what?"

"I'm not sure, anything. If you don't mind me saying, you seem a bit jumpy."

Valentine grinned, a wide headlamp smile that he knew he always reserved for such situations.

The buzzer sounded and the detective lunged for the handle and stepped inside.

"Saved by the bell, eh," said McCormack.

The stairwell was dark and dank. A mountain bike sat tethered to the railings of the banister; two stanchions had already been cut, and Valentine wondered how long the bike would last under such flimsy security.

"Here it is, this is us," said McCormack. She turned to face her boss, then spoke again with her hand poised over the door, ready to knock. "Will I do the honors, sir?"

Valentine nodded and took a step back, making sure his cell phone was switched off. They faced a faded net curtain in the door's window; its movement was almost imperceptible as the DS made two delicate taps on the doorframe and retreated to stand beside her boss. The musty smell that percolated the stairwell seemed to vanish as the door opened and Billy Cooper waved them in.

Billy's face was stolid as he closed the door behind the officers and began to run the palms of his hands over the sleeves of his T-shirt. He was nervous, clearly, but this was someone who had learned to deal with simple emotions and some that were obviously far more complex. He had survived a hurt that few would dare to imagine and there was nothing left for life to throw at him.

"Can I introduce myself – Detective Inspector Bob Valentine." He turned to face his colleague. "And this is Detective Sergeant Sylvia McCormack."

"My wife's through in the front room," said Billy.

"We'd like to meet her," said Valentine.

As they walked towards the living room, the detective became aware that he was not in a home. It was a shrine to the memory of a home. There were pictures on the walls, to a one they contained photographs of Janie Cooper. The sight of Janie stung Valentine's senses and a pain erupted in the depths of his chest. As the DI turned to Diane Cooper, where she sat huddled on a corner seat, she seemed held together by only a thin thread of life, which, under tremendous stresses already, threatened to snap.

"Hello, Diane," he said. "The pictures of your daughter are just beautiful."

30

The atmosphere of the house had the quality of a tomb. It was one of the last places where Janie Cooper was seen. Being there, in her home with her parents, made the realities of Janie's end seem only too real. Valentine felt his connection to the girl's passing intensify with each new second. He was tense, uneasy; would he be able to do this?

"Can I get you a cup of tea, Inspector?" said Billy. He stood in the doorway with his hands in his pockets, tipping his head towards a small kitchen where a kettle had just boiled.

"Erm." Valentine had no words.

"Yes, that would be lovely, thank you." DS McCormack seized the reins and moved herself between the detective and the deceased girl's mother.

Valentine positioned himself behind DS McCormack and tried to listen to the conversation, but the words became of little meaning after only a few moments. Valentine removed his handkerchief from his trouser pocket and dabbed at his brow.

"Inspector." Billy Cooper held out a mug of tea before him.

The DI spoke. "Can I ask you, Mrs. Cooper, did you ever have a feeling that there was anyone around you who would harm Janie?"

The woman's face tensed. Valentine wondered if he had overstepped a mark, gone too far.

"Did I suspect anyone, is that what you mean?"

The detective nodded. "We visited her school, before we came here, it looks a good school. But perhaps there was someone there, or on the periphery of Janie's life, who would have made you cautious around them."

Billy joined the others in the seating area. He looked like he had heard it all before, like the officers were going over old and very well-trodden ground.

Mrs. Cooper answered. "No. There was no one."

Valentine had conducted interviews with hundreds of grieving parents, but there was something strange about this encounter. He felt like he was visiting with grief — he felt their pained cries ringing in his ears like they were his own. The thought that he would intrude on such a personal hurt filled him with self-loathing and disgust.

"Why?" said Mrs. Cooper.

"I'm sorry, I don't ... "

Billy spoke, his voice a weaker force than it had been. "She means why did you come here? Has something happened?"

"We are investigating another case, a murder," McCormack's words were antiseptic, professional. At once the tone of the room seemed to be drawn back to a recognizable place. "We don't know if it's related, but one of the victims was questioned twelve years ago about the disappearance of Janie."

"He's dead?" said Billy.

DS McCormack nodded.

"Good."

"You don't know who it is, Mr. Cooper."

"What does that matter? If he was caught before and questioned about my daughter, he was nothing. Worse than nothing. I'm glad he's dead."

Diane Cooper sat perfectly still. When she spoke, the almost imperceptible movement of her lips seemed like a trick of the light. "Who was it?"

DI Valentine answered. "He was called Duncan Knox."

The name sat between them like a small explosion that dictated they wait for the dust to settle before dealing with the fallout.

"We don't know him," said Billy.

"Are you sure?" Valentine addressed the husband but kept his stare fixed on the wife. She remained still.

"Why would we?"

"There's no reason that you would. We just hoped."

Billy Cooper's color seemed to alter: he became darker. "You're on a fishing trip?"

"Excuse me?" said Valentine.

Billy got up, his inoffensive demeanor seemed harder now. He pointed a finger towards the detectives. "You came here with nothing and now you're leaving with nothing." He turned to his wife, who had her head bowed. "And it's the pair of us that'll have to pick up the pieces."

Valentine stood up. The blood was surging in his veins as he presented his open palms towards Billy Cooper. "I'm sorry. I know those words won't help a lot, but I do genuinely feel your loss."

Billy shook his head and shot a hand to the side of his face. His nails dug into the fleshy part of his cheek for a moment and then he lunged forward and closed down the detective. "Don't give me your shite!"

"Sir, can you step back, please." DS McCormack jumped to her feet and tried to get between the two men.

"Sylvia, it's fine. Sit down," said Valentine.

Billy stepped back, but his chest was still inflated, his eyes burning with anger. "You bastards don't care one jot about our loss, if you did, you'd have caught the freak that took our daughter."

Valentine was unable to hold Billy's gaze. He wanted to leave their temple to the memory of Janie, not because he felt unwelcome but because he saw now that it was all they had. Something precious had been taken from them, something more than their daughter, even — their will to go on.

Valentine motioned DS McCormack to the door. "I'm very sorry to have intruded like this. I hope you can forgive us." As he withdrew, a sharp pain shot up his left arm and he gripped it tightly.

In the hallway, Valentine heard McCormack's heavy footfalls on the thin carpet behind him, but his eyes were drawn to an open door at the far end of the hall. He tried to focus, but his vision blurred like he was underwater and he grew cold. With the next step, his knee locked mid-stride then suddenly gave way, his blurred vision disappeared into blackness as he fell first into the wall and then dropped to the hard floor with a thud.

Where he lay, Valentine saw the cornflower-blue walls in the facing room reflecting a luminous light that was streaming through the window. He took a deep breath as time slowed to the dull pace of a mill wheel and a small, white-haired girl appeared in the doorway of the room. Valentine stared at the girl, in a red raincoat, swinging a doll in her hand. She was smiling at him. He turned back to face the way he had come, hoping to see the Coopers, but there was no one there. When he spun back to the front, he felt a warm hand on his face.

"Boss." DS McCormack was before him, her voice loud in his ears. "Boss, are you all right?"

He gazed over her shoulder, towards the bedroom with the blue walls. The door was open but the room was empty now.

"Boss."

The Coopers appeared. "Is he all right?"

Valentine eased himself onto his feet, then pushed away from the floor with the flat of his hand. "I'm fine."

"Oh, I don't know about that, sir." McCormack placed a palm on his shoulder and withdrew her phone.

"What are you doing?"

"Calling an ambulance."

Valentine snatched the phone and eased himself off the ground; his head started to spin as he got to his feet. "You"re overreacting."

"Sir, you passed out."

The DI grabbed her hand and slammed the phone in it. "I'm fine!" Valentine staggered past her and opened the front door.

By the tenement's entrance, he was breathing hard and a glaze of sweat had formed on his forehead. He gulped for air as he stepped onto the front path.

Valentine was making his way to the edge of the garden as DS McCormack appeared. "Wait, sir, please."

He carried on to the edge of the road. Glancing back, he could see McCormack sprinting after him. He couldn't outrun her. He stroked his now aching chest as he settled onto the low wall skirting the communal garden.

"Where's the fire?" said McCormack as she caught up.

"We should never have gone in there."

"We needed to check it out."

"The last thing they needed was us stirring everything back up for them."

McCormack joined him on the wall. She unhooked the strap of her bag from her shoulder and balanced it on her knees. "We weren't to know. It was twelve years, sir."

Valentine turned on her. "Do you think that makes any difference?"

"No, but ... "

"But what?"

Her cheeks flushed. For a moment she looked like she might answer his question. "What happened in there?"

He didn't respond.

McCormack tried again. "I know something happened. I saw it in your face."

"Nothing happened."

She picked herself from the wall and stood before him. "I'll go and get the car." As the detective made to stand, McCormack planted her hand on his shoulder. "No, you stay. You"re in no fit state."

"I'm perfectly fine."

The DS took two steps before she turned and lunged at him. "You're far from fine." A curl unfurled itself from her hair and lashed at her brow. "And, I wish you wouldn't treat me like such a bloody idiot!"

31

Cameron Sinclair stood outside the Wellington Café watching the early evening punters shuffling onto the street with their fish and chips. There was a crowd and the ice-cream shop next door was picking up the passing trade. Sinclair checked his watch; his impatience was a display he couldn't have compounded with a fist shaken at the heavens. He moved away from the crowd. He didn't like the town, or the people. He had told his boss on the *Glasgow-Sun* – when he still had his job — that Ayr was too blue-collar for him.

"You're just a bloody snob, Cam," he'd replied.

"Well, what if I am, is there something wrong with having standards?"

"Yeah, there is, it's called looking down your nose at people, or being a snob."

"That's a reductive argument," he'd snapped, and had known at once it was the wrong tack to take with Jack Gallagher.

The older man laughed in his chair, rocked backwards, and pointed to Sinclair. "When you're at that big dictionary next, look up the word 'irony,' eh."

Gallagher had laughed him out of his office and the move onto the crime beat in Ayr was no longer up for discussion. Ten months, he'd slummed it with the proles now, and all it had earned him was a handful of page-one splashes and a dubious suspension for bending the rules when Gallagher had himself stated the rules were there to be bent.

"Nothing wrong with bending the rules. Getting caught bending the rules, now that's another matter." He could still see the ruddy cheeks, hear the raucous half-laugh, half-cough that rattled off the walls every time the editor found himself amusing.

"Bastard," said Sinclair. Gallagher would be laughing on the other side of his face when he brought in the real story behind the Ayr murders.

"Say something, mate?" It was just another commoner in a football jersey.

"Sorry, you got the time?"

"You just looked at your watch."

"It's bust. Battery must be flat."

The man seemed suspicious, but gave the time and walked away, glancing over his shoulder as he went. Sinclair nodded his thanks and made a brief wave that skated so close to the common touch that he thought he deserved congratulations. He was still waving after the man when he noticed Danny Gillon's white van pulling up outside the bus station on the other side of the road. He jogged towards the vehicle.

The passenger seat wore a dusting of white powder, plaster, perhaps. Who knows what he had been moving in the vehicle? It was filthy, chocolate bar wrappers and empty cans littering the footwell. Sinclair shook his head, hoped his tetanus shot was up to date, and moved inside.

"This is a bloody mess," he said.

Gillon grinned. "It's my office." He was holding a cigarette in his hand as he spoke, but he was also holding court, waving the cigarette expansively.

"Calling this an office doesn't lend legitimacy to your business." Sinclair spat the last word.

Gillon over-revved the engine and pushed through an amber light; there was a hail of loud horns as he turned the corner, with Sinclair gripping the dash. He smiled as the journalist straightened himself and brushed his hands on the front of his trousers. "Try and not get us killed."

"Oh, I'm always very careful in that direction," said Gillon, the grin returning to his face.

Sinclair caught himself staring at Danny Gillon's teeth: they were not like any normal teeth, but tiny yellow stumps, cracked and chipped like old headstones. Had he ever visited a dentist? How did these people live, here? He couldn't believe that he had grown up in the same country as some of the creatures he was brushing shoulders with now. They were a class above maggots, but only just.

On Racecourse Road, the conversation took a turn. "I hope you had a word with that whore of yours," said Sinclair.

Gillon pressed the cigarette to his lips and exhaled the smoke in his passenger's direction as he replied. "Oh, I had a word with her all right. But not the way you're thinking."

Sinclair contained the urge to laugh. "What would you know about what I'm thinking?"

"See that?" Gillon raised a hand from the wheel and drew a fist: his gnarled knuckles were bruised and reddened. "That's the only language she understands." He dropped his hand and grabbed his groin. "That, and this!"

Sinclair felt a queasiness rising in his stomach. He knew he had reached a new low with Danny Gillon, but he also knew that the pimp had something that he wanted. The whore had been reluctant to talk at their last meeting, but Gillon obviously had ways of getting information out of her that Sinclair didn't. For a moment he thought to ask of Leanne Dunn's condition, but he didn't care enough.

"This better not be another wild goose chase," said Sinclair.

Gillon was riled. "Are you saying I don't know what I'm doing? Are you saying I can't make one of my own whores say what I want them to say?"

"I'm sure you know your business very well, Gillon, but is the information going to be any use this time?"

He wagged a finger in the direction of the dashboard. The green Magic Tree air freshener hanging from the rear-view mirror came within reach and he pulled the tree down, crunching it in his hand. "Look, I told you she knew the fat pedo they found out at the track with a plank up his hole."

"We established that last time."

"But she knew the other one, the banker guy, as well. Urquhart. Not even the police know that. I could be getting myself into deep water just talking to you: it's two bloody murders we're talking about, here."

Sinclair turned his attention to the driver as he gesticulated above the wheel once again. "Keep your eyes on the road."

"Are you hearing what I said? They knew each other."

They'd reached the edges of Alloway, heading in the direction of Monument Road.

"And do you think the police haven't asked the Urquharts about that? It would have been their first question. What in the hell makes you think us turning up on their doorstep is going to make an ounce of difference?"

At the Urquhart's home, there was a man at the gate pouring petrol into a ride-on mower. He stared at them with cautious eyes.

"Yes, can I help you?" he said.

Sinclair peered down the bridge of his nose. "I'm sorry, and you would be?"

"My name's Bell. I'm a very close friend of the Urquharts."

"Then you had better let us in, Mr. Bell. We're here on a pressing matter."

The man retreated a few steps, seeming somewhat stunned to be greeted by Estuary English in such plain wrapping as a white Bedford van. As he placed the gas canister on the path, he released the gates and the van proceeded up the drive.

Sinclair waved regally as they passed the first hurdle and returned to his earlier conversation. "Well, you still haven't answered me."

Gillon brought the van to a halt in the gravel driveway. There was a screech of tires and he yanked on the handbrake. "I'm sure the police have asked the Urquharts if they knew Knox and I'm just as bloody sure they got a well-rehearsed answer." He paused to flick a cigarette butt out the window. "But have the police asked them about Leanne?"

Sinclair allowed a slow smile to creep onto his face. "You may have something there, Gillon."

"I know I have, and so do you, mate, or you wouldn't be coughing for the information in such a tidy manner."

When the pair met on the driveway, they faced each other for a brief moment until a wide grin spread over Gillon's face. He left the expression to hang between them for a moment like a statement of intent, and then he turned and made for the front door.

"I think you should leave the talking to me," said Sinclair.

"Why?"

"Because I do this sort of thing for a living."

"We don't want to mention what I do for a living." Gillon looked away, then turned briskly. "Or maybe we do."

"Just leave it to me."

Gillon kept his eyes front. There was the sound of door fastenings being moved, a key turning in the lock. "Whatever you say, Cam. Just shout if you get into trouble, if there's any rough stuff."

Sinclair had his reply paused on the tip of his tongue as the door opened and a figure he recognized as Adrian Urquhart took them in with a raking gaze. The young man seemed perplexed to see them at first, but soon gathered his composure.

"Yes?" he said.

"Hello, Adrian," said Gillon.

Sinclair stepped forward. "My name's Cameron Sinclair, I'm a writer, a journalist." The name didn't register on Adrian's face. "You might have been reading my stories in the Glasgow-Sun about your father's passing."

"I've nothing to say to you." The door moved towards the jamb; their view of Adrian Urquhart's features receded into a thin oblong.

Sinclair pressed the heel of his hand to the door front. "I think it would be in both our interests to talk."

Adrian's eyes widened as the door returned towards him once again; the shock of seeing a reporter on his doorstep had been compounded by the fact that they really didn't take no for an answer.

"Do you mind taking your hand off my door?" said Adrian.

"Oh, Jesus Christ." Gillon's guttural voice sounded enough to force the door backwards, but for the avoidance of doubt he pressed his shoulder to the heavy wood and stepped inside. Adrian started back-pedaling on the polished-wood floor.

"What the bloody hell do you think you're doing?" he said.

"Oh, stop playing the innocent," said Gillon, in the wide hallway. "We're here to talk to you about Leanne Dunn."

Adrian Urquhart's pallor lost some layers of its ruddy flesh tone. "I've no idea who you're talking about."

Sinclair stepped out of Gillon's shadow. "I think you might want to reconsider that stance once we set you straight on some stuff, Adrian."

Adrian backed up a few steps. His hands caught the banister behind him and he stopped still; only his gaze escaped down the hall towards the sound of a television playing the evening news theme.

"Look, my mother will be back soon, she'll go to the police."

Sinclair found himself turning to Gillon as if to share just how ridiculous the remark sounded; the pair started to snigger.

"Oh, I'm sure the police will be the last port of call in this storm, Adrian," said Sinclair, who nodded to Gillon. "What do you say, Danny?"

"Probably more chance of us calling them, once you hear what we've got to say."

Gillon headed down the hallway, in the direction of the blaring television. Sinclair took a few steps in the same direction, then turned back towards Adrian. "Come on, son, we've some talking to do."

32

DI Bob Valentine didn't know what had happened at the Coopers' home, and he wasn't even sure he wanted to, because the truth was it frightened him too much. There had been the stabbing pain that twisted like a hot wire all the way down his arm and into his middle finger, and then there was the loss of consciousness and the resulting visions. He was not right in the head: that was the only answer he had to the question of why he'd seen the young Janie Cooper again. He was losing it, seeing things. The job was pulling him apart, he was no longer capable of making sense of anything.

Clare brought through their coffees and placed them on the table in front of Valentine.

"You're doing it again," she said.

"What?" Valentine felt as if he'd been shaken awake.

"It's this case, isn't it?"

"Yes and no." He sat forward and retrieved his coffee cup. "I was thinking about Dad, among other things. Tell me what happened, again."

Clare watched Valentine press the cup to his mouth and then she followed his actions like a mime. "Well, there's not that much more to say: I took the book round and found him moaning at the bottom of the stairs."

"So, he must have fallen down the stairs?" Valentine raised a hand to touch his forehead. The information didn't seem to be going in, there had been too much put up there already, today.

"He didn't know, he was very groggy, but he didn't remember falling, so that's when I thought: stroke."

"And the ambulance crew, what did they say?"

"Nobody knew anything, Bob, that's why they've kept him in overnight. They'll do a scan and we'll know better in the morning when they see how he is."

Valentine noted how suddenly life brought these surprises to you: one day everything was as it had been and then there was a gear shift and all of the old markers changed at once.

"I should be at the hospital," he said.

"You can't, visiting time's over. If you'd had your phone on you might have been in a position to visit earlier."

"I'll go tomorrow."

"And you know what he'll say — why are you taking time off work?" said Clare. "He'll be here by the time you get in, and I'll call you if anything comes up, just see him when you get in."

"He probably won't be able to go back home to Cumnock, you realize."

Clare crossed her legs and balanced the coffee cup on her knee. "I know that. I've told the girls they'll need to share a room for a while."

"Oh, they'd have loved that."

"They were fine, actually. Well, Fiona was, thinks of it as an adventure."

He smiled. "And Chloe?"

Clare took up her cup, sipped. "I don't want to talk about Chloe. Not tonight."

"I need to know if there's anything wrong, Clare."

"She's still getting trouble at school, but ... "

"But what?"

"Look, can we do this another time, Bob? I can see you've had a long day and the news about your father isn't helping."

He shook his head. "No, Clare. I want to know."

She looked at her cup as she spoke. "She's being bullied. I went to see the headmaster before your dad and I told him how concerned I was, but he seemed to think it was all an overreaction." She turned towards her husband, her focus back. "I am not overreacting. I know my daughter."

Valentine rose from his chair and went to sit beside his wife. He placed a hand on hers as he spoke. "How is she?"

"I don't know. She's very quiet, doesn't tell me a thing. We'll have to wait and see what happens. The headmaster said he'd have a word with some of her teachers and see if there's anything amiss."

"It'll be OK, Clare. Chloe's tough."

"Like her dad?"

He didn't have an answer for that.

Clare picked up the thread of her conversation. "The other night you were trying to tell me something, about that girl in the picture."

"It's nothing."

"No, you said it was important."

Valentine withdrew slunk back to his seat. "It's not."

"No, you were agitated and I was tired."

"Clare, leave it."

"Leave it?" Her eyes lit with indignation. "I'm trying to help."

Valentine could see his reaction to Clare's olive branch had been to hack it down with a chainsaw. "I just don't feel like talking right now. I'm sorry."

She kept her eyes on him for a second, and then her face became a hard set of angles. "OK, fine." She stood up and turned towards the kitchen door. "I'm sorry too, Bob. I really am."

He listened to his wife loading a few items into the dishwasher and then he heard the light switch and knew she had headed upstairs to bed. It was early, even by Clare's standards. She would watch a little television and then, hopefully, nod off before he went up. Valentine realized he had started to avoid his wife, certainly any intimate contact. It wasn't that he didn't still care for her, but the relationship had changed, recently.

Valentine got up and went through to the dining room. His coat hung on the facing chair and he dug in his pocket for the cell phone that had been switched off earlier. He pressed the on button and watched the screen light up; a few seconds later, the missed-call icon started to flash. He ignored it and went to his contacts.

DS Sylvia McCormack"s phone was answered quickly. "Hello, boss."

"I thought I should give you a call."

"Really? Sounds ominous."

Valentine rubbed at his forehead with his fingertips as he spoke. "This situation we, I mean I, found myself in today."

"Uh-huh."

"I didn't want to say anything, at the time."

"Because you could see that I knew full well what was going on."

"I'm sorry." Valentine raised his head, lowered his hand from his brow. "I don't follow."

"When you took me on, I presume you looked at my files."

"Yes."

"So, you know about my previous cases?"

Valentine searched the recesses of his memory for the file he had skimmed on DS McCormack's background, but had to concede that he hadn't taken much of it in. "Sylvia, this case has been a belter, if I'd had the time to carefully go over every file that crossed my desk ... "

"Right, well, if you don't know, then I'll tell you now. I worked with Colvin Baxter on the Reece disappearance."

The Reece case was familiar to Valentine: she was a mother of five who had vanished, and several weeks later her children found out she was buried in a ditch. The other name meant nothing to him. "Who's Colvin Baxter?"

"He helped locate Karyn Reece. We had nothing on that case until he got in touch. We all thought he was taking us off on a wild goose chase, but we soon changed our minds. Anyway, I think the official term we use is a "precognitive," but you'd likely call him a psychic."

Valentine waited for the DS to stop speaking. When he was sure she had finished he felt a strange impulse to drop the phone and step away, but he resisted.

"I'm not sure that I see the ..."

"Oh, come on, boss, I saw your face." Her voice sounded high on youthful enthusiasm. "I know the look because it's the same one Colvin wore when he was in the zone."

Valentine sensed the consequences of what the DS was saying, perhaps in a way she hadn't given any thought to. He saw her claims seeping out into the public domain and panicked.

"No, Sylvia."

"Good officers, sir, senior police, went public with Colvin Baxter's help. Do you think that they'd expose themselves to that kind of scrutiny if they didn't think he was on the money?"

The DI's imagination lit up now: he was already under psychological assessment: he couldn't afford any more questions being asked about his mental health.

"I think you've got the wrong end of the stick, Sylvia."

"But, sir, you can trust on my discretion if ... "

"Sylvia, no ifs." He cleared his throat and raised his tone to signal the conversation was now closed. "The reason I was calling is I want you to go back to Glasgow tomorrow and speak to the officers on the Cooper case who interviewed Knox. If there are transcripts, bring them back."

"Yes, sir." McCormack's big talk seemed shrunken now.

"I have a sneaking suspicion what they might tell you, and if I'm right, we've found the link between Knox and Urquhart."

"Yes, sir."

He sensed his composure returning. "And Sylvia, keep your feet on the ground and remember who's running this investigation."

33

As Valentine stood with the keys poised before the car door, he watched the builders unloading sand and bricks into his neighbor's driveway.

"Hello, Bob," his neighbor Brian called out, as he navigated the building materials that sat between his lawn and his car.

Valentine nodded. "Looks like a bit of work for you."

Brian reached the wall and flagged a hand towards the goings. "We're opening up the space above the garage to give us a bit more room."

It was a double garage, and judging by the amount of materials the building work would be extensive.

"We could do with more space ourselves, now."

As if sensing his neighbor's discomfort, Brian changed the subject. "You were a bit of a celebrity down at the Chestnuts last night — they had you on the late news again."

"Look, I don't mean to sound short with you, Brian, but this case is ..."

Brian waved him off. "No need to explain."

Valentine nodded and got in his car. The drive to King Street station was a slow trial he set up for the prosecution of his own personality. He saw the evidence that he had isolated himself from his wife, children, father and colleagues. But the case that burned him the most was that of the Coopers; he knew he had served nothing by visiting them and conceded that Billy Cooper had had every right to attack him. As he walked into the station and headed for the incident room, the detective felt an empty void spreading inside him and he didn't know how to fill it.

Hanging up his coat, Valentine noticed CS Martin grilling DS McAlister, by the looks of things, over hot coals. The DS seemed to be feeling the heat, sticking a finger in the collar of his shirt and working the top button loose. He was nodding in line with the chief super's rapid speech as Valentine drew in.

"Morning," he said.

"Well, look who it is, Ayrshire's very own silver-screen star." Martin wore a smirk that could have passed for an incitement to violence.

"They'll be calling me DI Valentino next."

McAlister started to laugh, a deep gut laugh that he cut off abruptly as he assessed the chief super's lack of response.

CS Martin stooped over the desk. She closed a blue folder and straightened her back. "I'm glad you find it so funny."

The detective was in no humor for the chief super — he had far too much on his mind with the case and his visions of Janie Cooper.

He replied. "As you know, boss, I'm just the kind of arsehole to laugh at my own jokes. Most of the time nobody else will."

She seemed to be having trouble processing Valentine's self-mockery. "Well, now you're here, you can fill me in on the case instead of Ally."

"My office or yours?"

"Yours – lead the way."

The rest of the incident room was empty, except for McAlister and a couple of uniforms who seemed content to examine either the sheen of their shoes or the texture of the carpet.

"This better be good, Bob, because I don't have to tell you how anxious all this media attention has made me."

"I didn't know anything about the TV news report."

"The thing that worries me, Bob, is the fact that those city hacks are taking it so seriously. Normally they don't bother their backsides coming down here, but they think there's something sexy about the fact that a banker and a paedo have been impaled in my patch."

Valentine was drawing out his chair, he eased himself down before he spoke. "They mentioned Knox?"

"Had pictures and everything. Old case stills and a screen grab of him at the High Court."

"Christ almighty."

CS Martin had her hands on her hips: on anyone else it would appear like an affectation, but it seemed to fit her perfectly. "Can it get worse, Bob? I mean, is there anything else you should be telling me before I have to get on the phone to Glasgow and ask them to send us a lifeboat?"

He started playing with a pencil. "I have Sylvia McCormack in Glasgow today."

"Are you shunting that girl out of the way?"

"Not at all."

A ragged fingernail was pointed at the DI. "I mean it, she's to be given full responsibility. I don't want to have her scratching at my door next week telling me she's been sent for a long stand or a tin of tartan bloody paint!"

"Sylvia's exploring a link between Knox and a previous case — the disappearance of a schoolgirl in Shawlands, twelve years ago."

"Name?"

"Her name was Janie Cooper."

"It doesn't ring any bells, was it high profile?"

"It was a big case, yes."

"There were so many of them around that time, little girls snatched every other day of the week, you couldn't keep up. Anyway, what's the connection?"

The DI wet his lips with his tongue. "Knox was called in, they questioned him over the disappearance of the Cooper girl, but they released him." Valentine's voice became reedy and slow. "We haven't got anything solid yet, but Urquhart was living in Glasgow at the time and I think there may have been contact. I'll know for sure when I get the Knox interview transcripts today."

There was a moment of stilled silence in the room as the chief super started to pace towards the window.

"So, you're saying that Knox and Urquhart knew each other from before, from the Janie Cooper disappearance?"

"I'm saying I suspect that."

"You think we have a predatory pedophile connection to the killings on our turf?"

He allowed himself a half-nod. "It's possible."

CS Martin looked like she might shatter before him. "Well, if we thought we had some press attention before, what the hell's it going to be like when they get hold of this?"

"No, there's no chance of that."

"You don't know that."

"The only way they would know what I know is if they were involved in some way."

"Or had an inside track."

Valentine shook his head. His chest inflated as he rose from his seat and placed his palms on the desktop. "We had one mole, Paulo, and he got his. Nobody out there would be so bloody stupid to jump into his boots."

"You hope."

"Do you have some information you'd like to share with me, or is this just scaremongering?"

Her face said she didn't like the detective's tone. "I don't scaremonger."

"Then my original suggestion stands." He picked up the telephone's receiver. "Shall I call in the rep?"

Martin crossed the floor towards the desk. "Don't think about taking me on, Bob, or you"ll be back teaching cadets how to wipe their arse before the day's out."

He lowered the phone into its cradle — something told him he'd come too far with the investigation to risk losing it. The recent talk of Janie Cooper pushed her image back into his mind. "My squad's water-tight. I won't tolerate leaks and they know it."

"Glad to hear it." The chief super kept a firm stare on the DI for a moment and then turned for the door. As she reached for the handle, she called out, "I want a full report of what we've just discussed on my desk by close of play tonight. With Sylvia's transcripts from Glasgow. If it sounds at all promising, you might not have to look for your tracksuit and whistle again."

34

Valentine watched the chief super strut through the incident room and then stand and wait as the door was opened for her. When the door closed, he found himself following her footsteps into the main room. Some more officers had appeared now and he nodded to DS Donnelly and the uniforms he recognized from the murder scene at the racetrack. The DI stood before the board and took in the information. He picked up a black marker pen and drew a thick line between the two victims: Urquhart and Knox.

"Looks definite enough," said DS Donnelly.

"Bloody sure it is, Phil," said Valentine. "That pair were in cahoots: I can feel it in my blood. They knew each other, they were connected, and they preyed on children together."

"Whoa, step back a bit," said Donnelly. "We've got nothing to put Urquhart in the same league as Knox."

"He's textbook. He never had so much as a casual acquaintanceship with anyone he worked with. Kept himself to himself. Had no critics, but he had no admirers, either — wonder why? Because he was keeping a low profile, he was leading a double life and was frightened that if he revealed even a little of himself, he'd be found out."

DS Donnelly didn't look convinced. He seemed to be letting the DI speak himself out in the hope that he would say something he agreed with.

"Boss, I don't know. You always say we can't make assumptions; this just seems a bit against the grain."

Valentine turned from the board and replaced the top on the marker pen. He tried not to look at the DS because he knew his run of confidence might be shattered by a single glance. He dipped his head towards the desk. "OK, then, what have you got, Phil?"

"Well."

"Squat. Same as everyone else."

"Sir, I'm not playing devil's advocate here, I'm just saying show me the evidence."

"Are you saying that there's no evidence, just because we haven't found it?" He raised his head and took at the DI. "Because that doesn't wash either, Phil. In the absence of what we"d like, we have to make do with what we've got."

DS Donnelly raised his hands, holding them behind his head. It was a gesture that told Valentine he wasn't retreating any time soon; it also told him that if he was going to press the case against Urquhart then he was going to need more than blind loyalty to get the squad to go along with him. Was he losing it? Was he really letting his imagination take over from the rational part of his brain, the part that admonished officers like Donnelly when they made the kinds of lunging assessments he had just made? He was tense: the muscles of his shoulders ached. He was looking for answers where there were none, and he knew it. The earlier run-in with CS Martin had left him feeling pressured, and that was never a good way to be. Police officers under pressure made mistakes, made the wrong moves; he had done that once before and nearly paid for it with his life.

Valentine peered over at DS Donnelly and called out. "Ally, over here a minute."

The DS closed the top drawer in his desk and pushed out his chair; as he walked towards the two officers, he put his hands in his pockets. His expression was calm, blank, almost.

"Yeah, what's up?"

"Ally, tell us what you got with the club you were checking out."

He looked perplexed. "Club?"

"The model-railway club, the Wednesday night thing that Urquhart was supposed to be going to but never showed up at."

"Oh, the railway, sorry." He trotted back towards his desk and reopened the drawer he had just closed, when he made his way back to Donnelly and Valentine, he was carrying a notebook.

"Here we go." McAlister flicked through the first few pages. "OK, nothing from the first credit card. Well, it was used on a Wednesday night at the Tesco Express on Maybole Road."

"That's almost on his doorstep, doesn't tell us much," said Donnelly.

"At what time did he use it, though?"

"Ah, don't know. Have to get the file."

Valentine sighed. "Well, check it. If it's late at night it could be because he was coming back home from somewhere else. What about the other stuff?"

He turned the spiral pages over. "Yes, here we are, got a bank-card transaction on three successive Wednesdays at the liquor store on the Prestwick Road."

"Why's he going to a liquor store?" said Valentine. "I'm presuming these are nights he didn't make the railway club?"

"Yes, all those nights were no-shows. So, the question remains: where was he going with the booze?"

"He bought alcohol?" said Valentine.

"Yes, same every night – a bottle of Châteauneuf-du-Pape."

DS Donnelly tutted. "Very nice indeed."

"Well, I don't think James Urquhart has the type of palate to tolerate Blue Nun. He's drinking, but who with?"

DS McAlister turned a few more pages in the notebook, then shrugged, defeatedly.

The DI spoke. "Right, that's three Wednesdays on the trot he's buying expensive booze when he's supposed to be at some old-boys' model club. What the hell is he playing at?"

"It's a woman," said Donnelly. "It's got to be."

"I'd have to say you're right."

"But doesn't that rule out your earlier theory."

Valentine shook his head. "Are you saying he can't have an interest in women, too? He was married, you know."

"Yes, but that could be a front, boss." Donnelly positioned himself on the edge of the desktop. "If we're following your line of thinking."

"What's this?" said Ally.

Valentine flagged DS McAlister down. "In a minute." He turned back to Donnelly. "My point, exactly. This is a man, a predator, who likes fronts. Perhaps the wine was for someone who had something he wanted. A young daughter, perhaps."

Donnelly eased himself from the desk. "We need to check the rest of those cards."

The DI nodded. "And we want the CCTV footage from this liquor store and anywhere else within a country mile of Prestwick Road."

"We should run the same checks on Knox, too. I don't think for a second he's likely to have been as careful as Urquhart."

"You got that, Ally?"

DS McAlister returned to the notebook and stood poised with a pen over the paper. "Before I do anything, is someone going to fill me in on what we're talking about?"

Valentine patted Donnelly on the shoulder. "That's one for you, Phil, and when you're done with that, you can put a summary on the board. There's been far too little going up there of late and Dino's starting to get nervous. She'll be in here pissing on the table legs to assert her authority if we're not too careful."

McAlister and Donnelly were smiling as Valentine retreated to his office. His mind was racing with the possibilities. He didn't want to believe that he was being influenced by forces he didn't understand. He was being led by the thought that he might solve the Janie Cooper case if he could solve the murders of Urquhart and Knox. To a seasoned detective it was absurd, he was being led by instinct and avoiding the facts, but he couldn't deny that every significant development in the case had come as a result of following his gut.

As he sat down behind his desk, Valentine removed the blue folder that had the details of the Janie Cooper case that DS McCormack had compiled. He turned over the first page and skimmed the others until he found the photographs. There were pictures he had seen already, newspaper cuttings he hadn't seen before and a selection of lab pictures that were tagged and bagged, but only the one numbered 14 stuck out. The item was a small blonde-haired doll, a Barbie doll, like his eldest daughter had once owned. He had seen it before, though. Not one like it, not a similar one. It was the doll Janie Cooper had been swinging in her hands when he'd passed out in her parents' home.

"Christ."

Valentine picked up the picture and read the description on the label that was attached. The doll had been found a few streets from Janie's school on the day she disappeared. It was the last artefact to be uncovered before the girl was declared missing.

35

DI Bob Valentine tried to comprehend what his wife was saying, but the words wouldn't go in. He stood in the hallway with his coat still on and his briefcase in hand, as Clare grew to resemble a furious harpy before him.

"He's your father. How?" She shook her head and waved hands in a dramatic flourish. "Tell me how you managed to forget that?"

He didn't reply, because, although it was a question, he didn't feel an answer was required. When Clare became rhetorical it was for effect, and missing his father's return from hospital was an opportunity not to be passed up. Valentine took his wife's blows because they had little impact on him now, he shook them off in the same way he brushed raindrops from his shoulders. He wondered why his expression wasn't a giveaway to her. If it helped her deal with being Clare Valentine, then he could stand there and take it all night.

"Clare, I'm sorry. I intended to be home earlier, but I've had a very busy day."

She brushed her bangs from her eyes. "It's not me you should be apologizing to."

Valentine sensed an unscripted break in proceedings; he lowered his briefcase and started to unbutton his coat. "I'll go up now."

"He's sound asleep, they gave him tranquillizers."

"Is he OK?" The DI hung his coat on the banister.

"The scan was clear. It doesn't look like a stroke, but he's not a well man." She grabbed the coat from the banister. "And this is ready for the trash!"

Valentine snatched back his coat. "Leave it, Clare."

Chloe appeared in the hallway in dressing gown and pajamas. Her Bart Simpson slippers looked like she had stuck her feet into a pair of cuddly toys. Valentine smiled at the sight of his daughter.

"Hello, Princess."

She grimaced, turned to the side and waved over the glass of milk she held in her hand. "Oh, please."

He had an urge to scoop his daughter in his arms, but her teenage attitude flashed like a warning light. "How's school, love?"

She closed her eyes, let the lids hang in exaggerated fashion for a moment and then put a crick in her jaw. "I'm going to bed."

His sullen daughter squeezed past them and took to the stairs with heavy steps. Valentine saw his wife drawing a bead on him; he knew at once he had said the wrong thing, but his mind was so tired it required a back-up generator to keep body and soul together at this hour.

"I take it my dinner's in the dog?" he said.

Clare waited for Chloe to close the bedroom door. "Why did you say that to her? You know she's not having the best of times at school, and you know why."

He was re-hanging his coat on the banister as he replied. "I wasn't thinking."

"Well, perhaps you should start, Bob." His wife pushed him aside and followed Chloe up the stairs.

"Where are you going?"

"To see if our daughter's all right."

Valentine made to call out to Clare again, but something stopped him, an instinct perhaps, the thought that he could more than likely increase his trouble. He collected his briefcase, removed the blue file with the transcripts from the Knox interviews that DS McCormack had delivered, and headed for the kitchen. The downlights beneath the kitchen cabinets were burning, lighting the worktops but little else. He turned to the light switch on the wall and pressed it with his shoulder. There was a plate sitting out, holding what looked like dinner, but he wasn't hungry now. He made coffee and settled down at the dining-room table.

As he read the notes, the detective was nostalgic for the time when he would have filled out the same forms. The paper case files had lingered in a few of the smaller stations for longer than they should have. Everything was committed directly to computer, now, but the touch of paper felt more personal, reminded him of a time when the world itself seemed to care a little bit more. As he read on, however, Valentine realized his mind was just playing tricks on him: the world was a brutal place and always had been.

His thoughts were wiped clear by the sound of his cell phone. He reached into his shirt pocket and answered. "Hello."

"Are you reading the files?" It was DS McCormack.

"Just about to." He looked at the clock; it was nearly midnight. "I presume you're calling because you've found something."

Her voice speeded up. "Go to page nine, second interaction from DI Fitzsimmons. Have you got it?"

"Hang on." Valentine turned over the file and thumbed his way to page nine. "Right, what am I looking for?"

McCormack's impatience poured from every word. "Skip the top paragraph, read the next one."

The detective ran his gaze down the page to the point she had indicated. "OK, here we are."

"He's addressing Knox, by the way."

"Yes, got that." He read the DI's words: "Who are you working with, Duncan? You might as well tell us, because if they're on our books we'll be talking to them and they might not extend you the same favor . . ." Valentine was taking in the significance of the statement when DS McCormack spoke again.

"Sir, are you there?"

"Yes."

"Then you got that. You see what he's saying?"

Valentine rubbed knuckles into his tired eyes and felt a change in the rhythm of his thinking. "Fitzsimmons thought he had an accomplice."

"Yes, but he was looking for someone like Knox, a sex offender."

"They had no chance of finding Urquhart, in that case."

"They were looking in the wrong direction."

He pushed the folder away. If there were more gems worth unearthing, they could wait another day — he had the prize already. "How much of this have you read?"

"I'm well on with it, there's a few things we need to look at, boss."

"It's midnight, Sylvia, and I have a wife who thinks I'm a part-timer in this marriage as it is."

"Oh, of course. I'm sorry to call so late, I just thought ... "

He cut her off. "You did the right thing, I needed to know. I'm glad you called, but tomorrow's another day."

"I'm going to stick with it. I'm not tired and I'm all pumped up for this now."

He admired her enthusiasm and envied her youth. "Goodnight, Sylvia, I'll see you at the station tomorrow."

"I'll keep notes."

"Do that."

36

Danny Gillon over-revved his van on the road outside the doctors' surgery on Cathcart Street. By the time he had reached the Tourist Information Centre there was a cloud of black smoke following him onto the Sandgate. He didn't care what the woman waving her hand in front of her thought as he passed, because the town of Ayr was nothing to him. Who were they? Old scrubbers and junkies. Streets full of mug punters rolling drunk to the bookies or the Bridges Bar.

When he returned to the block of flats in Lochside, where he had set up his working girls, he parked and stilled the engine. The exhaust rattled a little after he had stopped and he knew that it would soon be costing him money. He gnawed the tip of his cigarette and stepped out, looking towards the rear of the vehicle: a sooty black cloud was hanging in the air. The exhaust pipe was still in place, but looked close to coming off. A bad speed bump or a clipped curb and he'd be forking out for a new one. He scrunched his eyes and tried not to think about it. There was the payday from the hack coming; all he had to do was get Leanne prepared for the next stage in Sinclair's little plan.

As he walked through the empty parking lot, Gillon kicked out at a stray can of Export and sent it into the air. The can spun all the way to the pinnacle of its grand arc and then plummeted onto the tarmac. The shaken remnants of its contents spilled onto the street in a bubbling foam that looked at home in the litter-strewn surroundings. When he reached the door of the flats, the pimp pressed the buzzer for Leanne's apartment, but there was no answer.

"Come on, Leanne."

He pressed the buzzer again, but there was still no answer.

"Come on!"

He stepped back and fastened his eyes on the kitchen window that faced out into the narrow courtyard: there was no sign of movement.

"Where the bloody hell are you?"

He had another girl set up in the same block. He returned to the buzzer and pressed for Angela.

She answered quickly. "Hello."

"It's me, Danny, buzz me in, eh."

"Danny?"

"Yeah, Danny. You wanting a picture sent up first?"

The buzzer sounded, the lock was released, and he walked through the door. The stairwell stank of urine and stale cigarette smoke. The combination was enough to put him off his Embassy Regal and he flicked it onto the floor. He grabbed the banister and loped up to the first floor of the flats.

Angela was waiting outside her door. "Something up, Danny?"

He grabbed her thin white face in his hand and pushed her back towards the door. "Who said you could come out?"

"I was just — "

He pointed at her as he walked to the foot of the next set of steps. "You were just getting into that flat and getting on your back. I'll be round after for my money."

The girl retreated into the dim hallway of the flat. She peered out from behind the narrow gap between door and jamb for a second, but as Gillon hit his stride on the steps she disappeared.

"Leanne." He battered on the door but there was no answer.

"Leanne, come on, open up." For a moment he had the notion that she might have collapsed. He leant down to look through the letter box but saw nothing unusual. The door to the kitchen was open, as it always was; the bedroom door was closed, but she never spent time in there unless she was on her back and there was no sign that she was with a punter. The place looked empty.

He banged on the door again. "Leanne."

It was a futile gesture, and he knew that. But at least she hadn't shot herself up and carked it on him. That would be messy: he'd have to take her to casualty and drop her at the door, or pay a cabbie, and that was never cheap these days.

Gillon punched out at the door again. The resounding sound of bone on wood rang through the empty hallway and brought a thin eye-slot to the neighboring door.

"Hey." Gillon ran towards the chink of light that had appeared by the doorframe. He could see the outline of an old woman. He pushed himself towards the door and she shrieked.

"Do you know where Leanne went?" He kept his hand pressed firmly on the front of the door.

"I don't know."

"Well, when did she go out?"

The woman smelled like an old chip pan, all burnt charcoal and dripping fat. "We don't speak."

"I didn't ask if you were best mates, I asked you where she went. When did you last see her?"

She raised a thin hand, and the spotted flesh hung over the bulbous fingers as she gripped the buttons of her cardigan. "She went out last night, I think. I never saw her after that and I haven't heard her today."

"Last night?"

The old woman nodded. She cast a glance into the stairwell as if looking for help. "Yes, that's right. I haven't seen her since."

Gillon started to drum his fingers on the door, a rough percussion that signaled his growing impatience and dissatisfaction with what was being relayed to him. "And was she alone, or with someone?"

"A man."

Gillon stared at the woman. Her eyes were moistening and she looked ready to keel over. He slapped the door and stepped back. She had the wood in the frame and the mortise turned in the lock by the time he could blink.

None of it made any sense. The pimp felt a mix of emotions and thoughts flushing through him. As he descended the stairs, he tried to put the facts together. She was with a punter, surely. But where had she gone? If the punter had turned up on her doorstep, then why hadn't they just done the business in the flat? It didn't make sense, unless he had a kink for the outdoors, but then she'd be back by now, would have been back last night, surely. He didn't see anyone paying for an all-nighter with a skank like Leanne: she was strictly disposable.

Gillon rattled the knocker on Angela's door once again. When she appeared, gripping a brown dressing gown around her thin shoulders, he felt the need to draw a fist. "Get inside."

Angela gasped for breath as he pushed her inside. Her face indicated she would have preferred to scream, but she knew that wasn't an option worth pursuing.

"Right, speak. Where's Leanne?"

"What?" She was trembling.

"That tart upstairs. She went out with some guy last night."

"I – I haven't seen her for a couple of days."

Gillon flashed his bottom row of teeth the second before he fired his fist into Angela's belly. She folded over and then collapsed onto the floor.

The pimp crouched onto one knee and grabbed her hair. "Am I supposed to believe that?"

She tried to speak, but merely spluttered.

"What are you saying to me?"

"I – I said it's true. Honest, Danny, I wouldn't lie to you." She brought her hands together as if about to pray. "Danny, do you have anything? Just a wee bit, just to see me through."

He smacked her head off the wall. As she yelped, her shoulders slid down the plasterboard.

There was a rage building in Danny Gillon's head and heart as he stamped down the steps towards the entrance to the flats. In the parking lot, the sight of the can of Export crackers sent him lunging with a kick once again, but there was none of the playfulness of his earlier shot. The can fired into the air and smacked off the side of the flats, dislodging some stucco with the force of impact.

"Bloody hell, Leanne. I will kill you for this."

When he reached the van, Gillon removed his cell phone from the inside pocket of his denim jacket and scrolled the contacts for Cameron Sinclair.

The reporter answered straight away.

"Yes, what's up?" he said.

"You're not going to like it."

"I don't think I do already and you haven't even told me what's happened."

"It's Leanne. She's jumped ship."

"What?" Sinclair sounded incredulous.

"You heard, she's done a runner."

There was a pause on the line. "I don't believe this."

"Believe it, I don't make up stories."

He could hear Sinclair sighing down the line. When he spoke again, his voice had an angry quiver he hadn't heard before. "You've done this."

"What's that supposed to mean?"

"You"re trying to bump your price up, aren't you." He sounded like he was speaking through gritted teeth.

"Wait a minute, I'm as pissed off about this as you, mate."

"I'm not your bloody mate." Sinclair ranted now. "And I'm not someone you can jack up for a few pounds. I told you what the deal was, Gillon: now, get me that girl or you won't see a bloody penny."

"Hang on."

"I mean it, Gillon. You think you can mess me about, you're in for a shock."

The line died before he had a chance to reply, but as he stared out of the dirt-scarred windshield into the fast-darkening Lochside ghetto, Danny Gillon knew there was nothing to say anyway.

37

Through the door that linked the living room and dining room, Valentine spotted his father's thin shoulders poking beneath the paisley dressing gown that must have been at least thirty years old.

"Hello, Dad," he said.

His father turned briskly to face the source of the greeting. "Oh, it's yourself. I was wondering if you still lived here."

"Don't you start!"

His father was smiling, an indication he had picked up Clare's earlier unease. Valentine looked the old man over: he seemed pale, gaunt. There was a little bruising on his forehead and white sticking plasters crossed his temple. He could sense his father's unease. He didn't want to be there, he wanted to be in his own home, but there was a weariness about him now that suggested he was tired of fighting the reality.

"Did you not get yourself some tea or coffee?" said Valentine.

"Oh, I'm not raking about in Clare's cupboards."

"Well, I know my way about. What can I get you?"

"Tea, remember how I take it?"

He shrugged. "I think Clare's got it written down somewhere."

"Milk and two sugars, and give it time to stand."

As he clattered with the cups and kettle, Valentine called through to his father. "So, how are you feeling, anyway?"

"Oh, you know."

His father was never a man to bemoan his lot, he would be half-starved before he'd ask for a scrap from another man's table.

"You don't remember what happened?"

"Well, I do and I don't."

The kettle boiled and Valentine popped his head round the door. "What?"

His father was rising from the chair, a pained expression crossed his face as his slow gait took him to the kitchen. "See, the thing is, I'd need to swear you to secrecy."

The detective felt like his stomach was dissolving into his backbone. "I don't like the sound of this, Dad."

He reached out a hand, slapped it on his son's shoulder and gripped tightly. "Oh, God, no. It's nothing like that."

The kettle boiled, prompting him to pour out the tea. "Well, what is it then?"

His father's long fingers, gnarled and toughened by a lifetime of manual labor, tapped the keys on an imaginary piano, then shot upwards to the waves of white hair on his head. It was clearly very difficult for him to find the words. "Well, son, you see I was given this gift. A beautiful gift it was, too, and I was very grateful for it at the time."

Valentine clattered the spoon off the counter with impatience. "Look, will you just tell me?"

"It was the slippers."

"What?"

He sighed, reached out for the cup and turned for the dining room. "You see, Clare bought me these lovely slippers the other day, grand they were, nice and comfy with the fur inside ... but ... "

The two men sat facing each other over the table. "But?"

"They were too big, son. I didn't want to hurt her feelings, but I did myself a turn in them."

Valentine started to laugh. "You tripped over your own feet?"

"Oh, bugger off. They're size tens, I'm only an eight. I took a nosedive down the stairs."

"And you didn't want to tell Clare."

"God, no, she'd be heartbroken. It was a lovely thought."

The detective looked at his father, delighted that there was no serious damage done. The thought of the old boy going for a day of scans and having to keep his mouth shut for Clare's benefit was comical to him.

"You know she has you shipped upstairs for good?"

"Oh, Christ, you'll have to set her straight."

"Me?"

He drew his hands from the sides of the cup. "I need my own space, I can't be stopping in the youngster's room."

Valentine took a sip of coffee, then made his way back to the kitchen to collect his coat and briefcase, but kept his stare on his father. "I'll see what I can do. I don't think you're getting off that lightly, though, she'll keep you under observation for a bit longer."

His father was on his feet, waving him off as he opened the back door. "Aren't you going in a bit early?"

"I've got a lot to do, Dad. I'll see you tonight. Mind how you go, especially on those stairs!"

"Bugger off."

Hillfoot Road was so quiet that Valentine gave serious consideration to leaving the house at an earlier hour every day. There were still plenty of Glasgow commuters about, and maybe even a few late starts to Edinburgh. To a one, they were Mercedes or BMWs, the odd Audi, with a suit jacket hanging in the back window.

As he reached King Street station, Valentine took the stairs to the incident room and slid backwards through the swing door as he wrestled himself out of his coat. The lights were out. He fumbled for the switches on the wall and soon the room was flooded with brightness. On his way to the far end of the incident room, the detective glanced at the whiteboard to make sure DS McAlister had added the results of the credit card and CCTV sweep: he hadn't.

"Bloody hell, Ally." He would call him on that later — if the chief super hadn't already. She was becoming more than a worry to the DI now. One more piece of bad press, or another line of inquiry drawing a blank, and she was liable to wobble. He'd seen it before, and when she did it he knew to get out of the way or she would use him to break her fall.

As he reached the office at the end of the incident room, Valentine's eyes were drawn to a set of blue folders. He flipped the first one open: an old VHS videotape was inside with a yellow Post-it-note attached. The note was in Ally's spidery scrawl: "Interesting viewing, boss."

Ally had indeed come up trumps, after all, the credit search showing two more successive Wednesday-night purchases attributed to James

Urquhart in the same locale. But it was the CCTV footage from a Prest-wick Road twenty-four-hour garage that intrigued him. Valentine took the tape and slotted it into the TV-recorder in the corner of the room.

"Right then, Ally, let's see what you've got here."

The tape was set a few minutes before the point of interest that had been marked by the DS. Valentine watched the grainy image of the petrol station forecourt. There appeared to be one car parked at the pumps and another just arriving, but making its way to the parking bays next to the bags of charcoal and the long-past-their-best bunches of flowers. He thought he recognized the second car from somewhere, but he couldn't place it.

"Interesting."

The screen changed again: a white band descended diagonally, split-ting the image in two and merging with a new screenshot of the interior. A clock in the lower left corner ticked away the hours, minutes and seconds. It was 7.15 p.m.

"Hello."

The first man to the counter was stocky and broad-shouldered, but carrying a heavy paunch. His hair was short and cropped close to his scalp. As he handed over his money to the teller, there was no mistaking Duncan Knox.

Valentine nodded. "Very nice work, Ally."

He let the video play a little longer and watched Knox leave the shop, and then the screen flipped back to the forecourt and he watched him getting into his car and driving away. He reached out to pause the video recorder. For a moment, the detective let his thoughts breathe. This was evidence placing Knox and Urquhart in the same vicinity at the same time, but it was far from the conclusive stamp he needed. Valentine knew Knox and Urquhart were connected — to have his suspicions almost confirmed was tantalizing, but added little to his overall knowledge. Would it be enough, even, to convince the chief super of a link? He doubted it. What it presented was an interesting proposition, a list of more possibilities, but little else.

He returned to the blue folder on his desk and removed the yellow Post-it-note on which DS McAlister had written the next screen time he wanted him to view. He pressed the fast-forward button and watched the counter. As he pressed play once again, the picture had jumped back out to the forecourt but was obscured by two jagged diagonal lines. He could see the door of the other car — the one he thought he recognized — opening and a figure stepping out. The screen jumped again, back to the interior, and Valentine leaned forward to better view the figure going into the store and approaching the counter. He had his head down, towards the counter, the rim of a tweed cap obscuring the man's face. He was buying cigarettes. He paid cash and then, as he collected his change, he tipped his head towards the camera.

Valentine leapt to press pause on the video recorder.

As the screen stilled, there was no doubt in his mind the man in the tweed cap was James Urquhart. He stared at the face and tried to process the information. His thoughts were already buzzing with the possibility of what it might say and what it might mean, not only for the investigation, but for the Janie Cooper case.

38

DS McAlister and DI Valentine stood facing Adrian Urquhart across the threshold of his late father's home, like opposing forces meeting in no man's land. The second he had opened the door, Adrian lifted his gaze skyward and sighed — all that was missing was a stamped foot to complete the image of petulance.

"It might be better if we came inside, there are some new developments we need to talk about," said Valentine.

Adrian stepped back into the hallway and flagged them in.

"It shouldn't take too long," said McAlister.

Adrian didn't acknowledge the DS, just closed the door and turned to face Valentine. "Will you need to speak to my mother? She's in the kitchen."

The detective nodded. "If it's no trouble."

"I'll get her. Just go through. I'm sure you know the layout of the place by now."

The officers proceeded down the hallway towards the living room and stood before the fire. It was a large room, elaborately and expensively decorated, but the chintzy feel belied any real personality. Had the room been decorated from pictures in magazines? There was no feeling of a home about it at all. As he looked around and gauged that the footprint of his own property might fit comfortably into this one room, Valentine conceded a bias for what was and was not a home.

"Hello, again." Mrs. Urquhart was rubbing her hands on a tea towel when she appeared from the kitchen.

The officers turned to face her and nodded in unison.

"You could have taken a chair, gentlemen," she said, directing them towards the sofa and flicking the tea towel over her shoulder.

Adrian joined her on the adjacent sofa. The additional bodies did nothing to diminish the room's extent. There was a lulled silence that sat heavily between them. The four faced each other like opposing teams. Valentine wondered why. He was still searching for a killer and it was too soon for the conclusion of hope. In his experience, the families of victims tended to reserve resentment until a case was closed without a proper solution being found.

Valentine leaned forward, clasping his hands above his knees. "How have you been, Mrs. Urquhart?"

She tilted her head to the side; her reply came in a drawl. "Did you come here to inquire after my health, Inspector?"

The DI's face tightened. "If you don't mind me saying, Mrs. Urquhart, I detect you might be a little uncomfortable with the investigation."

"Oh, really." She crossed her legs and snatched the tea towel from her shoulder. There was no disguising her anger and frustration as her hands clasped the tea towel and twisted a tight coil.

DS McAlister spoke. "Have we come at a bad time?"

"Oh, for God's sake," said Adrian. "My father has been murdered; do you think there is a good time for any of us?"

Valentine unclasped his hands and waved McAlister down. The tone of the interview had been well established now; he hadn't expected it to reach rock bottom so quickly, but the turn of events presented an interesting possibility for a more direct approach. "We won't take up too much of your time. I hope you'll appreciate that this murder investigation is a top priority for us and there are certain aspects of the case that have caused us some concern, recently."

Adrian snatched the tea towel impatiently from his mother's hands and slapped it on the arm of the sofa, out of her reach. "Such as?"

"When we last spoke, you may recall I mentioned the name Knox."

Mrs. Urquhart's voice pitched higher. "Yes, the other unfortunate victim."

"That's one way of describing him."

"Well, how would you describe him, Inspector?"

Valentine watched as a scowl crossed her face. He kept his words low and calm but avoided a direct answer. "You said you didn't recognize the name."

She cut in. "I've had no cause to change my opinion."

DS McAlister spoke. "We didn't ask if you had."

The Urquharts turned to each other, but no words were exchanged. They seemed to both be concentrating on saying as little as possible. Their actions might have been rehearsed, but that was unlikely, thought the detective.

As Valentine assessed the pair, he leaned back in his chair and rested his chin on the back of his knuckles. He could tell that he had crossed a line with them, but he had no idea where it was or what it represented. Was it a personal animus or a more vague scattering of disapproval in his direction? Either way, he didn't judge them for it — when he found himself perplexed by people, he knew the only route to understanding was observation. As he prepared to pose his next question, there was a sound like cups clattering in the kitchen and then the heavy wooden door opened.

Ronnie Bell looked to be dressed for country pursuits, a shiny wax jacket and Chelsea boots beneath corduroy trousers. He walked to the middle of the room, then approached the mantle, where he stood facing the officers, firm-footed and sure.

"Hello again, Mr. Bell," said Valentine. "I hope you'll appreciate we're in the midst of a delicate discussion."

Mrs. Urquhart interrupted. "No need to bother about Ronnie. He's fine where he is."

The neighbor removed his outdoor jacket and flung it over the back of a chair, then joined the others on the sofa, sitting stiff and proud. He smiled to Valentine but did not open his mouth.

"All right, if you're content with the situation," said Valentine.

"I think it might be best if you asked what you came to ask and were quick about it," said Ronnie. "This family has been through enough, and what with all the media attention, it's been far from pleasant."

"Media attention?" said McAlister.

Adrian stood up, his voice rising like a slow siren wail. "Look, what is it you want?"

Valentine's shoulders tightened. "We'll try not to take up too much more of your time." He motioned to the sofa. "If you don't mind please,

Adrian."

He shook his head and sat back down.

The DI picked at the edges of composure. "Mrs. Urquhart, do you think there is a possibility your husband may have known Duncan Knox, from your time in Glasgow, perhaps?"

She massaged her wrist. "Well, I can't see how."

DS McAlister spoke again. "The Inspector asked if it was possible, Mrs. Urquhart."

"Well, anything's possible in theory. Are you asking if I knew that my husband was an associate of this Knox person when we were in Glasgow? I don't know. I certainly don't think so." She dropped her wrist suddenly. "I told you before, I have no idea who this man is."

Valentine saw the answers were not going to change, no matter how he posed the questions. "This model club that your husband attended on Wednesdays."

"Yes, what about it?" Her voice edged higher.

"He went every week?"

"Yes. Why?"

"And you're sure of that?"

"Yes, I told you before, he went every week."

Valentine glanced at McAlister and the DS seemed to sense the passing of the baton. "That's not what the club told us," said Ally. "In fact, he was rarely there at all. Have you any idea where your husband might have been going on those nights?"

Adrian reached over to touch his mother's hand. "Why are you doing this to us?"

"I'm sorry?" said Valentine.

"You're upsetting my mother. This is an interrogation. Don't you see we're the victims here, as much as my father?"

"This is all routine questioning, Adrian. We're trying to establish the facts, that's all."

It was Ronnie Bell's time to stand up now. He pushed away Adrian's hand and made to grab Mrs. Urquhart's elbow. "I think that's enough for one day, gentlemen."

The Urquharts raised themselves from the sofa in time with Ronnie, and the police officers followed suit. They all stood facing each other across the broad room.

"I'll ask you to leave, now," said Ronnie.

"Thank you for your time," said Valentine. As he started to fasten his coat, to walk for the door, he turned. "We have James Urquhart on camera in the vicinity of Prestwick Road on one of those Wednesday nights. Any idea what he might have been doing there?"

"No. None." Adrian's voice was blunt.

Valentine held his gaze. "Duncan Knox was there, too."

"It's a very small town, Inspector," said Adrian.

Ronnie stepped between them. "Right, that's it, no more questions. If you keep pestering this family, then I'll be directing you to a legal professional."

Valentine retreated to the door. In the hallway, the DI spoke out once more. "It is, indeed, a small town, Adrian, and secrets aren't kept long in small towns. I'll be in touch."

"I'm sure you will, but my mother is leaving for the Highlands in a little while."

"The Highlands?"

"She wants some peace and quiet. You don't grudge her that, do you?"

"Not at all," said Valentine. "That's not something I would grudge anyone."

39

The diluted blue skyline was a dreary indicator of DI Bob Valentine's mood. The detective stood in front of his desk, staring out to a street being washed in rain. People were being hurried and harried by the elements into shop fronts and winds — and not a glance was exchanged between them.

When had it become like this? At what point did we all become so atomized? No one wanted to be part of this society. We wanted our homes and our flat-screen televisions, to escape into self-delusion. If we were honest, at this point, we didn't even like each other.

Valentine couldn't look out the window anymore. The world outside repulsed him. Just a short time ago, he had been dead. No longer of this world. He tried to remember why that wasn't a good thing.

DS Sylvia McCormack was standing outside his office. She seemed to be holding some files, the thick blue files that they stored the case notes in, but also a collection of loose sheaves of paper. In her left hand, pressed tight to her side, was a mug that looked like it might contain coffee. Valentine crossed the floor and opened up the door.

"You weren't thinking, were you?" he said.

"About the handle you mean?" She nodded to another mug sitting on a table by the door. "I made us coffee; can you take this?"

"Yeah, sure."

The detective took the mug from her hand and watched her wrestle the bundle of files onto her hip; she retrieved the other mug and walked through the door. The job of closing it behind her seemed to require another set of arms, but she didn't look fazed or in any way like she might welcome assistance.

"I take it you heard about the trip to the Urquharts?" said Valentine.

She placed the folders on the desktop and flicked her fringe from her eyes. "I saw Ally in the lunchroom. Pretty grim, eh?"

"Oh, it's that all right."

"I wouldn't let it get to you." She dropped herself in the chair and watched as a swirl of coffee was evacuated from the brim of the mug. "Shit!"

Valentine grinned. The DS was what his late mother would have called "soulish." He had met precious few people who had set him in mind of his mother.

"Are you OK there, do you need a hanky?" he said.

She shook her head and sneered at him over the bridge of her nose. "I've survived worse."

As he took in her scowl, he knew she wasn't milking the moment for herself. "I'm sure you have."

Valentine retreated behind his desk and removed the chair. As he sat down, he raised the coffee mug and tested it for warmth. As he returned the mug to rest, he rifled the files and the pile of paper on top.

"What's this?" he said.

"The full Knox transcripts from Glasgow. I've marked up the highlights." She crossed her legs and balanced the coffee on her knee. "That other stuff, the bundle of papers, is just something I thought might interest you."

Valentine picked up the top sheet, which looked to have been printed from the Internet. The website seemed official enough, but the content of the page was an excursion to new territory for the detective. As he read the top line and glanced over a sidebar, he knew the DS was dragging him towards something he didn't want to face.

"Look, Sylvia." His words trailed off as he was caught in her eyeline.

"I'm only trying to help, sir."

Valentine lowered the printout and gripped the tip of his chin. "So, tell me about this Reece case, the mother of five."

The DS smiled. "God, where to start? We had nothing until Colvin showed. He had images in his head of Mrs. Reece in a field, he knew she was dead, but that was it. Most of the stuff he gave us was fragmented, patches of words and pictures of her children crying, and so on."

Valentine had heard of instances in the past where quite incredible messages had been delivered to police from people with no apparent knowledge of the case at hand; they had always struck him as slightly suspect or, worse, as frauds.

"Was he looking for money?"

"No, not a penny. He made that very clear from the start." She tilted her head at a strange angle, as if searching the far reaches of her memory. "The thing was, he was desperate. It was like he had to get this out of his system because it was, I don't know, haunting him."

The detective shifted uneasily. He didn't want to be drawn into believing in psychics helping police with their clear-up rates, but something about McCormack's story poked at him and drew his attention into new areas.

"So, you took him on?"

"More like took him in. As soon as he got close to the investigation, the information just started spilling out of him."

"He found her, then?"

She retrieved her coffee mug and took a sip. "No, sir. She was dead."

"Not a great success."

"How do you mean?"

"Well, the crime had already been committed. Murder, I presume."

"No, you miss the point. The investigation was cold. Colvin saw where the victim was buried and led the squad there. We'd never have found her remains without him."

Valentine stared at his coffee. The grey liquid seemed uninviting, but he raised the mug to his mouth again. He didn't want to reveal how he truly felt. The overriding feeling, he noted was embarrassment.

"Sylvia, I don't know what you think you saw at the Coopers, but..."

She raised a hand, as if to punctuate his sentence for him. "Boss, I know what I saw."

"Sylvia."

"Wait a minute." She reached forward and clattered the mug on the desktop. It was still quite full and some liquid ran down the side. "Have a read of the notes I printed for you — sudden precognition is a well-documented occurrence in near-death survivors."

Valentine forced a smile onto his face. He felt his attention drawn to the activity outside the office; he hoped no one could lip-read. DS McCormack stood up and headed to the door.

"Just read the notes, boss," she said. "And if it doesn't ring true, then I'll say no more."

He doubted that was true. "Oh, really?"

"Keep an open mind, sir." She reached for the door and paused, and a smug gleam entered her eye. "And remember, there are more things on heaven and earth than are dreamt of in your philosophy."

If she had appended a wink to the statement, Valentine couldn't have been more unsettled. He felt like she had something on him now, a hold over him. He knew, however, that DS McCormack's intentions were pure — decent, even — but that only added to the tension crushing him.

The DI fingered the edge of the paper printout for a moment longer and saw himself reading it, perhaps even digesting the contents, and then he withdrew his hand. He returned to the window and the sight of the grey and rain-lashed streets of Ayr. For the first time, Valentine realized he was trapped: trapped in the town, trapped in his marriage, and trapped in a career he had no right to in his current condition. Most of all, and certainly the most worrying for him, was the fact that he was trapped in a mind and body that he no longer felt in full control of. It worried him in ways that DS McCormack seemed incapable of grasping. It was not a matter of glimpsing a quite useful and seemingly productive sixth sense, it was a matter of whether he could stop it interfering with his sanity long enough for him to solve the murders of James Urquhart and Duncan Knox and the disappearance of Janie Cooper. Valentine felt his chest tightening, his heart beating so hard that he had to press the flat of his hand to his breastbone. As he reached out to steady himself on the window ledge, his vision became blurred and blotched. The detective knew he had to bury these feelings soon, because if he couldn't, the danger was that he would lose his job, or worse.

40

D I Bob Valentine came to the conclusion that the only option left to him was to resign from the force immediately. As he kept his gaze on the rain-battered windowpane, the view beyond became a blur of indistinct shapes. He thought about the situation he now found himself in, and the move he knew he must make increasingly seemed like the only honorable course of action. He had failed to find a way through the mess. His focus was gone.

What mattered was his family and that they would be kept safe. If he came clean, admitted his physical and mental failings, then he would be granted a medical discharge.

Valentine walked through the incident room in a daze. He tried to maintain his usual posture, he kept his hands in his pockets and gave the odd, slouching nod to those who crossed his path, but he wasn't present. His mind was already in with the chief super, delivering his resignation. By the time he reached the brassy nameplate that bore the name CS Marion Martin, his heart was pounding.

He knocked once and reached for the handle. As he stepped inside, he felt a flash of heat in his chest and then he saw the chief super lowering the telephone in the most careful manner. Her eyes were wide, her skin pale and shiny, and her mouth a thin point that threatened to reveal a recent hurt. She sat down and slowly pushed herself away from the edge of her desk.

Valentine was first to speak. "Something wrong?"

She remained still. A slow trail of words seemed to be coming from somewhere else. "We have another one: a young girl out in Mossblown. Running club just about trampled over her." She looked up, stared into the DI's eyes. "Did you hear what I said?"

He nodded. "Is it the same MO?"

She shook her head. "No spike. Uniform say the scene looks like it was abandoned in a hurry."

Valentine found a juggernaut of thoughts driving over his earlier intentions. As he looked at CS Martin, felled in her own office by yet another murder, he knew there was no one else who could carry the load. Resignation seemed his most insane thought now — how could he abandon the investigation to Martin? He was lurching from pillar to post, but there was another victim to consider, now, and perhaps it would reveal some secrets that had so far remained hidden from the investigation.

"Mossblown? The others were in Ayr. That's worrying, a widening spread."

"Probably thought the town center was too hot, now."

"No. If it's a different MO then the intention will be different – Urquhart and Knox were impaled on spikes to attract attention, taking a body into the countryside says concealment to me."

The chief super nodded. "Why show off with the others and not this one?"

Valentine shrugged. "I don't know. We don't even know that they're linked."

"Oh, come on, we treble our annual murder count in a matter of weeks and it's not the same perp?"

"Maybe the motivation's different." He reached out and leaned on the desk. "Maybe this girl was done over because our killer wanted her out the way."

"It's possible."

Valentine felt his energy levels increasing. He pushed himself away from the desk and turned for the door. "Running club?"

"Bloody Ayrshire Harriers. Twenty-six names taken by uniform."

"Crime scene will be a mess."

Martin shook her head. "I'm more worried about the potential for press leaks. Won't take long to seep out with twenty-six tongues wagging."

The DI gripped the door handle, he felt like he was entering a different station to the one he had crossed a few moments ago to offer his resignation. "I'll get out there and see what's what."

She didn't reply. Valentine knew this was virgin territory for the chief super, and if there had been a clock ticking on his efforts before, it had just sprung into the red zone. He returned to the incident room and took a brief pause, once inside the door.

"Can I have your attention?"

The room seemed to go into slow motion and then freeze. A cup clattered onto a desktop like the last bell in a pub and then the only sound was that of the photocopier. A uniform reached out to remove the paper tray and silence fell.

"Thank you," said Valentine. "I've just been in with the boss and have to report we have another body on our patch."

DS McAlister called out, "Another one. Where, this time?"

"Mossblown, Ally. The details are still sketchy, but we'll know more when we get out there."

"Right, then," said McAlister. "We should get going."

The room's volume was suddenly turned up a notch, some shuffling and animated facial gestures spread through the enclosed space.

Valentine walked to the rack and retrieved his coat. "Right, Ally and Phil, you can follow me out. Sylvia, you're with me." He pointed to the DS and then he curled up his index finger as if reeling her towards him.

"Yes, sir."

The sound of the squad's feet on the stairs came like a stampede. Jim Prentice looked up from the front desk and a woman struggled to hold onto what looked like a lost dog; it started barking as Valentine rushed past.

"What's all this?" said Jim. "It's never another one."

The detective held the door for DS McCormack and the others and managed to sneer towards the desk sergeant. "Jim, try and keep it zipped."

In the car, Valentine pulled out before McCormack had a chance to put her seatbelt on. A red light illuminated on the dashboard and then a chime started to ping.

"It won't go off till you've got the belt on," said the DI.

"I haven't sat down, yet." McCormack turned towards the door and reached out for the seatbelt. Cars halted on the approach to King Street roundabout as the trail of police vehicles accelerated. They were halfway to the Tesco superstore before the conversation began again.

"What do we know about this one, sir?"

Valentine changed lanes. "Female and not the same MO."

"How far out's this town?"

"About ten or fifteen, depending on the road. There's nothing to the place. A few council houses and a couple of pubs. Farms all around and, if I remember right, a nursing home."

"Sounds beyond glamorous."

"It's beyond the beyonds. Nobody goes to Mossblown unless they have to, and even then, you'd try to avoid it if you could."

The traffic lights turned to green and the left lane cleared enough for Valentine to put the foot down. They'd passed Tesco and were well on their way to the bypass before the weather turned again. He put on the wipers and wound up the inch or so of window he had left open.

"Sylvia, about that little chat we had earlier."

She turned towards him. "What about it?"

"I know you think you saw something, and I know you think you're helping me, but ... "

"There's always one of them, isn't there?"

He glanced towards her. The expression she wore was the one he expected, a mix of disappointment and sadness tinged with no little hurt. "I'm grateful to you for your concern, obviously."

"Oh, obviously." The tone lapsed into polished sarcasm; the change didn't suit her.

"All I want to say is, let me deal with this in my own way."

She looked towards the wet fields in the distance. "And you'd like me to mind my own business, I suppose."

"Sylvia." He didn't think he had said anything to merit this reaction, were they talking at cross purposes?

She turned to face him as the car came to a halt. "It's OK, boss, I know when to bite my tongue." She looked away again. "You've no need to worry about that. Consider your secret safe with me."

41

Clare Valentine removed her wedding ring for the first time in nearly twenty years and stared at the white band of skin beneath. She grasped the ring between finger and thumb and held it up to the light — myriad tiny scratches glinted before her eyes. Each scratch was a memory, an experience — they existed, perhaps more than she did now.

Clare returned the wedding ring to the dresser and stared at it. It looked so insignificant, tiny. She remembered the day she and Bob picked the wedding bands from the jeweler on New Market Street. Her mother had a wide gold band that signaled solidity. She wanted that, too.

"Isn't it a bit big?" Bob had said. "It's not going through a bull's nose."

How could she bury those memories? Did she want to?

Clare turned away from the window and half-rose from her seated position, then decided to sit down again. She felt weary, like all vitality had been drained from her. She dropped her face into the palm of her hands and started to cry. The sobbing lasted only a few moments before she shook herself back to reality.

There was not much left to pack: two cases were more than enough. There was just her coat, and she could wear that. As she stared at the bulging suitcases on the bed, they seemed to press on her mind, light the landing torches that were summoning in a descending guilt.

"Get a grip."

The girls were older now. They were hardly children — more like young adults. They would understand. They might shed a tear for her the first night she was away, but that would be all. She'd seen their friends talking about their parents' separations like it was a trip to the shops; it was all just another rite of passage, these days.

She flicked her fingers away from her face and tried to ball a fist. It was a pathetic-looking symbol of anger, but she felt the need to press it into her thigh and attempt to spark some anger.

"You did this, Bob." She shook her head. "Not me."

She turned back to the bed and latched her grip on the handle of the suitcase. It was heavier than she imagined, or perhaps she was weaker.

Clare couldn't alert Bob's dad to her leaving because she couldn't stand the explanation she'd have to give.

She descended the stairs and made her way through to the living room, where the old man was sitting. The television was silent, the only sound was from the builders in the neighbor's garden.

"I think they must be putting up the Taj Mahal next door," said Bob's dad.

"Lucky them." Clare moved towards the window and peeked through the blinds.

"I was saying to Bob, I'll not be under your feet much longer."

Had her husband put him up to this? He was always very good at reading the advance signals of her intentions, but she didn't think he had been paying that much attention lately.

"Don't be silly."

"It's been very nice of you, but you need the space. You're a family, after all, and I'm just a visitor."

Clare felt his words were so pointed they might have been scripted. Her lip trembled and she fought to prevent a single teardrop being released from her eye. She touched the window ledge and tried to hold her composure as she spoke towards the blinds. "You're part of the family."

There was a pause. "Not really."

Clare turned around and wiped her eyes. She knew at once that her father-in-law suspected something wasn't right.

He lifted his gaze from the carpet and fixed his eyes on Clare. "Is everything all right, my dear?"

"Quite all right." She'd managed to inject some steel into her voice. "Look, why don't you nip down to the Spar and get yourself a paper?"

"I'm not bothered about a paper, love, there's very little reading in them these days."

She smiled. "Well, stretch your legs then, the fresh air will do you good." She turned back to the window again. "It's a lovely day."

"Maybe you're right."

The old man raised himself from the sofa and strolled through to the kitchen. As Clare turned, she caught sight of him removing the cap from his jacket pocket and maneuvering it into place on his head. When he had wrestled the jacket on and negotiated the awkward zipper, he turned and tapped the tip of his cap to her.

Clare ordered the cab and was told to expect it in ten minutes. She collected her coat first: putting it on was an act of resolve. But she couldn't believe how heavy the cases were; the castors screeched and bumped each step of the staircase.

As Clare waited for the cab, she could see through to the living room — the pictures of the girls in their school uniforms seemed to scream to her. Her nails started to tap off her lips. She hadn't realized how hard this was going to be.

The doorbell went.

"Right, taxi. Hold it together," she told herself.

As she checked herself in the mirror, Clare recognized only a passing resemblance to herself. Her cheeks were red and puffy, her eyes spider-webs of burst capillaries.

She opened the door — her breath sank into a sigh — she was staring at her father-in-law.

"There's a taxi here, love," he said.

She couldn't explain herself. "I thought you were going for a paper."

He held up a copy of the Daily Record. "Builder next door gave me a lift there and back." He peered round her shoulder and obviously caught sight of the suitcases. "Clare, are you going somewhere?"

42

DI Bob Valentine crouched low to the ground and examined the pale corpse, damp now, with the rain. She was no more human than the bed of dirt she lay on. He felt cold inside — he felt the coldness of her loss.

"Look at those bruises," said DS McCormack.

"On the neck or the arms?" said Valentine. "The ones on the arms are older."

"She's a junkie."

She was a drug user, there was no mistaking it, but she was also someone's daughter. She'd meant something to someone: if not now, then once.

He lowered himself on his haunches and picked a wet leaf from the white flesh. The contusions continued down her arm. "She's been battered about."

"Repeatedly, I'd say for some time. Look at the stomach distension, sir."

"She's a hooker, I'll bet money on that." Valentine rose and motioned to one of the uniforms. "We got her printed?"

"Yes, sir. Going through now."

"Well, that's something. With any luck we'll have her on our books and get a name before too long."

DS McAlister and DS Donnelly approached the crime scene. They were ducking under the blue and white tape as Valentine turned away from them to take a closer look at a silver chain around the girl's neck.

"What's that, boss?" said McCormack.

"Don't know. Some kind of pendant."

As he knelt down again, Valentine removed a yellow pencil from the inside pocket of his sports coat. He pointed the pencil towards the girl's neck and slotted the tip beneath the silver chain; as he rummaged for the pendant, he saw a tangle of mulch around a silver clasp and then the item was sprung onto her chest.

"A cross," he said. The detective almost felt like laughing. "Where was her God?"

"It's just a cheapie," said McCormack.

Valentine stood up and turned his gaze to the heavens. "Maybe He was pissed at her for that?" The DI shook his head. "I mean, there's some things worth splashing out on."

DS McCormack seemed unsure how to interpret the detective's words. She held herself still as the wind took stray tendrils of hair in front of her face. Valentine turned away and walked towards the blue tape.

"A bloody cross."

He didn't know why he had got so worked up by the sight of the small silver cross. It just seemed so out of place to him, so ridiculously trite. She was a young girl who hadn't had a chance from the day she was born, a prostitute who pumped her veins full of poison to numb the pain of being alive: what use did she have for God? He knew her story all too well, because it was the story of every young girl like her. Pain in childhood, and pain in bigger portions the older she got. There was no escape, no savior for her. As he reached the edge of the clearing, he felt his throat constricting with unwanted emotion.

"Sir, have you seen the tracks?" One of the uniforms pointed to the broad-rimmed tire marks in the wet ground.

"You better get those cast," said Valentine.

"Looks like a big vehicle, sir. A large sedan or maybe even a truck"

The detective looked at the tire prints; they were clear and fresh, and the vehicle seemed to have spun a little in the wet mud. "Looks like they were in a hurry to get away."

"Might have been the running party. Maybe saw them coming."

Valentine turned back towards the crime scene. The crime scene team had started to unfurl a white tent, and a noise like wind in a sail sent a wood pigeon scrabbling from the branches of a nearby tree.

The detective pointed to what looked like a steep gash in the ground.

"What's that, there?"

"Some kind of hole, sir. We think it's fresh, too."

"A grave."

"Could be, sir."

The DI had seen enough to know he didn't need to see any more. He turned for the car with his face in the wind. "Tell the others I'm going back to the station."

"Don't you want to wait for the fiscal, sir?"

He didn't think the question deserved an answer. Was the fiscal going to deliver some insight? Was the fiscal going to tell him how to do his job, how to solve another murder? As he reached the road, Valentine unlocked the car and kept his head low, facing off a fierce wind, until he had reached the vehicle. He got inside just as the rain was starting up again and sat with his hands in his lap. As he stared out of the car's window to the row of grim council houses, he saw the stacks of chimneys stalking the grey horizon like weary sentries who wished to be anywhere but here. An old man stood in front of his home, leaning on a dilapidated garden gate with folded arms. Valentine stared at the man for a moment, made an unfathomable connection with his dark eyes and felt them share a mute understanding of a world that had long ago ceased to make any sense to them both. The detective put the key in the ignition and set off.

At the station, Valentine approached the front desk and called out to Jim Prentice. The desk sergeant turned and nodded; he was holding the receiver of a telephone, but the conversation seemed to be coming to an end. His expression suggested there was a fence that needed mending sitting between the two men.

"Sorry to be barking at you this morning, Jim," said Valentine.

"It's all right, I know how it is." He momentarily clamped his mouth shut. "I take it that's another one to add to the tally?"

The detective nodded. "Young girl. She's a hooker, and lucky if she's seen twenty summers."

"Well, she'll not see another one." He shook his head. "What's this bloody place coming too? What happened to the days of lost bikes and kids raiding orchards?"

"Long gone, Jim."

As he made his way onto the stairs, Valentine caught sight of the chief super's thick ankles on the floor above him heading for the incident room. The thud of her footsteps suggested that she had some important news to deliver.

Valentine upped his pace and made leaps of two steps at a time. As he jogged in behind CS Martin's footfalls, he was breathing heavily.

"Oh, you're back?" she said.

"Just."

"Couldn't have been there long."

"Long enough. She's a prostitute, a well-worked one by the looks of it, so she shouldn't be too hard to ID."

The chief super raised her right hand and pinned a pile of papers to Valentine's chest. "Get your laughing gear round that. We have an ID."

"The prints?"

"Yes, indeed. We've pulled her up more times than a shithouse seat."

Valentine removed his gaze from Dino, peeled the paperwork from his chest and scanned the contents. The printout wasn't the best quality: a grainy black and white photograph of the girl that looked to have been taken during a booking. There was no doubting her resemblance to the girl he'd just left lying in a cold field.

"That's her," he said.

"You sure?"

"Certain." Valentine held up the papers and slapped his other hand off them. "The corpse in Mossblown is Leanne Dunn."

43

DI Bob Valentine spread Leanne Dunn's file over the desktop in front of him. His thoughts moved quickly as his eyes took in the details. She was an Ayr girl, had always lived locally, if you could apply that term to how her days had gone. He couldn't hide his sympathy for her; it all seemed such a tragic waste. The poverty and the deprivation she had endured since childhood had been compounded by a drug-addicted mother. She'd had little success with foster parents from an early age and ended up in care homes. He knew the types of places, had heard all the names before: they were the region's hate factories, churning out the types of conveyor-belt criminals he was depressingly familiar with. She suffered, under what the social workers called a "constellated disadvantage," a life of casual drug use and less casual criminality. Her death in a field before the age of nineteen could almost have been written in the poor girl's horoscope from the day she was born. What the detective also knew, however, was short lives like Leanne Dunn's were remarkable in being defined by their chaos. Murder victims mostly knew their killers and the likes of Leanne didn't mix with master criminals: they were the bottom feeders, the pond life, the scum that always left a sticky trail in their wake. He would find Leanne's killer because experience had taught him that unravelling the murder of a penniless prostitute was much easier than that of a wealthy banker. Whoever her killer was didn't know it yet, but the DI was prepared to gamble on wrapping up more than one murder now; in that regard, Leanne Dunn's short life and brutal death might yet serve some wider good.

Valentine had called the other detectives back from Mossblown and now they started to appear in the incident room.

"What you got there, boss?" said DS McAlister.

The DI took the page containing the picture of Leanne Dunn and pinned it on the board; he nodded to Phil and Sylvia as they arrived.

"This is our body in the wood," he said. "Leanne Dunn, a prostitute who is well and truly known to us."

"Local girl, then?" said Ally.

"Born and bred." Valentine stood square-footed before the others. "Right, you know what I want and you know I want it done yesterday."

DS Donnelly stepped out from behind the filing cabinet he was leaning on. "So, she's Ayr: then that narrows down the options." He turned to Ally and showed his hands like he was testing for rain. "We're talking one of Big Madge's girls or someone like Finnegan or Gillon."

Ally nodded, but Valentine halted him from speaking. "Dunn was a prostitute according to her record, so that rules out Madge. I want all known bedsits, flats, bloody lay-bys used by Finnegan's girls and Gillon's looked at by uniform right away. I want the word out on this that I'm taking them all in, every last one. I want no hookers in Ayr in any doubt that we will bust heads on this."

DS McAlister seemed pensive, deep in thought, as he pushed his way to the front of the board and stood there.

"What is it, Ally?"

He pointed to the board. "Here, sir: the tip murder, we were trying to trace a white van."

"And?"

McAlister turned to face the team. "Danny Gillon drives a white van."

DS Donnelly nodded. "He does, too, calls it his shagging wagon. And, boss, we had something like van tracks out at Mossblown, as well."

Valentine stepped away from the board and cut a path through the squad as he made his way towards the desk with the rest of the notes. When the DI collected the page he was looking for, he picked up his coat and started to slot his arms into the sleeves. His voice came loud and firm, followed by a wide-eyed trawl of the room: "Right, Ally and Phil, I want you to take Danny Gillon's place right away. Get the word out to uniform, too: I want all his known haunts dug up, and while we're at it, every pub on the port. The Ship, Smugglers, the Anchor, the Campbell-town; anywhere I've missed, try there, too."

"Yes, sir." The pair moved towards the door.

"Sylvia, you're with me," said Valentine.

"Yes, sir." She gripped the strap of her bag and turned to follow the DI as he made his way to the top of the stairs. "Where are we going?"

At the first rung of steps, Valentine locked eyes with her. "Leanne Dunn's last known address. It's in Lochside."

DS McCormack tipped her head towards her shoulder and gripped the banister as the DI started to descend the stairs at speed. "Right behind you, sir."

The officers trailed the marked cars out of the station parking lot. A man with a dog made a sour look as he was flagged from the road, he leapt back to the pavement and the dog was jerked fast to his side by a tight leash.

The persistent rainfall of earlier had diminished, but the road was still wet, and waterlogged potholes became short-lived geysers as the cars' tires crossed them. Valentine spun the steering wheel awkwardly and gunned the engine to keep pace with the marked cars. The houses and flats they sped past sat shrunken beneath an oppressive grey sky. A few heads turned, mouthed some words, but soon moved back in step with their drudge trails towards the town's center. No one was heading to Lochside, it seemed, apart from the police officers; the grim council scheme was a place you went when all other options were no longer open to you.

Valentine glanced towards his passenger. DS McCormack's eyes flitted about the streets, eager for information. As they turned into the final road before Leanne Dunn's flat, an old man gave them a gummy smile then halted in the street and delivered them a V-sign salute.

"That'll be the welcoming party," said McCormack.

"We're as welcome as a dose of the clap around here." He turned sharply into the parking area outside the flats and a spray of water was evacuated from a deep declivity in the road. As he parked up and exited the car, Valentine felt the tips of his fingers pulsating after the rapid friction of his movements. He broke into a jog as the uniforms congregated outside the door to the flats.

"What the bloody hell are you waiting for?" he called out.

The uniforms exchanged blank glances among each other.

"Put the door in, for Christ's sake!"

An officer in a high-visibility stab-vest and protective helmet swung a small battering ram in front of him and charged the door. The rotten wood splintered and the weak lock retreated as if backed by explosives. The squad piled onto the stairs.

"Right, up to the next flight," said Valentine.

The sound of their boots on the stone steps sounded like an army maneuvering. A door opened and a head popped out, then quickly retreated. The action was mimicked several times as they approached the flat that had been occupied by Leanne Dunn.

"That one." Valentine brought the black mass of bodies to a halt outside the door. He moved to the front and battered with the heel of his hand. There was no reply. He made way for the officer with the battering ram once more.

"She's not in!" The words came from the flat next door. An old woman with a cardigan clutched tight to her chest stood in the lobby.

Valentine raised his hand to halt the uniform. "Wait." He approached the woman. "What's that you say?"

Her hair was as white as cotton wool, sitting in limp curls around her heavily lined face. The long fingers worrying the seams of her cardigan were attached to liver-spotted hands. Her voice came quieter the second time she spoke. "She's not there, hasn't been for days."

The detective approached the old woman. "This is Leanne Dunn we're talking about?"

She pinched her mouth. "I don't know what her name is."

Valentine removed the printout with the photograph from his pocket. "Is this her?"

She nodded. "Yes."

He looked back to the team and ordered them to go in. The sound of the wood splitting in the door caused the old woman to shrink further. The detective stepped forward and adjusted his vision to take her in again. "Can I ask, when did you last see her?"

"There was a man round asking me that yesterday. He was screaming like billy-o."

"A man?"

"He'd been round before."

The sound of the officers in the next flat came through the thin walls, and Valentine felt a pang of sympathy. Is this how we treated our elderly? A rathole flat with prostitutes turning tricks a few feet away. As his mind totted up the column of new facts, he knew at once who he was dealing with. "A tall man, quite stocky?"

"Yes, he'd be about thirty or thirty-five."

The DI left the old woman. "Thank you. I'll send an officer round to get your details."

As Valentine was entering Leanne Dunn's flat, he was distracted by movement in the corner of his eye. When he turned, he spotted someone on the steps, staring at him through the stanchions. She knew she had been recognized immediately and slunk back, running down the stairs.

"Hey!" Valentine ran to the top of the stairs and called again. "Stay where you are."

The thin girl in the tight blue dress froze on the spot. As the detective reached her, he took the last few steps slowly.

"Where do you think you're going, Angela?" he said.

The girl folded her arms, but seemed uncomfortable in the stance and unfolded them again quickly.

"I'm not saying nothing."

Valentine's chest was rising after chasing her. "You know the drill, Ange: you can say what I want to hear now, or you can say it down at the station."

"You'll get me killed, you will."

"Oh, really. Like Leanne, you mean?"

Angela screwed up her features. "What? I don't know what you're talking about."

"That right? Funny you should say something like that when I've just seen Leanne cold as stone out in the wilds of Mossblown."

Angela's mouth opened a little, but the corners stayed closed, stuck together by a heavy application of red lipstick. She stared at the detective for a few seconds then pressed her hand to the wall.

Valentine reached out to steady her. "Here, sit yourself down."

She folded her arms again. "I need a cigarette."

"Wait a minute." He called out to the squad in Leanne Dunn's flat. DS McCormack came running, one hand in her bag removing a packet of cigarettes. Valentine caught the box of Benson & Hedges as she threw them and then nodded for her to join him on the stairs.

"Here you go, love," he said.

Angela's long, thin fingers, the nails bitten to the quick, shook as she opened the packet and took out the pink plastic lighter inside. She drew out a cigarette and pressed it in her mouth."

"Had she been arguing with Danny?"

The girl looked up; her eyes didn't seem to be able to focus. Valentine knew she would be needing a fix within an hour; her shoulders started to shiver as she spoke. "No. Danny was with me."

"Angela, I never asked you if Danny was with you."

She flicked cigarette ash on the stairwell. "But he was, all day and night."

DS McCormack was moving her head from left to right as Valentine looked up from the stairs. He placed the sole of his shoe on the step Angela was sitting on and leaned forward. "Look, Angela, I want you to think very carefully about what you're saying."

She jerked her gaze towards him. "He was with me."

"Ange, I'm not buying that. It sounds too rehearsed to me."

"I'm not saying any more."

Valentine stepped away. He straightened his back and motioned for DS McCormack to follow him to the foot of the stairs.

"What do you make of that?" he said in a whisper.

"She's lying."

"No kidding. Do you think Gillon's put her up to it or is she acting on instinct?"

McCormack turned to look at the prostitute. "Hard to say."

"Get her down the station and let her sweat for a bit. She'll be scratching at the walls for a fix soon enough. We'll try her again then."

44

Valentine was loading Angela in the back of the car, his hand pressed on the crown of her head to guide her in, as his mobile started to ring. He closed the door but kept an eye on her; she looked so thin and frail that he wondered if the handcuffs might slip off her delicate wrists.

"Yes, Valentine," he said.

"Boss, we got him." It was DS McAlister.

The DI turned away from the car. DS McCormack was getting into the passenger seat; she halted with one foot on the tarmac.

"Tell me you're talking about Danny Gillon." He made a thumbs-up sign to McCormack.

"Picked him up at the Auld Forte. Had the van parked outside, which was a bit of a giveaway."

Valentine thought to allow himself a moment of elation, but it soon passed; the squad was still a long way from where they wanted to be. "Ally, what about the van?"

"What do you mean?"

The detective shook his head. "The mud, Ally, was the van covered in mud from the field in Mossblown?"

There was a pause on the line. "I can't see from here, boss. Do you want me to check it out?"

"It should have been the bloody first thing you checked." He reeled in his temper. "Look, just get back to the station and fill me in there, but if there's mud on that van I want samples and I want it soil-matched with the tire tracks at Mossblown."

McAlister's voice dropped. His initial enthusiasm seemed to have been drained away. "Yes, boss. I'll do that right away."

Valentine hung up. As he pocketed his cell phone, he caught DS McCormack's gaze. He turned away from her and opened up the back door, the one through which a few minutes ago he had maneuvered Angela. He raised his voice loud enough for everyone to hear: "Good news, Ange. We have Danny to keep you company down the station."

Her red mouth drooped. She seemed ready to allow words to pass her lips, but then she closed them tight and dropped her head towards her hands, which were cuffed in her lap.

"Nothing to say, Ange?" said Valentine. "Well, I'm sure Danny will have plenty to say, that's always been my experience of the man, wouldn't you agree? Likes to try and talk his way out of trouble, Big Gillon, doesn't he?"

Angela sucked in her cheeks. When she turned to face the DI, she looked ready to spit. "Leave me alone."

"Oh, come on, Angela, you know there's no chance of that. It's murder we're talking about now, not just streetwalking." He leaned back and slammed the car door shut. As he walked around the front of the vehicle, he kept his gaze firmly fixed on the prostitute.

Valentine got in the car and yanked on his seatbelt, then started the engine. He looked in the rear-view mirror as he spoke again. "You better have a think about what you're doing, Ange. If Danny Gillon's going down for murder and you're telling me lies, then you'll be going with him. Think about that, and while you're at it, spare a thought for your friend, Leanne, because if anyone needed looking out for, it was her."

He turned the wheel and pulled out of the parking lot. He could see Angela staring out the window towards the block of flats and the group of uniformed police officers gathering in the street below. He tried to interpret her expression, but her face was unreadable. The detective knew things could get messy, now: he was looking at hours wasted in interview rooms stringing together the stories of accomplished liars. It was a way of life to the likes of Gillon and Ange: their first instinct was to suppress the truth, even if it was in their own interest to reveal it. What he had in his favor, though, was the fact that they were both as likely as each other to sell out their own mother if it would save their skin.

Valentine followed a monochrome road beneath a blackening sky all the way back to the station. No words had passed between the occupants of the compact Vectra, and when he parked, it seemed almost an invasion of the enclosed space to open his mouth. He exited quickly and took two steps towards the back of the vehicle, where he motioned for Angela to get out. She slid herself along the back seat.

"Come with me, Angela." DS McCormack emerged from the car, beckoning the young woman towards the station.

DS McCormack separated the prostitute from the other detectives and uniforms who had Danny Gillon in handcuffs at the main desk. He seemed cocky as the officers booked him in. Valentine raised his hand and signaled to DS McAlister to separate from the group and join him by the stairs.

"Hello, boss." He smiled and tipped his head towards the crowd he had just left. "Nice result, eh?"

"We don't know that yet."

"Well, we got him anyway. That's a start."

"How's he been?" said Valentine.

McAlister inflated his cheeks and exhaled slowly before answering. "Honestly?"

"I wouldn't want a lie."

"Well, he's been playing the big innocent and being really shirty with it."

"What do you mean?"

"When we clocked him in the pub he didn't even move, never got off his stool. He thought we were there for someone else."

"He's acting it, Ally."

"I don't know, boss, he looked rattled when we took him out. Quite a contrast to how relaxed he looked when we spotted him. If he's putting on an act then he's bloody good at it."

Valentine shoved his hands in his pockets. "I'll be the judge of that when I get him in the interview room."

"You taking him down for questioning, sir?"

"In a minute. Let them get the pair of them sorted first."

DS McAlister turned back towards the others. "OK, I'll get on with it." As he went, he pointed a finger to the ceiling. "Oh, and his van was clean."

"How clean?"

"Spotless."

Valentine shook his head and headed for the stairs. "Yeah, straight-from-the-car-wash clean, I'll bet."

As he ascended the stairs, he met the chief super on the mid-landing. She seemed confident, almost jaunty. He didn't want to be the one to dispossess her of the notion, since it was the first time in living memory he could recall seeing her this way.

"Good work, Bob," she said. She was two steps past him and staring back up the stairs before she spoke again. "I really didn't think you had it in you."

He resisted a response, because he had more important matters on his mind.

In the incident room, Valentine rounded up the case notes and photographs he wanted for the interview with Danny Gillon, and then he made his way towards the interview room. Outside, a uniformed PC stood with DSs McAlister and Donnelly. The PC held out a packet of Club cigarettes and a box of Bluebell matches for the detective.

"Thanks," said Valentine. "You pair set?"

They nodded, and McAlister spoke. "I'll come in with you, sir."

"Right, then let's get on with it. Phil, you and Sylvia get what you can out of Angela."

"Yes, sir."

As Valentine turned the handle on the door, he saw Danny Gillon raise his head and let out a tut.

"I thought you were finished," said Gillon.

Valentine slapped the folder down on the table. "You thought wrong, son."

Gillon straightened his back and reclined in his chair, eyeing the cigarettes.

"So, what's all this about?" he said.

"What's it all about?" said Valentine. "Are you taking the piss, Danny?"

The stocky pimp rolled his gaze upwards. "I told this one here that I don't know what any of this is about."

"You might want to rethink that statement." Valentine opened the folder and removed a picture of James Urquhart's corpse. He let the bloody and scarred flesh sit before him for a moment and then he removed another picture of the corpse of Duncan Knox and, finally, the picture of the corpse of Leanne Dunn.

Danny Gillon stared at the pictures, he seemed to have lost some of his assurance. He opened and closed his mouth and then he pushed the pictures away.

"Not pretty, is it, Danny?" said Valentine.

Gillon was staring at the cigarettes. The detective picked up the pack and started to remove the cellophane wrapping. "Where were you last night, Danny?"

He looked away. "I was with Ange. You know that."

Valentine started to laugh; McAlister joined him on a lower volume.

"Yeah, you can laugh, but she'll back me up on that."

"Do you think I care if you have a junkie streetwalker standing alibi for you, Danny?" said Valentine. "This is a triple murder investigation, not a counter jump at the BP garage."

Gillon stood up and hit his palms off the table. "I don't know anything about that!"

The detective opened the box of cigarettes and slowly extended a single filter tip from the packet. "Calm yourself down, Danny," he said. "Here, have a cigarette."

Gillon snatched the packet and walked away from the table. When he had lit up, he returned to his seated position and placed the cigarette box on the edge of the table.

"Ange's word's as good as anyone's," said the pimp.

"How do you work that out?" said DS McAlister.

"It just is. I mean, it's her word against yours."

Valentine leaned forward. "She's a drug-addled prostitute and you are her pimp, who has form for beating the living daylights out of her. What court are you putting this proposal to, Danny?"

Gillon drew on the cigarette and the detective pushed the photographs back towards him. "Think about it, Danny, think very carefully about what you're saying to me. Look at those pictures: three lives have been taken and we have to account for them. Now, so far, I've got your face with a bull's eye on it pinned to my board and unless you convince me otherwise, "'m sticking a dart in you."

Gillon drew deeply on the cigarette. A grey trail of smoke escaped from the elongated ash tip. "I told you, I was with Ange."

Valentine reached out for the photographs, collected them up and shuffled them into position in the folder. As he closed the blue folder completely, he pushed out the back of his chair and rose. He didn't look at Danny Gillon again. He turned to DS McAlister.

"Can you believe this idiot?" he said.

"You just can't help some people."

"He thinks he's bulletproof, but he's more like the Yorkshire Ripper using Rose West as an alibi."

McAlister laughed out. "He's going down for the lot, boss."

"Oh, I think so, Ally."

The officers headed to the door and Valentine knocked twice. The PC opened up.

"Let us out, we're done with him."

45

DI Bob Valentine stood outside the interview room and pressed his back to the wall. His shirt provided little insulation from the cold plaster and a shiver seemed to pass straight into his shoulder blades and down the thin sweat-line below. He widened the spread of his feet to add strength to his stance, but the detective didn't feel in the least way steady or confident. He'd thought he had something on Danny Gillon, but now he wasn't so sure. Gillon didn't have the intelligence to bluff and yet he was defensive in his answers. There was no reason for him to keep what he knew to himself in the circumstances, unless it was because he was afraid of greater consequences or was protecting someone. Neither of those two options made any sense to Valentine; there was no greater consequence than life imprisonment for three murders, unless you counted death itself. And Danny Gillon didn't regard anyone, save himself, as worth protecting; he wouldn't put his own neck on the block for anyone.

The DI paced the hallway between the interview rooms. There was a stopwatch on him now, he knew that. The latest murder in Mossblown would be latched onto by the press sooner or later, but if they got to it before tonight's news bulletins then he would face the likelihood of a full-scale press scrum in the morning. Dino had been on a high since they'd pulled in Gillon, but that would become a crushing low if it yielded the wrong outcome.

"Time to give Ange a rattle," said the detective. He headed towards the interview room where DS Donnelly and DS McCormack had taken Angela. As he walked, he flicked through the blue folder, trying to locate the one image that would deliver the most impact.

He thrust down the handle and the door screeched loudly as DI Valentine entered the room. He took firm strides towards the table where the interview was underway.

"Right, I am not pissing about with you anymore," said Valentine. The heavy bass of his voice rattled round the room. "Tell me how this happened now or I'm putting both you and Gillon away." He slapped down the image of the bloodless face of Leanne Dunn.

Angela turned away; her hands shot up to her face and she began to sob.

"Don't start with the bubbling, love," said Valentine. He picked up the picture again and stuck it in front of her face. "Do you see anyone crying for that girl?"

"Get it away." She got out of her chair and took two stumbling steps towards the shuttered window frame. Her arms went out to steady herself when she reached the ledge.

Valentine followed her. "This is Leanne. You remember her, don't you? Leanne Dunn."

Angela sobbed harder. "Yes."

"Then tell me where Danny Gillon's been and what he's been up to."

She looked up through her reddened eyes. "I don't know."

"Say again."

She straightened her arms in front of her. "I don't know. All right? I don't know where he's been."

"So, you were bullshitting us?"

"Yes."

"Once more, loud enough for us all to hear."

"Yes. I made it up. I wasn't with Danny."

Valentine turned away from her. As he paced towards the table, he slapped the photograph of the corpse of Leanne Dunn back on top of the folder and paused before the officers. "Get her cleaned up and get some coffee into her."

"Yes, sir."

"Then get out on that street and start rattling cages, all Gillon's known haunts. If he's been seen in the last few days, I want the where and when in writing and I don't care if you have to smash teeth or heads to get it."

Valentine left the room, closed the door firmly and returned to the hallway, where DS McAlister was waiting. The DS had his hands in his pockets and quickly removed them as he spotted the detective; he looked like he was getting ready to break into a run.

"Everything OK, sir?"

He pointed to the room where Danny Gillon was. "Follow me."

Valentine's footsteps sounded loudly on the floor as he entered the room. He closed the short distance between the door and the table where Gillon was seated – Valentine snatched the burning cigarette from Gillon and threw it at the wall.

"Right, Danny, seems like Ange has had a change of heart. You've lost your alibi."

He sniffed. "So?"

"Not good enough for you?" He turned to McAlister and held out his hand for the blue folder. "OK, we've got more. Greta Milne, Angela's neighbor, has ID'd you as the bloke knocking ten bells out of her door the other night." He slapped down the folder. "Speak to me, Danny. Now."

Gillon looked at the wall, and his eyes latched onto the point where the cigarette burned on the floor. For a moment, Gillon's mask of assurance slipped and he looked alone, without a friend in the world. An almost imperceptible tic started in his left temple and then he wiped at his mouth with the back of his hand.

"I want a lawyer," he rasped.

Valentine shook his head. "You give me what I want."

Gillon looked up, a grey tongue flashed on his parched lips. He shrugged. "What's that?"

"Everything, Danny. From start to finish."

The pimp turned away again; his shoulders drooped now. He seemed to be physically shrinking before Valentine's eyes.

"I want to know, if I tell you, that none of this comes back on me."

"Danny, I'm not trading favors here. You start speaking or I walk out that door. It's your choice."

Gillon took a deep breath and looked at the table. As he started to speak, he sounded like he was reading from a prepared manuscript detailing his confused thoughts.

"See your murders, the guy from the bank and the other one."

"Knox?"

He nodded. "Yeah, well, Leanne knew them."

"What do you mean knew them?"

Gillon fidgeted on the chair. "I want to know I'll be looked after if I talk."

"No deals, Danny."

He slumped closer to the table. "She knew them from way back: the Knox one from when she was in that home place."

"She knew him as a child?"

He nodded. "She might have known them both, then." He looked uncomfortable, as if detailing secrets that the dead would have preferred to take with them. "They used to come around, like years back, when Leanne was, you know."

"When she was working as one of your prostitutes?"

He crossed his legs and started to finger the hole in the knee of his jeans. "Well, not really. She was only young."

Valentine moved away from the table and retrieved the chair. "Let me get this straight, Danny: you procured an underage Leanne Dunn for Duncan Knox and James Urquhart?"

"No, it wasn't like that. She wasn't working properly then. Just them, she knew them both from before."

Valentine's palms started to sweat. "So, your involvement was what? Estate agent? Hotelier? This went on in your property, I take it?"

He grimaced. "She went to work there in the end, yeah."

The DI watched as Gillon avoided all eye contact. He was trash, worse than that. Valentine wanted to raise him from the chair and clamp his hands around his neck. He spoke about a young girl's life being ended before it had begun as if it were just another transaction. He cared more about his shabby van or being kept in cigarettes than he did Leanne.

"Was Leanne the only girl you got them?" said Valentine.

"I didn't get a girl for them. Look, it wasn't like that – I don't deal with beasts."

"Was there another girl, Danny?" The anger in his voice was unmistakable.

"No way. Never."

Valentine let the pimp's blood cool. He looked agitated, pensive as the DI spoke again. "Who killed Urquhart and Knox?"

"I don't know who did that. How could I know that?"

"You don't know?"

"Of course I don't."

"But you seem to know a great deal, Danny. Why am I only finding this out now?"

"What do you mean?"

Valentine leaned forward and flattened his palms in front of him. "I mean you've known about these pedos for years and never told a soul. Were they paying you hush money?"

"No. I kicked them out. I didn't want any part of it, but they kept coming round to see Leanne behind my back. I told her it wasn't bloody on, but they had some hold over her."

"What hold?"

"I don't know, just a hold — she said they were her keepers." Gillon seemed tired, his voice trailing now. He had the look of a man who felt repulsed by the discovery of his involvement with people he had nothing but contempt for.

"Why didn't Leanne come to the police?"

He snatched an answer. "I don't know."

"I don't believe you."

Gillon looked up from his misery. "She wanted to. I – I ... "

"What? You stopped her?"

He nodded.

"Why would you do that?"

Gillon shrugged, his foot started an uncontrollable tapping on the floor.

"Oh, come on, Danny, you must have had a reason, there must have been something in it for you."

He stayed silent. Valentine understood how the criminal mind worked. He had spent years of his life dealing with people like Danny Gillon and knew he could second-guess them. There was no need to coax out a motive or search their psyche for reasons why or how — it was all about opportunity — if it existed, they would take it.

"I'm going to ask you again, Danny, because I can tell you want it off your chest. Why didn't you let Leanne come to the police when Urquhart and Knox were killed?"

"I don't know."

"But now you know that was a mistake."

He shrugged again. "I suppose."

"No suppose about it, Danny. If Leanne Dunn had told us what she knew about those murders, you wouldn't be sitting here. And Leanne might not be in the mortuary."

He looked up. "I wanted money for her."

"Who from?"

"I thought, the papers."

Valentine's palms tingled as he got up from his chair and approached Gillon. "You went to the papers: who?"

"Just some guy."

"Who?" Valentine's voice rose again.

"Just a hack. He said he would pay. He spoke to Leanne a few times, I thought he would pay up."

"A name, give me his name."

"His name was Sinclair."

The detective noted the name but felt a strange urge to object. When it came, his voice didn't sound like his own: "Cameron Sinclair? From the Glasgow-Sun?"

Gillon chamfered the table's edge with his fingernail. "That's him, yeah."

"You spoke to him about Leanne?"

"Well, yeah. But she spoke to him, too."

The DI couldn't take in what he was hearing. His thoughts were working in reverse, moving backwards to the press conference where he'd seen Sinclair, and the post he'd left on his daughter's Facebook timeline, then through to the bribery affair that had led to DS Rossi's suspension.

"When did you last see him?

"I don't know. Few days ago. I spoke to him on the phone. I told him Leanne had done a runner."

"He knows she went missing?"

"Yeah, I just said that." He leaned onto the edge of his seat. "I didn't know she was dead."

The DI struggled to rein in his thoughts. Nothing seemed to make sense. He headed for the door.

Gillon's voice rose. "Hey, where are you going?"

Valentine banged on the door with the side of his hand, and as it opened, he turned to Gillon and pointed. "Don't worry, I've not finished with you, not by a bloody mile."

The DI pushed the door. The feeling of getting close to a killer that had gripped Valentine when he'd first approached Gillon had gone now; he felt like he'd been dunking for apples in an empty barrel.

DS McAlister appeared in the corridor, fanning a lapel nervously as he spoke. "Well, boss, what do you make of that?"

"There's nothing to bloody make of it, Ally."

The sharpness of the DI's words hung between them. "Do we bring in Sinclair?"

Valentine nodded. "Of course we do. Now, Ally."

The DS turned and broke into a jog. "Yes, sir."

"And, Ally, Get onto his paper. I want to know what kind of copy he's been filing lately. And if the editor's thinking of running anything like Leanne Dunn's last interview, then read him the bloody riot act — he'll be grateful he got it from you and not me."

46

The skies outside King Street station were already darkening as Valentine stood at the window, stroking a deep ache inside his ribcage. He watched an old man navigate the road as the wind picked up, blowing a stray newspaper that attached itself to his leg. Another man, younger, made to wrestle the paper from him. The scene was almost comical, had the quality of slapstick, but the detective felt too raw to be amused.

DI Bob Valentine knew his options were rapidly running out. He couldn't count on Danny Gillon to reveal any more information, and what he had revealed was limited. If Gillon was to be believed then Leanne had been abused in care when she was still a child, and the timing was close to the disappearance of Janie Cooper. There would be another case now: a cold investigation of the children's home and the broad sweep of Urquhart and Knox's associations. The detective's main target had to be the murder investigations that were in hand; the rest would have to wait.

He turned from the window and walked back towards the main incident room. DS McAlister crossed the floor towards the board.

"What's that you're sticking up, Ally?" said Valentine.

McAlister turned around to face him. A dull glaze settling on his eyes. "The Sinclair stuff, sir."

"Give me that." He snatched the papers from his hand. "We'll keep that to ourselves, for now."

"But — "

Valentine cut him down. "No buts about it, Ally, if Dino gets wind of Gillon's ramblings then she'll be on us like a dog eating chips."

McAlister agreed. "I called the paper and spoke to the editor."

"What did Jack have to say for himself?"

"He hasn't heard from Sinclair since his suspension over the bribery allegations."

"Did you believe him?"

"Well, I'd no reason not to. He didn't go as far as calling Sinclair a square peg, but I got the impression he was a bit surprised that I seemed so interested in him."

"Just because he's a public schoolboy doesn't make him as pure as the driven snow, Ally."

"I know. Anyway, Phil and Sylvia checked out his flat and he's not there. They're going to check a few hacks' bars on their way back."

"He's not there?"

"Yeah, he gave a forwarding address of a guest house in Queen's Terrace, but he was only there for the one night."

Valentine raised himself onto the edge of the nearest desk and listened to the hammering inside his head. "Right, get onto all your snitches, even the ones you haven't seen for a while, and find him. Bloody Ayr's not gotten that big and he isn't the invisible man."

"Yes, boss." McAlister stood splay-legged for a moment. "What's going on, sir?"

Valentine threw up his hands. "At this stage, Ally, who knows?"

"Do you see Sinclair in the frame?"

"What's his motive?"

McAlister shrugged. "Well, it's a cracking story, whichever way you look at it."

"That's taking manufacturing the news a bit far."

"Maybe he had some connection to Urquhart and Knox that we've not seen. We've not been looking at Sinclair."

"So, he's an unknown factor to us. So are you, Ally, we haven't looked into your background on this one: does that make you a suspect?"

"Get real, sir."

Valentine smirked. "Who's to say you're not on the right lines, Ally? The truth of the matter is, right now, we don't know. There are too many variables. Has Sinclair been up to something? Yes, I've no doubt. And has Gillon been up to something, too? Yes, I've no doubt about that."

"So where do we go from here?"

"Where can we go? We can't magic up extra variables to the mix, we have to wait and see."

"Dino will love that. She went out that door tonight expecting us to have it wrapped up by the morning."

Valentine shook his head: the mere mention of the chief super's name struck an exposed nerve. "She's bloody deluded."

"You know she's going to drop the bomb tomorrow morning."

"Not if we don't give her the chance."

"Meaning?"

The DI raised himself from the desk and headed for the other end of the room. "There's more than one way to skin a cat. Get onto those touts now, and don't expect to get home tonight!"

DS McAlister collected his jacket from the back of his chair and headed for the door as Valentine stepped into his office.

The blue folder containing the details from the Janie Cooper case was still sitting on his desk. He turned over the cover and saw the picture of the little girl staring back at him. The image of the doll was there, too, sticking out from beneath a sheaf of notes. She had been swinging the doll and smiling at him when he passed out at the Coopers' home. Since that day he had tried to push the image from his mind.

As Valentine allowed his gaze to take in the full extent of the incident room, he spotted DS Donnelly and DS McCormack walking through the door. He tapped on the windowpane to beckon them in. As he checked the clock on the far side of the room, he knew the evening news headlines were just about to start. He was leaning over to switch on the television as the officers came in.

"Hello, sir," said DS Donnelly.

"Well, what did you turn up?" said Valentine.

Donnelly sighed and motioned to DS McCormack.

"Not good, sir," she said.

"What do you mean?"

"We did the usual points of interest. Nothing. No one's seen hide nor hair of Sinclair for days."

"Have you rung the B&Bs, checked the hotel bookings?"

"Yes, boss, we tried that," said Donnelly. "What are the odds on him booking himself under his own name? He's not stupid."

DS McCormack spoke up. "And he obviously doesn't want to be found. Apparently, he was a regular in the Phoenix – there every night — but two days ago he vanished without trace."

Valentine flagged the officers down. "Right, shush. I want to hear this."

As the news headlines played on the small portable screen, he reached down to turn up the volume. The familiar face of the early evening news anchor read out an abridged snapshot of the day's events: a fatal road accident on the A9 was followed by a Royal visit to Deeside and a factory closure in Broxburn. There was no mention anywhere of the west coast of Scotland; for once, Ayrshire was gratefully ignored.

"Well, that's something," said McCormack. "Gives us some breathing space."

Valentine flicked off the television. "Maybe twelve hours, if we're lucky."

The officers looked at each other with heavy eyes.

"So, what now, boss?" said Donnelly.

Valentine's answer was short. "Nothing."

"Come again?"

"Unless you're hiding something that's going to spark my interest, Phil, then nothing. You might as well both go home."

They glanced at each other again.

McCormack pitched up her voice. "Well, we can keep searching the town for Sinclair."

"And what makes you think you'll do any better than uniform? It's like Phil said: he's smart and doesn't want to be found."

"So we just give up?" said Donnelly, his voice following the same peaks as McCormack's.

Valentine shook his head. "I didn't say that. I said you both go home and get some rest, it's been a long day. If anything changes, I'll let you know. I'd sooner have you both fresh for tomorrow."

Donnelly inflated his cheeks and exhaled slowly. He turned for the door and waved farewell to the others. When he had left, DS McCormack lowered her voice to a near whisper. "Is everything OK, sir?"

Valentine turned back to the television screen and pressed the on switch. "Perfectly, Sylvia. Go home." He turned to wave her out of his office. "You heard me, give me some peace to catch the headlines on the other channel."

The detective reclined in his chair. He stared through the blinds towards the bottom of the incident room and watched Donnelly and McCormack put on their coats and make their way through the door. As he returned to the television screen, he lunged forward and flicked the channel to the other side. He felt sure that both stations ran with much the same output, but wanted to check. He sat through twenty minutes of trivia masquerading as news-entertainment, a schedule of football fixtures aimed at the recently lobotomized and a weather report by a glamour model in a cocktail dress. When he was sure Ayrshire was not making the headlines on any of the main stations, he switched off the television set and closed his eyes, before lowering his head onto the desk and giving in to his exhaustion.

DS McAlister was arriving back in the empty office when Valentine next looked up. The large incident room was empty, with only the hum of strip lights and the occasional gurgle from the coffee machine attempting to suggest otherwise. McAlister didn't seem to notice the detective until he called out on his way to greet him.

"Any luck, son?" said Valentine.

McAlister stood silently as he shook his head.

"Not a thing. I don't know what to say, boss."

"You don't need to say anything."

Valentine pulled out a chair and directed McAlister to sit down. He reached out for another chair and dragged it by its castors towards him, then sat with his chest leaning on the chair's high back.

"Look, Ally, I know you want this bastard as much as I do. I can see it: that's why I bumped you up to DS when Paulo lost the plot."

"You're not wrong, boss."

"But I don't want you to think you owe me for that. You deserved the promotion and it was coming your way sooner or later."

McAlister looked perplexed, shrugging and showing his palms. "OK."

"You see, I'm going to ask you to do something, but you don't have to say yes."

"Do something. What?"

"Now, remember you're under no obligation. You can say no and I won't hold it against you."

"I understand what you're saying, boss."

Valentine decided he might be more comfortable standing. "You've got your whole career in front of you, son, and you have to think about that, but if you're game, and you trust me, I think we can close this case tonight."

McAlister pressed the palms of his hands firmly into his trouser pockets. "Well, I'm in. Just tell me what you want me to do."

The detective reached a hand out and placed it on DS McAlister's shoulder. "Good, lad."

47

DI Bob Valentine knew things weren't quite as they should be at home. He had taken on the case and returned to active duty without even consulting his wife, and she had every right to object. When he thought about Clare receiving the call to say her husband might not make it through the night, his reserves of strength left him. She was fragile, she always had been. She would always be highly strung or one of those types people spoke of as suffering with their nerves.

Valentine raised the telephone receiver and dialed home.

The ringing on the line filled him with the same dread it always did now. There were simply no words to reveal to Clare that the job had won again, that he was not coming home as planned. She would be angry, at best; offhand with him at worst. Did it matter which? Sometimes the short burst of belligerent temper was preferable to the stony silence that left him wondering just where and when the blow would come.

"Hello," he said. The line stayed silent.

It wasn't his wife who had answered. "Oh, hello, Bobby."

"Hello, Dad, where's Clare?"

He heard the old man negotiating the windowsill where the phone sat, unravelling the wires and taking a seat. The puffed cushions sighed at his back. "She's, erm, taken a bit of a lie-down, son."

Something didn't sit right with him. "What did you say, a lie-down?"

His father's tone changed. "It's just me and Mr. McIlvanney here now. Not a bad book, Strange Loyalties."

It was one of those perfectly honed skills of the experienced police officer to be able to detect lies, white or otherwise. "You wouldn't be changing the subject on me, Dad?"

He sighed, exasperated or too aware of the futility of his stance. "Clare, as you know, has her little moments."

"What's happened?"

"Look, nothing's happened, she's fine." His voice slowed into a reassuring drawl. "You know how she gets: well, she had one of those days, but we had a little chat and now she's fine."

Valentine read the gaps in his speech more than he did the actual words. He knew his wife, but he also knew his father"' way was to adopt a less-said-soonest-mended philosophy. But something had happened, he knew that much, and it worried him.

"All right, Dad, if you say so." He paused briefly. "If you see her, tell her I'm thinking of her and I'll be home as soon as I can be. She's not to worry."

"Yes, son, I'll do that," he said. "Goodbye now."

Valentine lowered the receiver into its cradle and stood staring at his desk for a few seconds; he wasn't quite sure he had handled the situation effectively, but he knew there were few other options available. He would see Clare later and explain things. If he could make her see what he had been through, maybe she would understand.

DS McAlister paused outside the door and gently tapped his knuckles off the glass. "Is now a good time, sir?"

"Yes, come in. Sorry, Ally, I had a personal call to make." He let his previous lines of thought scatter.

"It's all right, I understand." McAlister took a step inside and closed the door behind him.

"So, about this grand plan of mine." Valentine raised the blue folder from his desk and turned it towards the DS. It sat between them, commanding the room like a model army. "Take a look at that."

McAlister leaned forward. "A tire cast."

"From Mossblown."

The officer looked at the pictures and read the accompanying notes. "Lab boys say it's not from Gillon's van."

"That's right." The DI paused. "Which means it's from another vehicle."

McAlister lowered the file. "Which means he's not working alone."

"Exactly." Valentine leaned his back against the window, and the Venetian blinds crumpled. "Danny Gillon isn't going to win Mastermind any time soon, but he's not a complete idiot, either. He knows about self-preservation and he knows when to keep his trap shut."

"I think I see where you're going with this, sir."

"Do you?" He eased forward. "I mean, Ally, do you really? I wasn't joking when I said I was asking you to put your job on the line."

The DS remained silent. He pressed a crease into the corner of his mouth: it was a glimpse into a mind that had ran the list of consequences and couldn't care less what they brought. It was the outcome alone that concerned him.

Valentine nodded when he saw Ally was onside. "OK then, if you're game, here's what I'm proposing. We give Gillon his freedom tonight — let's see where he leads us."

"Oh, Christ." He nervously pinched the tip of his nose. "I mean, yeah. Let's do it."

"Are you sure, Ally?" He took another step forward, fixed him with a flat, expressionless look. "You won't get a chance to change your mind."

"Sir, the way I see it, if we don't, then in the morning we've lost the case, and if Sinclair's still in town, this is our last chance."

Valentine held out his arms, then brought his palms together in an ear-splitting clap. There was no going back now. "OK, then. We let the bastard out for a few hours."

McAlister smiled, cautiously at first, but widening with a growing confidence he still seemed uncertain of. "Yeah, but he's not to know that."

As the DI walked towards the door, he snatched his coat from the back of his chair. In the main incident room, his strides were purposeful but his stomach churned with the uncertainty of the action he was taking. If he was to make this gamble pay off, however, he knew he had to convince himself otherwise. There was no room for the distraction of doubt. It was all or nothing, because if he looked at what was on the line, it was already over.

On the stairs down to the cells, Valentine turned to catch sight of DS McAlister: his face was ashen and immobile, making him look younger than his years. The image struck the detective like a body blow; he knew there was more at stake than his own washed-up career, and the heavy responsibility unsettled him. He knew he needed to push all his cares and concerns away; however, the idea of gambling on such a grand scale without the nerve to back it up was lunacy.

Outside the cells he looked at the desk and summoned the custody sergeant. It was Alec Laird on duty, his deep tan and lightened hair proclaiming his recent visit to warmer climes. He eyed the two officers and tipped his head in a knowing nod. Valentine hoped the holiday high hadn't worn off yet.

"Hello, Bob," said the sergeant.

"Alec." He picked up the duty log and ran a finger down the column of names and cells. "Right, number four can breathe easy."

Sergeant Laird recovered the logbook and presented Valentine with a narrow, searching stare. "That's Big Danny Gillon. Thought he was in some hot water?"

The detective shook his head and snatched a pen from the desk without returning the look. "Gillon's always in hot water. Not bloody hot enough this time, mind you." He scratched his signature in the book.

"Danny's always been a daft boy." The sergeant looked down at the logbook for what seemed like an eternity. If he chose to be difficult, thought Valentine, then everything would be ruined — the plan would go no further. He jerked back his head as the sergeant took the logbook and hung it on its brass hook. "Danny's problem is that he likes to run with the big dogs — but he's just a bloody chihuahua."

McAlister and Valentine emitted the usual drone of enforced laughter that was the accustomed response to such a remark and turned for the door. The DI spoke: "He's got a van in as well, give it back to him. We won't be needing it now the trail's run cold."

The sergeant nodded and raised a hand, still smiling at the plaudits to his humor. "No bother. Goodnight, lads."

On the way out to the parking lot, Valentine's knees were loosening, but he tried to keep his wilting resolve from McAlister. He knew he needed to convince him that their mission was at least partway capable of success.

"Alec seemed to buy that well enough," said McAlister.

"Why shouldn't he?"

The blunt rebuttal buoyed the DS. "No reason, I suppose."

On the way to the car, Valentine extended the keys and the indicator lights flashed at the vehicle's corners. It felt like a flag waving, a beacon: they were really doing this. When they got inside, the detective rolled down his window and craned his neck. The air was cold and still.

"I can see Gillon's van from here," he said.

"Where do you think he'll lead us?"

Valentine turned towards McAlister; the assuredness of his voice surprised him. "Well, I'll be bloody disappointed if it's back to the Auld Forte bar."

"You and me both, sir."

The night air defeated him and he turned up the window again, but kept a few inches of it open in the hope that some of the car's tension would escape. He had no reason to believe that things would go their way, but tried to tell himself that the bigger the risk, the bigger the reward.

"No matter what happens tonight, Ally, don't let Gillon out your sight."

"Christ above, I don't even want to think about losing him, sir."

"And I don't want you to, either. But if things go tits-up for whatever reason, stick with him."

"Yes, sir."

As they readied themselves for the night's eventualities, they seemed to come crashing down upon them like a violent hailstorm. There was no room for preparation now. The station doors swung open and a thickset figure in a faded denim jacket emerged into the darkness. He stood for a moment lighting a cigarette and then he loped down the steps, followed by a plume of white smoke. Danny Gillon looked over his shoulder as he walked towards his van, then spun the keys around his finger and started to jog. He looked cocky, confident.

"Seems keen," said McAlister.

"Let's hope so, let's hope he's bloody keen and bloody worked up."

As Gillon started the van and moved onto the road, he indicated a right turn on the roundabout ahead. Valentine pulled out behind with a sense of dread building in him. The white van followed the pothole-pitted road round to the traffic lights and took a left onto the one-way system of the Sandgate. As the van proceeded through the next set of lights and chuntered uphill towards Wellington Square, the route seemed to indicate the next move would be in the direction of the plush mansions of Race-course Road.

"Where the hell is he going?" said McAlister.

"Well, it's not to any kip-house or B&B. Unless it's a very nice one."

"He's heading out to Alloway."

Valentine grabbed a glance at McAlister as the van crossed a box junction and proceeded past the desolate playing fields. The road widened, presenting snatches of shoreline and blue sea. From time to time the cloud-wreathed Isle of Arran came into view, as wide driveways blinked between Victorian villas. By the time the white van had passed the entrance to Belleisle golf club, it was clear Gillon was either leaving town or heading to an address the officers had visited themselves only a short time ago.

"This is very odd," said Valentine.

"I didn't expect this at all."

"Well, why would you? There's nothing to suggest Danny Gillon's had any contact with the Urquharts. But here he is." His fingers rose from the wheel and pointed, palm up, towards the unfolding scene. "Pulling into their drive."

Valentine brought the car to a standstill behind a drystone wall and watched as the van rolled to a halt, spluttering black smoke onto the driveway. Gillon stalled momentarily, seemed to be gathering wit or wile. He exited the vehicle quickly, slamming the door behind him, and pro-ceeded to the front of the property, where he started banging on a window.

The two officers followed his action from the car.

"He doesn't look too happy," said Valentine.

"Well, you wanted him worked up." Ally twisted in his seat. "Should we get out?"

"No, we'll wait and see."

As the door to the property opened, Gillon gesticulated wildly, waved his arms and banged a fist off the window ledge. The sound of raised voices, both men's, was heard by the officers, but from where they sat it was impossible to see who the other voice belonged to. As the men went inside a second door slammed, but the loud yells were still detectable in the street beyond. For a second, Valentine allowed himself to feel he had done the right thing by releasing Gillon, that he might actually get somewhere with the investigation, and then some long-lost philosopher's lines about hope prolonging the torments of man came back to him.

"Should we go in, boss?" said McAlister.

"Not yet."

The raised voices could still be heard from the road. The DS stepped out of the car and made his way towards the edge of the garden. As he leaned onto the wall, Valentine left the car and joined him in the cold, dark street.

"It sounds pretty nasty in there, boss."

"You're right." He looked down the broad, rain-washed street. It was empty. He knew they had brought a disturbance to the neighborhood, but not a curtain twitched.

The row of trees lining the driveway started to sway in the wind and the large, old house etched its bulk against the moonless sky. The shouting stopped as abruptly as it had begun. Valentine felt the night air enclosing them as he watched McAlister brace himself against the wall. As the detective focused on the property it ceased to be a home and became a keeper of secrets. In the dim light, the souls of the past were stirring.

"I'm going in," said Valentine.

"Right, I'm coming with you."

"No, you stay here." He knew at once how ridiculous such a bold statement sounded from a man in his condition.

"You've got to be kidding. Do the sums, that's two against one."

Valentine put his hand on McAlister's arm and turned him away. "Think about it: if they drop us both, who's going to raise the alarm?"

The sharp sound of a door slamming came from the house. "Someone's coming."

Valentine peered over the wall, he wasn't prepared to see Danny Gillon striding back towards his van. He moved quickly, had the engine in motion and the wheels churning up the drive before he closed the door.

"Someone's in a hurry," said McAlister.

"He's not the only one." As Gillon maneuvered the van through a rough three-point turn in the driveway, Valentine pressed his car keys into McAlister's hand. "Right, follow him, and whatever you do, don't bloody well lose him."

The DS looked unconvinced by the sudden decision, like he was searching for the right words to object. "But ... "

"No buts, Ally." The van screeched past them and into the road. Valentine pointed the DS towards the car. "Get going before you lose him!"

McAlister turned for the car, he was no sooner inside than he had accelerated wildly in the direction of Danny Gillon's van. The back wheels lost some traction on the smooth, wet road and the car fishtailed for a few yards before righting itself.

As Valentine stood in the street, peering over the wall towards the large and uninviting house, his heart stiffened and the blood grew heavy in his veins. A dull ache set itself up in his chest and spread in numbing rings throughout his body. It was instinctual — he had not been in a confrontation since taking a knife in the heart. Images of his wife and children came flooding in. As he took his first step towards the Urquhart's home, Valentine's heart pounded so hard in his chest that he felt sure a cardiac arrest was coming.

48

DI Bob Valentine buttoned his coat to ward off the rain and leaned toward the approaching gable. When he had driven up to the building before, he hadn't taken the time to be awed by its stature. The place seemed to belong to another time, surely by this point it should have been subdivided into half a dozen flats or adopted as the headquarters of a government quango.

Valentine passed the first window and glared in: everything was as it should be. The flickering colored shadows from the television screen leant a familiarity to the setting. He didn't know what he had expected to see. Human sacrifice? Pentagons drawn in blood on the walls? Whatever it was that waited for him inside, he knew it contained an answer. That's what he was there for, that's what he had risked his career for and was prepared to risk his life for now.

Valentine's cold breath appeared in white bursts as he neared the front door of the mansion house. He could feel the icy fingers of the night on his chest and in his lungs. The rain had fooled him again, his shoulders were soaking, his hair stuck hard to his brow. At the foot of the steps he saw the door was open, only a few inches, but enough of an invitation for him. As he touched the door, he expected noise, but nothing came. He felt almost welcome, like he was walking with destiny. He stepped in and the squelch of his wet shoes on the hardwood flooring compensated his eardrums for their earlier disappointment. The sound rang out in the still emptiness. There was no sign of anyone. The staircase leading skyward was fully lit, as was the lobby entrance leading towards the living room. The detective stood still, picked up the minute burr of his breathing, but nothing else. He was certain no one had left through the front door, they would have to pass him on the driveway, so whoever had been arguing with Gillon must still be there.

There was a third hallway to the rear that he had seen on previous visits but never explored before. Where did it lead? Valentine gave in to his curiosity, the unknown was now his favored option. A trail of watery footsteps went with him as he approached the dark corridor. His mouth was dry as he reached out for the door handle and slowly, almost wearily, opened up.

The room sat in silence, almost a tableau of an old-fashioned study. There was a desk, a leather-backed chair on castors and a brass reading lamp burning away. It was James Urquhart's, no doubt, and the sight of the large and detailed model railway encompassing three-quarters of the floor space confirmed it. There were no trains in motion, but he saw them there, in the station where tiny people huddled behind newspapers and children rushed about the concourse. The sight of the miniature railway gripped the detective; like a strange message from childhood, it seemed to call out to him to take a closer look, to come and play. How many others had felt the same compulsion? He resisted. His attention had already turned towards the open hatch bleeding light from the floor.

There was a door from the hatch pressed up against the wall, and as he approached, he could see there was a bright light burning in a room below, a wooden staircase leading all the way down. It looked like a cellar, or a basement perhaps, but why was it necessary to keep it out of sight? The rolled-up carpet that came out from the wall had been tugged and torn and now sat in a crumpled mass beside a hessian-backed rug. Valentine's chest tightened as he stared into the secret world below. As he paused, he sensed a presence; he made to turn, but a heavy blow struck the back of his head.

Falling was a strange experience: the sudden loss of vision, the blurring of the familiar into the unfamiliar, and the way time seemed to slow down. Valentine stretched out his arms to break his fall on the stone floor. A loud crack, followed by shooting pain in his wrist, alerted him to a broken bone. The pain arrived at once, in a sharp, agonizing burst that repeated itself over and over, extending further along the arm and into his shoulder.

Valentine lay flat on the stone floor. After his arm, his nose and mouth had taken the brunt of the fall, and blood rushed from both. He spat it out: a mouthful at first, and then more drooled onto the dusty floor. There was a strange smell in the basement: not damp alone, something else, like burning kerosene. He tried to raise his spinning head, to regain his blunted senses. The next to return was his hearing, warning of the sound of footsteps. He was jerked backwards by a hand on his shoulder and spun round to face a pair of wild eyes.

"You've broken my arm." The remark was instinctual. When he heard it, he thought it might elicit a laugh, such was its absurdity at this point. When his vision drew the dark shape in front of him into focus, he could see laughter was not going to be an option.

Adrian Urquhart was holding a knife in his hand. It looked like a dagger or a bayonet as he leaned forward and placed its tip on Valentine's shirtfront. "Why are you here?" he said.

The detective's eyes flitted between the blade and Adrian's hardened, immobile features. He saw there was no reasoning with him: he was a maniac in the making.

"Think about what you're doing, Adrian." Each of the detective's words fell between short bursts of pain.

Adrian removed the knife and stepped back. His dark gaze was too far away to read. "Get on your feet, Valentine."

The detective eased himself against the wall and slowly got to his feet. When he managed to stand, he took in the full extent of his sur-roundings for the first time. Adrian watched him, tapping the dagger off his leg like it was a stick he itched to throw for an impatient dog. He was anxious, but not in any normal way; his anxiety was a burden. He'd carried this weight for so long that it had become part of him — the option to release it was irresistible now.

"You want to know what this place is, don't you?" he said.

He raised up the blade and pointed it at Valentine's chest once more. His mouth split into a nervous grin as he spoke. "It's your final resting place."

Valentine's gaze flitted about the room once more. In desperation he sought an escape, but his attention fell on a tiny red coat, a child's coat, hanging on the wall. As he stared at the coat, he knew he had seen it before, but he didn't want to believe it matched the connection in his mind. He felt himself drawn away from Adrian; the dagger became an irrelevance as his eyes fastened on the wall, on the child's coat and the pictures. There were photographs stuck on a large frieze and more in boxes on a table. He turned from Adrian, pushed away the knife and walked over to the images. They were children. Their pale bodies exposed to the flashbulbs looked so thin and frail, but it was the pained cries on their faces that reached out from the prints and stung Valentine's eyes.

He turned back to Adrian, his voice a growl. "What the hell is this?"

He didn't answer. Valentine saw a small pair of sandals on the table: they were tan with buckles, like the kind very young children used to wear to school. He thought he had seen the sandals before. He felt compelled to touch them, and as he did so he felt their inert power pass through his fingertips.

"Oh, God."

A schoolbag, an old-style leather satchel, sat next to the sandals, and its buckles were opened. Valentine reached out for the bag and picked it up with trembling fingers. Inside were jotters, little notebooks from a children's school. All the pale, age-worn dusty books had the same child's name on them: Janie Cooper.

A flash of heat engulfed his head as he took in the name and then he dropped the satchel back on the table.

"Janie."

In the box of pictures beside he saw a little girl wearing the red coat and carrying the bag, but it wasn't Janie. He picked up the top photograph and held it up.

"Who's this?"

"You know her too," said Adrian, his voice was monotonous.

Valentine turned to face him. "Who is she?"

"It's Leanne Dunn . . . in Janie's clothes."

The detective turned back to the picture and stared. He could see some hint of the young girl Leanne was then, but there was very little of the child left in her. She was aged, old before her time, her eyes wide, staring into a world she didn't understand but knew she was trapped in. The look she wore was of sheer pain and helplessness; it was beyond any of the hurts a childhood could bear or move on from.

"You see, don't you?" said Adrian.

Valentine steadied himself on the table. He tipped out the box of pictures. There were more images. Piles of them. Pictures of children with men. In focus, out of focus. Color-bleached or bright, black and white. They covered decades: odd reminders of times past appeared in the backgrounds. A teak-trimmed television, a star clock, bright-red Kicker boots. One thing that never changed was the children's misery and pain: it was etched on their little faces like a first taste of fear. Valentine brought his uninjured hand to his mouth and gripped tightly; he couldn't look away. He tipped over the box and spread out the pictures; it wasn't long before he alighted on the evidence and held it before Adrian.

"This is your father," he yelled.

"It is." He didn't move. A low-pitched sigh started to flow from deep inside him, like he was dredging for a dead emotion. "That was my father."

The detective understood; he didn't need to hear an explanation. The silence said it all. How could it be explained, anyway? There were no words for this. The true revulsion could never be expressed. He knew why the man before him couldn't face the shame of what inhuman acts had taken place, of the monstrous events his own father had participated in, the man whose blood he had running in his veins.

Valentine's heart pounded as he took in the sight before him; a million cruel images burned in his mind. He swayed as he wiped sweat from his heavy brow. "What happened to Janie Cooper?"

"You think I know that? I know she died. I know Knox took care of the remains. They kept her coat and things. I think they dressed Leanne in them to remind them of her. She was special to them." His voice was so flat, so devoid of emotion that he could have been dictating a shopping list — not the brutal abduction, rape and murder of an innocent.

Valentine looked down at the picture in his hand of the little girl and felt a fierce wave of anger engulf him.

"But why Leanne, why would you want to kill her?"

Adrian brought the dagger up to the side of his head, his eyes dark pits of anguish. "I didn't want to kill her. I had to."

"You had to?"

"She was going to talk to that bloody reporter, wasn't she?"

"So Sinclair paid you a visit. You should have lapped that up."

"What?"

"Oh, come on, Adrian." Valentine put down the picture and moved towards the murderer. "That's what this has all been about, isn't it? Well, I've seen it now, and everyone will know about your father's secret."

"It wasn't about that: they needed to pay."

Valentine fronted up to him. "Leanne Dunn didn't need to pay, she'd already paid, her and Janie Cooper and all the rest of those kids."

"Leanne was in the way. I didn't want to kill her, but she was going to talk to Sinclair."

"And steal your bloody thunder. That's what you resented, isn't it, Adrian? Leanne was going to expose your father and you wanted to be the only one to do that."

"No. You're wrong." He steadied himself before the detective and brought the knife towards Valentine's chest once more, pressing the point of the blade right into the flesh.

"Did you really think he'd hurt you more than those girls?"

"Shut up! Just stop talking now." He pressed the knife harder.

Valentine backed up, fear and painful memory rising in him. He tried to lift his injured arm to fend off Adrian, but a greater pain overtook him. "You've got what you wanted, this is what it's been about, the whole world will see him for what he was, now. Everyone will know about your father, everyone, Adrian."

The sound of police sirens started to wail through the house, diluting the intimacy of their talk, bringing back the outside world. Adrian looked up to the rafters for a solution but was greeted by the sound of pounding footfalls above. Yells and roars came on the back of the study door opening, and louder footsteps were heard on the boards of the staircase. Adrian jerked his eyes to the detective, but Valentine severed the gaze between them and looked up to see DS McAlister descending the stairs.

Adrian gripped the dagger tighter. He was lost in himself now, haunting the room with all the other ghosts.

"Adrian, come on, it's over. Your work's done."

He raised his hands towards his face and let the knife fall to the stone floor. Valentine reached out to him and brought his head onto his shoulder. The young man creased up and cried, deep in anguish and misery, for the father he never had.

"It's all over now, Adrian."

Epilogue

DI Bob Valentine had enjoyed another uninterrupted night's sleep. The weeks since the conclusion of the case had served to build his spirits. The worries he had once carried back and forth on the Tulliallan road had faded into insignificance. He was not the same man, but the thought simmering in his mind about who Bob Valentine was no longer mattered. He had surrendered to himself and to the world he lived in.

The road to Glasgow was dry and fast, some late sun spreading through the cloud in crimson bursts. There were still glass-topped puddles twinkling in the sunlight by the side of the road, but they were only there to reflect the day's glory.

"Isn't it lovely," said Clare. "It's too lovely for a funeral."

Valentine glanced towards his wife. "It's not a funeral."

"I know, but it feels like one."

The detective wanted to agree, but he knew he couldn't. It was the one hurt he harbored from the investigation: that he had been unable to recover Janie Cooper's body for her parents. That secret had gone with Urquhart and Knox to their graves.

"You look so smart in that jacket, Bob."

It was good to see Clare smiling again. He hadn't given her much to smile about lately — it was his father's intervention he had to thank for her being there at all. He knew his devotion to the case had nearly cost him his wife and family, but that was going to change, now.

He raised his bandaged arm from the wheel and offered the nap of the cloth. "I'm still not sure about pinstripes."

"They suit you. They're distinguished."

Valentine started to laugh. "I liked the old sports coat, you know, it had seen me through many a tough time."

Clare frowned. "Let it go, Bob, the old dog-tooth's where it should be — bloody landfill."

The mention of the dump stalled the detective's thoughts and brought him back to the grim find on the outskirts of Ayr that had led him to this day. He felt no remorse for the passing of James Urquhart, or even the indignity of his death. His sympathies lay with the man's wife and the children he had abused in life; wherever he was now, the world was a better place without him.

"That's our turn-off," he said. His eyeline followed the dotted-white lines at the side of the road as it merged into the slower, more sedate pace of the city limits.

The contours of parklands soon gave way to streets of shop fronts and pedestrians. The kirkyard, when it came into view, was dominated by a red sandstone tower, almost spartan in its simplicity.

"There's Sylvia and Phil," said Clare.

As Valentine parked the car, he was greeted by DS McAlister. They hadn't spoken properly about the night in James Urquhart's basement or in any great detail about how the DS had trailed Gillon to where Sinclair was holed up. He knew they were both still reeling from the gamble they had taken; it might be years till they fully digested the investigation and shared their thoughts. Today certainly wasn't the time or place. "Hello, Ally."

"Boss."

"Looks like we're all here."

"All except Dino."

The detective smiled. "Don't tell me she's developed a sense of herself."

"It's your show, sir, everyone knows that."

"No, Ally, it's that little girl's show." He turned to the rear of the car and opened up the boot. Inside was the box containing Janie Cooper's red raincoat and sandals; her satchel sat beside them.

DS McAlister looked into the box and quickly removed his gaze.

"I can't look," he said.

"You have to, son. You have to face it for them." Valentine nodded to the Coopers as they waited by the edge of the burial plot.

"They're just the tip of the iceberg, the ones in plain view."

"We can't bring any of them back, but there'll be no more now, not from that evil pair."

McAlister leant into the boot and eased the box towards him. "Here, let me."

Valentine shook his head. "No, it's my job."

As he wrestled the box onto his hip and walked towards the others, the DI eyed the Coopers being joined by the minister at the burial plot. The sun was high in the sky above. The mood was of perfect stillness.

"Boss, why did Adrian Urquhart kill his own father?"

"He hated him. Hated what he was and what he stood for and how the world knew nothing of the father he knew."

"But he was his father."

Valentine's thoughts turned to his own parents for a moment. "It's a good thing you find it difficult to grasp, Ally." He halted his stride and turned to face the DS. "I read a line in a background report once, I think it came from a German philosopher: when one has not had a good father, one must create one."

McAlister stared back at the detective, seemed to be digesting the comment. "Do you think Adrian was abused, too?"

The DI shrugged. "It seems more than likely, but who knows?"

"He sacrificed what was left of his own life."

"Do you think he felt like he had a life? He despised himself, too: he was his father's son. He had the beast's genes."

As they got closer to the grouping, Valentine could see the pain etched on Diane Cooper's face. The inevitable tears traced the outline of her cheeks, but it was the far-away glare in her eyes that haunted him the most.

"Don't get me wrong, boss, I'm not crying for any of them, except Janie and the others." McAlister shook his head and squinted towards the sky. "Just why did the bastard have to kill Leanne?"

"That sticks with me, too."

"She'd been through enough."

"Her whole life was suffering, and I think Adrian Urquhart saw that, he knew the territory. Maybe in some perverse way he thought he was doing her a favor, putting her out of her misery."

"That and he wanted the spotlight."

"I don't doubt it, Ally, but there's more goes on in here" — he tapped his chest — "than we"ll ever know."

Diane Cooper's husband seemed to be holding her up, one arm around her back and the other grasping her shoulder like she might blow away. When he saw the detectives, Billy Cooper looked up and showed a slim smile that poured alms on any fears Valentine had that they were intruding.

"Hello," said the DI, his voice a soft whisper. "I've brought all we have."

As he placed the small box down beside the freshly dug hole, the minister hurriedly took to arranging the little red coat, sandals and satchel in the ground. He peaked the coat's hood and then placed the satchel below the line of the coat's hem; finally, he rested the two sandals beneath the bag. There was a girl who had once owned the carefully arranged items and it was not difficult to imagine her returning for them now.

A hand touched Valentine's arm.

"Thank you." Diane Cooper was holding out something to him: at first it seemed only a blur in his peripheral vision, but as she raised her hand, he saw it was her daughter's doll.

"Are you sure?"

She nodded, and the wind fluttered the edges of the white handkerchief in her hand. "She loved that doll."

"Then she should have it." He knelt down and placed the doll beside the satchel, as if placing it in Janie's hand.

A final pained smile passed between Valentine and the Coopers, and then the minister gathered his hands together and stood beside the artefacts of the dead in solemn prayer.

About the Author

Tony Black is the author of more than 20 books. He has been nominated for eight CWA Daggers and was runner up in The Guardian's Not the Booker Prize.

He has written four crime series, most recently DI Bob Valentine, published in the US by Bold Venture Press.

An award-winning journalist, he still writes regularly for the press.

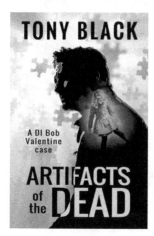
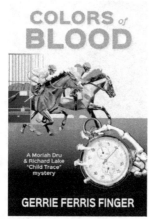

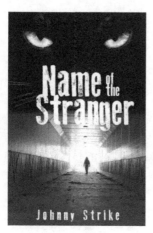
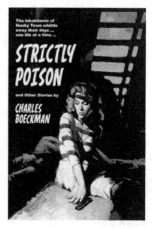

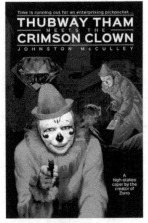

CPSIA information can be obtained
at www.ICGtesting.com
Printed in the USA
BVHW092137110819
555624BV00017B/2219/P